The Code

A NOVEL

J. R. Klein

Copyright © 2020 J. R. Klein.
All rights reserved.

No part of this book may be reproduced in any written, electronic, recording, or photocopying without written permission of the publisher or author.

Although every precaution has been taken to verify the accuracy of the information contained herein, the author and publisher assume no responsibility for any errors or omissions. No liability is assumed for damages that may result from the use of information contained within.

Publisher: Del Gato
Editor: Nick May
Cover Design: Robin Vuchnich
Library of Congress Control Number: 2020906655
ISBN: 978-1-7339069-8-2
ISBN: 978-1-7339069-9-9 (ebook)

Also by J. R. Klein

Frankie Jones
The Ostermann House
To Find: The Search for Meaning in Life on The Gringo Trail
A Distant Past, An Uncertain Future
The Visitor

This is a work of fiction. Names, characters, places, and incidents are drawn from the author's imagination or are used fictitiously. Any resemblance to persons, living or dead, events, or locales is coincidental.

"Grounded in the natural philosophy of the Middle Ages, alchemy formed a bridge: on the one hand into the past, to Gnosticism, and on the other into the future, to the modern psychology of the unconscious."

— Carl Jung

Part I

The Room

1

History, it is said, is written by the victors. Or is it?

Detective Mike Smith sat in his unkempt office at the Covington Police Station, flummoxed, staring hard at Officer Robinson.

"What do you *mean* Clara Parker is dead?" Smith said after a long pause. "She's the president of Graebner College for Christ's sake. You make it sound like your parakeet just died." Smith buried his face in his hands and groaned. He looked at Robinson. "What am I supposed to do now! Parker was my last lead…my very last lead."

2

Nick and Katy discover a secret passage to an altar chamber deep below the Graebner College library

"Ready up," Katy Malone said. "I brought something tonight."

Reaching into her backpack, she produced two stubby LED flashlights. She handed one to Nick, pushed the button on the other, and shined it around the third floor reading room of the Graebner College library. A stream of cold white light bounced off the walls and ceiling. The evening was late. The room was empty. Katy glanced at the wood panel that hid the passage Nick had found in the corner of the room.

Nick Sanchez needed no explanation. He knew exactly what Katy had in store. He ran a hand impetuously through his wavy black hair, by no means convinced this was a good idea—not by a long shot. But he knew all too well it was useless to try and talk Katy out of it. Nick's druthers were to grab their bags and head across campus to the Ratskeller, the Rat as it were, in time for a pitcher of beer. Maybe two if they hurried.

Katy Malone walked across the room. "Go check the hall."

It was empty, not a soul, not a sound.

This time Nick knew how to trip the latch on the door. All he had to do was slip the screwdriver of his Swiss Army knife into the space between the bookshelf and the panel and give a quick twist. He did. The latch let out a soft click. The door swung open on a set of hidden pivots.

Nick stared into the empty black portal. "All right now. If we do this, if we go in there, we need to close it up behind us. You know what that means. It means we better be sure, and I mean *damn* sure, we can get our asses back out again," he said, speaking as much to himself as to Katy.

As Nick saw it, the sooner they wrapped this up, the sooner they'd be on their way to the Rat. He looked at Katy and stepped inside.

"What do you see?" Katy asked.

Nick flashed his light across the back of the panel, searching for a latch to open it from inside. He ran his fingers over the surface. "Okay, here it is—I found it. It's up near the top. And there's a small ring to pull the door shut, too. So, what we need to do is run a test. Stay there and close the door. I'll open it from here. If it doesn't open, use my knife. Got it?"

Katy pushed the door until it clicked. Nick waited briefly, then pulled on the trigger. Nothing happened. What if it wasn't part of the latch? Worse, what if Katy couldn't get the door open? A door does two things. It keeps you out—or it keeps you in.

Nick tried again, tugging harder, fully expecting nothing to happen, fully expecting to be trapped inside. But this time, like perfect clockwork, the door popped open. He watched as it rotated effortlessly outward. "Hot shit," he croaked.

Backlit by the emerald-green glow of the library table lamps, Katy stood smiling and speechless.

Nick pursed his lips, drew in a slow, deep breath, and exhaled. "You ready for this?"

Katy wasn't so sure now, but she gave an unequivocal nod nonetheless. She stepped inside and set both backpacks on the floor. Nick grasped the ring. He looked at Katy and pulled the door toward him. This time the latch echoed minaciously. They stood in the black chamber, waiting for their eyes to adjust to the dark. Their two white LEDs probed the abyss like small crisscrossing searchlights at a miniature Hollywood movie opening.

Katy trained her light down a long passage; pure thick darkness gobbled up the feeble stream. She stooped down and ran a finger across the smooth flagstones that made up the floor beneath her. Three feet overhead, a craggy ceiling tapered down onto sidewalls like a Byzantine arch in a monastery cloister, just wide enough for a line of people going in opposite directions. Two centuries ago when the school was a theological seminary the students would have used the passage to enter the upper floors of the building. It was not hard to imagine them filing orderly and silently through the corridor. But now it was closed off—closed off to the world. Or so it seemed.

"Big stones," Nick said, reaching up and running his hand across one as a large as a rough-cut bowling ball. Tiny flakes of mortar sprinkled his hair.

Katy proceeded into the passage, her silhouette turned a pale nocturne, then a dark midnight, then vanished off into oblivion.

"Hey, not so fast there," Nick called. He looked around, calculating where they were. "Okay, all right, now I get it. We're in that dead space. You know the one that runs along the wall between the reading room and the corridor. It never made sense to me till now."

A set of stairs angled down. Anchored onto the walls were large iron candle holders with thick candles. Years of soot coated the stones next to them. Nick pulled off a piece of dripped wax and rubbed it between his thumb and finger. He smelled it the way a Frenchman puts his nose to a new glass of wine. "Beeswax, pure beeswax. Liturgical, same stuff they use in church, the Catholic church," he said, spoken as one who knew.

He waved his LED across the steps and looked at Katy, who was standing not more than three feet away but bobbled in shadows. "What do you think? We need to make it back before Kojak shows up to close the place down." Kojak, the library guard with a shiny globe of a head. The spitting image of the old TV character, all but for the lollipop. "What time is it?"

Phones up in their backpacks, Katy guestimated it to be about twelve-fifteen, somewhere thereabouts. The library would be open until one a.m. A little farther couldn't hurt.

Katy led the way, intrepidly panning the steps with her light, going down until they came to a landing with an empty window case made of fine granite that rose ecclesiastically to a point at the top. The glass was gone. The entire window was forever sealed off on the outside with stone and mortar.

A second tier of stairs flanked by candles led down to a turbid corridor. Katy crept along, moving sedulously. A fluttering breeze washed across Nick's face, blowing up a sprig of hair. How could this be in a place so still and stale there was barely enough air to breathe? Had he imagined it? Could have, but he didn't think so. Or was it the freaky passage itself screwing with his thoughts. Just being there was enough to do that. He turned and looked around, feeling as though they were not alone, thinking that someone was nearby just off in the desolate darkness, watching them, following them.

Another steep and stark staircase took them to the ground floor, the vestibule of the ancient building. A metal door confronted them. Katy gave a tug. Its hinges delivered a painful squeak, yielding yet more stairs. These, little more than three feet wide, led deep underground.

Katy tracked the wall with her hand as she worked her way down step by step, ready to skid into an empty and endless pit of darkness, into a place as black as a cast-iron skillet. At the bottom of the steps was a partly opened door. On each side of the door, sitting on a small platform as though guarding the entrance, was something round—carbolic gray. Katy already had a troubled feeling. Moving in closer, she aimed the cone of light from her LED onto one of the forms. She stopped and gasped, pulling her hand to her mouth. Taking a quick step back, she collided into Nick. They inched forward.

Katy had never been this close to one before: an actual bone-dry skull. Big empty square eye sockets, jaw turned up at the tips as though caught in a jocular moment at the last second—at the very end. She lifted it from the pole. Realizing she was holding the braincase of some long-gone person, she passed it quickly off to Nick and wiped her hands on her jeans.

Above the door, a stone plaque delivered the imprimatur *Mors Vita Est* and the number 322. Nick touched the elaborate gold script. He spoke the words, first in Latin, then English: "Death is Life…or Life is Death, take your pick. Three twenty-two. Genesis 3:22, 'Then the Lord God said, Behold, man has become like one of us, knowing both good and evil.'"

"Good grief, you're a virtual encyclopedia of knowledge."

"Catholic stuff. Don't worry, exorcised long ago," he proclaimed as he panned light across the numbers. "Three twenty-two. Three and two and two is seven, a number tied to the Illuminati. The Illuminati and the occult…and a whole lot else."

They entered the room as if drawn in against their will. Nick waved his light onto walls stippled with dirty plaster. In the center of the room was a thick stone slab that rested on four heavy pillars. Katy ran her hand across the stone, smooth as a perfect pearl. A ceremonial altar perhaps. On the edges all the way around it were carvings of grotesque human faces. A cross of fine black wood dangled upside-down from a chain above the altar. It swung motionless in the stale drought air—thick air with the chalky odor of the brittle plastered walls.

Set into the walls around the room were bas reliefs of the Stations of the Cross. Nine stations, not the usual fourteen, placed in reverse order going counterclockwise from the entrance of the room. Fourteen candle holders, each with thick candles, grabbed the walls.

"What, God forbid, is going on down here?" Katy said, as she climbed on the altar. Hands over head, feet spread out. A momentary tingling sensation rippled through her, head to foot...so it seemed. She cringed and climbed off.

"Damn creepy place," Nick uttered in little more than a whisper. He looked at Katy, her soft blue eyes now big and dark as a gazelle's. On the far side of the room was a small wooden door. Thick forged hinges secured it to the wall. A large iron ring hung in the middle. Nick grasped the ring and snapped a tug. The door rattled but didn't budge. Putrid odors seeped from behind the door. Rot, decay—death.

"Whew! Bad smell." Nick swept his hand in front of his face. He looked at the altar, looked at the black cross, looked at the door in front of them, looked at Katy. "All right, seen enough. We're outta here."

Getting up the stairs and back to the panel door was no easy task. It seemed to take forever. They were breathing hard by the time they arrived. Nick flipped the latch. The door swung obediently open. Confronting them was a dark room. The green globes on the tables had been turned off. Fragile opaline light from outside trickled in through the tall stained-glass windows. Nick closed the door, pressing it hard with both hands, making sure everything was safely behind them.

Katy retrieved her phone. "Aw, geez! One-thirty…the library's closed down."

3

Nick and Katy spend the night in the library

One thing for sure, there would be no pitchers of beer at the Rat that night. Another thing for sure, Nick and Katy were trapped in the library. They couldn't leave, not without tripping the alarms on the way out.

Should they risk it? Try to get out fast and head for the hills? If they were spotted, though, caught in the act by campus police, it would be hard to explain. Two ace students breaking into—or out of—the library after hours. Not the dean's list either of them sought.

They walked along the third-floor hallway and down the stairs to the vacant second and first floor rooms where the stacks and study areas were. Only red neon light from the EXIT signs at the end of the corridors split the darkness. The circulation desk was shut down. The metal gate in front of the doors was closed and locked. Kojak was probably deep into Miller Time by now.

"We wait till morning; that's all we can do," Katy said. "Then we slip out after the library's been open a while. Make it look like we came in early and left."

They went to a room on the second floor at the end of the hall, which was filled with biology, chemistry, and math books. Graebner had dumped tons of money into its library. Every imaginable resource existed. If you needed a reference, a textbook, anything at all, it was in the library.

They set their packs on the floor and sat cross-legged facing each other. "I've spent a lot of time in this place," Katy, the math major, boasted. "Cripes, I can tell you something about every math book on the shelf."

To say Katy and Nick's backgrounds were similar was to say giraffes are nature's midgets. Nick had come up through the school of hard knocks. One of three children of Mexican immigrant parents in Houston, he had graduated at the top of his class at Lamar High School. A full scholarship to Graebner (and a half-dozen other schools) was his reward. He was in his senior year now. One more semester, three more courses, three more A's, and he'd be on his way to medical school.

Katy, in her sophomore year at Graebner, had sailed through life as if on a skateboard that whizzed her past every haphazard rut with not so much as a skinned knee or a sprained ankle along the way. Bright and cute and crafty, she had grown up in the posh Chicago suburb of Hinsdale.

"Got a long wait ahead of us," Nick said. He looked at his watch, just past one-thirty. The library staff would arrive shortly before the library opened at six. A few diehards would show up right away: the top-notch students who burned the midnight oil, slept a couple of hours, then started the day with a visit to the library before heading to class. Nick knew that crowd. Katy did too.

"Hungry?" Nick asked.

Katy shrugged and nodded.

Nick pulled a bottle of water and a pack of Cheetos from his bag. "Not much but better than nothing."

The room was filled with tempered light. A large fireplace, the inside blackened from years of use, was spread across one of the walls. Once a necessity, now a fire hazard, it hadn't been stoked in decades. Each floor had two of them made of ornately carved stone.

An hour crept by. Katy and Nick talked about their gruesome discovery. This was Graebner College tucked away in the sleepy hamlet of Covington, Vermont. Everything about Graebner—its past, its present—was known. Warts and all. Graebner had no secrets to hide. No secrets that had not already been revealed and purged from its dashing history. The last bad thing to happen at the school, and it wasn't long ago, was when Marv Friedman hung himself in his dorm room. It had caused a big stir because Marv was not someone you'd expect to do that, but he did. He skipped his morning class of English Lit, slipped a rope over his neck, attached it to a hook on the ceiling, and gave his neck a twist. And that was it. Too bad about Marv. Destined to be the next Norman Mailer everyone said. But then things like that happen at all schools.

What Katy and Nick had found did not fit into the perfect brand that Graebner College was peddling to the world. Or could it be that this was the real story behind the legendary tales that circulated endlessly in dorm rooms late at night? Stories dating to the time before the school was Graebner College, when it was Schulenmeister Theological Seminary two centuries ago. Stories of Satanic worship right where young boys were being trained to go out into the towns and boroughs and villages to preach the gospel. Stories of a spate of unexplained illnesses that spread through the nearby towns quick as brush fire. People coughing up blood—hallucinating. Illness came on fast and within days people were dead. Dead or possessed…Salem, Massachusetts redux. The Covington residents and farmers, blaming the seminary, frantically rounded up a group of faculty and hanged them on the front lawn of the campus. Was the altar chamber an ancient relic of those grisly days? Maybe, but was something foul going on deep in the bowels of the old library now? What Katy and Nick had seen was more than some relic of the school's ancient past. It was as real as a toothache.

"What do you think's going on down there?" Katy asked.

Nick shook his head. "Doesn't look good, that's for sure."

They talked about going back down and taking another look, now that they were sealed off in the library, now that they had hours to kill. But neither wanted to. Time was needed to absorb what they had seen.

Katy brushed hair from her somnolent eyes. "You know, if someone's going there on a regular basis, they'd have to do it at night when the library's closed, like now for example. Unless there's an entrance no one knows about."

The idea of a second entrance wasn't an altogether absurd possibility. The old building could have underground tunnels that had been shut off to the outside long ago. Like the old sewer system under the streets of New York. The catacombs under the streets of Rome. In the early days of Graebner, they may have once been used to get from building to building without having to navigate the wet Vermont winter.

Another hour crept by. Nick got up and stretched. He pulled each ankle to the back of his thigh one at a time and walked to the window and looked out. The misty fog that had descended on the campus earlier in the evening had turned into fine powdery snow, one of the first of the season. It covered the walks and bushes and trees and made the light from the lampposts float in midair. The campus was deserted but for an occasional student who slipped past the building and vanished into a wall of whiteness. Nick came back and sat next to Katy.

"Hey, what's that?" Katy said quickly, with a touch of urgency.

"Shh! Someone's coming," Nick whispered.

The sound of muffled footsteps and barely audible voices coming down the hall in their direction.

"Quick...here, over against the wall. Keep it quiet." They picked up their bags from the middle of the room.

"Kojak...you think?" Katy said.

Nick held his fingers in front of his lips; he shook his head.

The footsteps passed the entrance of the room and faded away down the hall.

"Couple of people...two, I think. That's what it sounds like," Nick uttered.

"Uh-huh, going up to the reading room."

Nick nodded. "And down to where we were, I bet...down below. Geez, made it out just in time."

"What do we do if they come in here?" Katy said.

"Just sit tight. We have no idea who else is with them. Or how they got in here for that matter. We'll deal with that if it happens. The chains on the door, the alarms, yet somehow they managed to get in without any trouble." Nick looked at his watch. "Three o'clock. Pretty damn late for a little rendezvous down under."

Time dragged. Total stillness filled the library. At four o'clock, almost an hour later, the footsteps returned. Muted voices passed the doorway as the visitors moved down the hall.

Nick and Katy held tight. They faintly heard the sound of the front gate closing and the chains being reattached.

"That's it, they're gone," Nick said, letting out a deep breath. He crept to the window just in time to see two people moving quickly down the steps. "Two of them," he reported as he watched them vanish into the misty snow-washed night.

4

Nick has a portentous dream

Exhausted from the jagged events of the night, Nick and Katy fell into a deep sleep in the early hours of the morning on the hard parquet floor. Almost immediately a dream came over Nick—one of those weird-ass dreams he would get when he was stressed. Vivid to the point of being starkly real, they seemed to carry arcane telltale messages.

He was standing with Katy in a half-lit musty room full of sour and noxious odors. Two candles delivered pale light that trembled on the walls: walls of ocher and vermillion. Katy couldn't leave; Nick couldn't leave. An uncontrollable force commanded their presence. Free will was gone. Freedom to move was eliminated. There were others there with them: students, some to Nick's left, some to his right. Dozens. Others behind him.

A vague, cloudy form floated before them. The room was uncomfortably warm. Perspiration broke out on Nick's face. He tried to raise his hand to wipe his forehead but couldn't. He was wearing jeans and a T-shirt…then shorts…then nothing, without a stitch…then jeans again. His arms were covered with small purple bruises.

The form in front of him hovered close to a wall—a breathing wall. No, wait, a moving curtain. The form took on a misty and diffuse shape. Human, perhaps. A long thin hand projected forward like a wispy wand that aimed out to the group standing nearby. It moved across, signaling to each person one by one with great and determined purpose.

Then came a voice. A voice that resonated with a dull echo. "Red Rover, Red Rover, send Melisa over." Once again. "Red Rover, Red Rover, send Melisa over."

Someone from the group stepped out and walked forward and vanished through the wall.

The air, foul and putrid, rolled across Nick. He could even feel it. There was the shuffling of feet, the occasional impatient movement of the awkward gathering. Nick looked down. He had no feet. It was terrifying for him to see this. His heart fluttered. Was he crippled? Decayed? Christ, were the rancid malodors coming from him? Then his feet were back—his body reconstructed.

Again, the words: "Red Rover, Red Rover, send Jason over." With that, a person to Nick's left pulled forward, walked to the wall and passed through.

And: "Red Rover, Red Rover, send Katy over."

Nick watched as Katy stepped forward. She stopped, looked at Nick, then passed through the wall.

The air was warm. Chalky and warm.

Now: "Red rover, red rover, send Nick over." He started forward. As he reached the wall, as he was about to pass through, the dream ended. He opened his eyes, momentarily terrorized by the dream. The gray light that had covered the library room was gone. Rich streaks of sunshine broke through the windows.

Nick listened for a moment then leapt up. "Katy, Katy, get up, the library's open! Get up! Quick!" She sprung to her feet, still dazed. They gave their hair a quick fluff and sat at the library table, pretending they had been there for half an hour.

Not a minute passed before the first student drifted in and sat down. "Eye, yi, yi," Nick droned, realizing that just minutes before they had been snoring away on the floor.

They waited a while, then got up and ambled down to the first floor, looking as dumb as Benjamin Braddock in *The Graduate* as he crossed the hotel lobby in front of the desk clerk holding his toothbrush. Nick gave the circulation librarian an awkward smile and a nod. She watched, confused, shook her head and returned to work.

5

Nick and Katy make a return trip to the altar chamber

A fortnight later, Nick and Katy were again in the third-floor reading room—same bat time, same bat channel.

Of all the rooms in the old library, the reading room was Nick's favorite. Inlaid parquet floors that creaked and croaked when you passed across them. Tall bookshelves of old sapele mahogany that bore a natural patina from two centuries of human contact. Deep sills shrouded twelve stained-glass windows of lustrous green, brilliant red, vibrant blue, and sparkling purple. An antique Gustav Becker grandfather clock stood majestically in the corner. Large and imposing and in perfect working order, it ticked off the seconds, chimed the hour and the half hour. Green globes on the library table lamps shed comforting light throughout the room—effective but not intrusive light that was kinder on the eyes than the harsh fluorescents on the first and second floors.

They waited for the last student and the last member of the faculty—Professor Linkley, the gaseous one—to leave. You always knew when Byron Linkley was around. Boy, did you ever! And that hair, oh God. Nothing wrong with old Linkley that a good flea dip couldn't fix. And that stupid plaid bowtie, even at eleven o'clock at night. At long last he rose up and tacked out of the room as Gustav Becker rang once, halfway below the eleventh hour. This left Nick and Katy with plenty of time, a good hour or more, to get in and get out and still have thirty minutes before Kojak cycled through. They had no desire to be trapped in the library yet again.

"So tell me now, why exactly are we doing this?" Nick said, doggedly hoping for a better answer.

"You'll see," was all he got.

Katy slid her books in her pack and went straight for the panel. She opened the door, set her things inside, and waited for Nick, who tagged reluctantly along like her kid brother. She closed the door. Within five minutes they were in the altar chamber, this time lit by the beam of a DeWALT 12-volt that Katy had brought. Sickly whiteness bounced off the chocolate brown walls. They stood in front of the plain wooden door with the wrought-iron ring on the front. Katy recovered a set of keys from her pack.

"Where in the world did you get those?"

"Antique store in Covington," Katy said, fiddling with a ring of large skeleton keys.

"You don't *really* think you're gonna open the door with a skeleton key, do you?"

"And why not? Here hold this." She handed Nick the DeWALT. "A little light over here, Poncho, you're shining it on the wall."

Katy tried each key one at a time. Some went in part way. Some not at all. A few went in but did nothing. Then, miraculously, one key turned the bolt and unlocked the door.

"Son-of-a-bitch," Nick yelped, causing Katy to eke out a short laugh.

Katy gave the door a tug. It swung part way open on heavy, dry hinges. She pulled again. Greeting them was a long narrow corridor full of old, stale odors. It was just big enough to proceed claustrophobically down, two abreast. But unlike the stone and mortar of the passages leading underground, this one was covered with five-inch pale-green ceramic tiles and a floor of thin hardwood strips, dark and dirty with age. A light switch connected through a metal tube to a row of fluorescent lights that ran down the ceiling.

Nick flipped the switch. Harsh blaring light surrounded them. Heading down the corridor, they came to a half-open door. Katy poked it with her foot and aimed the DeWALT inside. In front of them was a room with the same green tiles across the walls and ceiling and the same wooden floor. It had the appearance of an early operating room from days gone by. Something akin to the infirmary of Philadelphia's infamous Eastern State Penitentiary. Piled waist high in the corner were human skulls.

"So this is what's behind door number two," Nick mumbled. He walked inside and examined the skulls. "Get a load of this will you, these clowns have been trepanned, every last one of them." He took the DeWALT from Katy and aimed the beam into a grizzly wound about the size of his thumb and looked at Katy, her face lime-green from the walls. "Trepanned. You know, that thing people used to do to release evil spirits and other bad stuff from the brain," he said, bobbing the skull up and down in his palm like a sixteen-inch softball. "Lucky bastard—dude survived. See, the wound is totally healed...smooth edges."

A pair of rusting white cabinets stood against one wall. In the center was a surgical table that was little more than an old gurney. Attached to the ceiling, a crude operating room light aimed down. Nick flipped the switch, expecting nothing. Unforgiving brightness filled the room; he shielded his eyes and killed the light.

Bolted to the table was a metal fixture with stiff, decaying leather straps. Something to immobilize the head no doubt. Nick opened the tin cabinet. Inside were steel drill bits, a hand drill, a butcher's saw for cutting bone.

Katy picked up a drill bit.

"Uhm, I do not believe I would do that, Madam," Nick said. "No telling what's on those things. Like Confucius say: That which won't kill you, make you sick as hell." Several old rubber balls, cracked and dry, sat on the shelf. "Wow! Now check this out. They give you a pair of these babies when they're boring into your skull. The whole thing is done while you're awake. The brain doesn't feel pain. But, yes, the mind knows what's going on. You can be sure of that!"

On the back wall was a narrow door, unlocked and opened a crack. Nick gave it a shove and aimed the DeWALT down a long thin corridor made of the same green tile and dirty hardwood floors. No telling where it went, but there was no time to find out.

6

Sam Whitney meets with Clara Parker, the Graebner College President

As women go, Clara Parker, the Graebner College president, was on the tall side—every bit of five ten. But if you were standing next to her, you could easily be fooled into adding another inch. Her mere presence drew attention. She was aware of this and made sure it was balanced with a kind and reassuring voice that was never abrasive. What's more, she had a perfectly intoned laugh that she delivered at just the right moment in response to the most inane joke. It sounded believable and made you think she was locked onto every word that was spoken. It was an acquired skill, and Clara Parker used it skillfully.

Parker's face, her countenance, was that of a scholar, unbattered by the skirmishes that confront most professional people her age: the lawyers, the doctors, the businesswomen. It was the face of someone who had devoted a life to reading and thinking and writing. And now, it was the face of someone who had succeeded at the top job in one of the country's leading liberal arts colleges.

In her sixth year as president, she was liked by most, feared by some, hated by a few. Of course, there were those who felt it their mission to challenge her every word, every decision she made.

Parker didn't mind—it added a touch of spice to her daily routine. They would come to her office mean as a rattlesnake and leave gentle as a kitten. Parker's strategy was simple and effective. She let them rant as long as they wanted, never challenging them, usually agreeing with them, offering a smile and a nod until they could muster no more verbal barbs to fire in her direction. She would assure them their concerns were real and that *she* was the one who could and would mend the problem.

Sam Whitney, a big donor to the school, sat in Clara Parker's opulent first-floor office in the central administration building. Whenever Sam Whitney visited, Parker treated him like he was a head of state in the Oval Office. Each held a snifter of Remy Martin Louis XIII, as good as it gets.

Clara had known Sam from her first day on the job at Graebner. Their friendship had grown ever since. He had been her confidant through thick and thin. Clara unloaded to Sam. Not being part of the college, he could take it all in—could offer a word or two of advice that was untainted by personal motivation.

Clara's eyes drifted over to the window. How many times had she stood there looking out across the campus, her kingdom, like some great queen pondering her vast holdings from her castle? She looked at Sam. "You know, I like my job. I think we're a good match...me and Graebner. Eighty percent of what I do is a snap, just keeping the rusty old gears spinning, the wheels turning, at a pretty damn good school. The other twenty is pure nonsense. You have to kiss a helluva lot of ass to run a place like this, let me tell you. Suck up to a lot of rich old biddies so you can tap into their checkbooks." She took a small sip of cognac. "And, of course, then there's the board of trustees, who when you get right down to it make all the real decisions anyway...not me. And the faculty senate, who ridiculously think they run this place—ugh, God, bunch of idiots! Nobody runs this place—nobody! The inmates run it, that's who." A dreamy half-smile crossed Clara's face. "Sometimes I feel I should have a big sign plastered on the wall here with that quote from Kurt Vonnegut: 'True terror is to wake up one morning and discover that your high school class is running the country.' Take out country and put in college and there you have it." She thought about that for a second. The corner of her mouth curled as if she wanted to laugh.

A touch of inner joy always bubbled up inside Sam when he listened to Clara's rants. It's much more comforting to hear about someone else's woes than to deal with your own. Sam found it absorbingly enjoyable, and he knew that Clara reserved her most torrid revelations for him— those black secrets that every school holds close to its vest.

"Be clear, we here at Graebner want to keep everything as good as possible for you, Sam," Clara Parker said. Not that Sam needed much more from her, what with the Whitney name already splattered across buildings everywhere you looked: the auditorium, the student union, the Whitney School of Business, the Whitney Activity Center—The Whit, to the students.

Sam Whitney's visits with Clara were meant partly for enjoyment, partly to reconfirm Clara's commitment to him as she had done almost from the moment she took on the job as president of Graebner. It had to do with one rare and special privilege that Clara afforded Sam. One hand washes the other, and it was hard to know who made out better on the deal.

Sam Whitney raised the snifter of cognac to his lips. He breathed in the sweet sharp fragrance of the amber cognac and took a sip. "You sure know your liquor, my dear," he said. "As for things with us here at Graebner...I couldn't possibly ask for more."

Clara Parker may not have known all the details, but she had a pretty good idea what Sam was up to at the school. It had to do with an underground room in the library, and it was tied to the occult—to something known as the Sanctus Codice. The Code as they called it—a word that always gave Parker shivers.

But beyond that, she stayed safely out of the loop lest the lid were to blow sky-high off the whole affair and Clara suddenly found herself surrounded by a roomful of buzzing reporters and photographers. She already had a plan if, God forbid, that were to happen. She would say: "Well yes, sure, it happened on my watch, but I knew nothing about it, *nothing*. Colleges are complex entities. No one, not even the president, has knowledge of everything that goes on." That would be her defense. And yes, she would throw Sam under the bus were it to come to that.

As for Sam, if he could continue undisturbed, the arrangement was fine with him because what he got out of it was something so incredible that even he could barely believe it.

Bill Walker, Parker's executive administrative assistant, knocked on the door, opened it quietly, and entered with a sterling silver tray bearing a cup of imported caviar on a bed of crushed ice. Two mother-of-pearl spoons. A small stack of crackers. He set the tray on the table and left.

Parker waited for the door to close. "So, how's Linkley been? Is he helpful?"

"Who? Oh, Byron Linkley. Sure, he's there when we need him. He's our…our point man you could say. Our eyes and ears."

"Fine and dandy, but keep a sharp eye on him as well," Parker warned. "Like a lot of the others around here, Linkley can be a royal pain in the ass. But after running a psycho ward like this, you come to realize you need people like Linkley. They're your gophers. Dumb clown will do anything. He's one of the goons that is perpetually worried about his job, even though they have tenure. Getting rid of someone like that takes a meeting of the full UN Security Council…and then that's usually not enough."

Parker waited a second and added, "And anyway, the students like Linkley. Actually, the guy is no moron; he knows his stuff, and he tells good jokes in class. Makes the kids laugh. You do that and you've got them in your pocket. But I guess the question is, are you sure he can be trusted?

He probably knows more than you might expect, about the…" she couldn't quite get herself to utter the word, "…that thing you folks are doing. What's your feeling? We damn well don't want anything getting screwed up here now, do we?"

"Not to worry, everything is under control," Sam said assertively.

Parker sighed. She knew that if what Sam was doing at Graebner became public knowledge, heads would roll for sure. Reputations would be destroyed. The conversations between Sam and Clara always took place in Parker's office, a place considered to be the safest. Yet even Sam Whitney took no chances. He periodically had the room examined by *his* security detail, making sure that nothing was being surreptitiously recorded. Not that he didn't trust Clara, but to make sure no one else had been nebbing around, that's what he told Clara. Trust among crooks does not run deep.

7

Lenore Simenson discovers The Code—a medieval ritual of alchemy and sorcery

Forty-four, tanned and trim, with green eyes that were as mysterious as they were beautiful, that was Lenore Simenson.

She had been Sam Whitney's business partner for more than two decades. It was Lenore who had stumbled onto a description of The Code in the rare book collection in the Graebner library, the Velvet Room as it was called.

The library was internationally noted for its first edition and rare books, including one of the forty-eight remaining original Gutenberg Bibles, kept hermetically sealed in a locked, fireproof cabinet. The Bible had been acquired at a Sotheby's auction by an anonymous benefactor for an undisclosed amount and donated to the school. It had happened on Parker's watch, a fact that had seared her reputation with the board of trustees.

Lenore was a frequent visitor to the Velvet Room, which was actually three small rooms, two with tall bookshelves and a ladder that slid effortlessly across the front on a track. Each room had soft, purple, velvet-covered chairs, from which the rooms acquired their name. Antique tables of fine rosewood, ash, hickory, and elm.

The third room had locked glass-fronted bookcases with the rarest of the books, and the cabinet containing the Gutenberg. Just standing there filled your head with images of Johannes Gutenberg placing each tiny Latin letter in rows, painting them with ink and pressing them onto the parchment.

Gentle indirect light, easy on the eyes, reflected off the ceiling from behind crown molding. All in all, it was as quiet as an empty cathedral.

Walking along the shelves, Lenore retrieved an original copy of James Joyce's *The Dubliners*, a collection of his short stories that had taken nine years and dozens of rejections before it was published in 1914. She read parts of several stories, then placed it back on the shelf. Further along, her eyes landed on three books about the history of Graebner.

For no reason but pure curiosity, she took them to a chair and began paging through one. It described the origins of Schulenmeister Theological Seminary in 1801 before the school had become Graebner College in 1867. It was at Schulenmeister that the first Code had been performed. She read about it carefully and methodically—an occult ritual that was bizarre, amazing, and flat-out frightening. The information was sketchy. It had been performed by a group of Schulenmeister faculty and a few students somewhere deep in an underground recess below one of the buildings.

8

Lenore tells Sam about The Code

Two days later, Lenore sat in Sam's office, one leg draped over the arm of the chair, her skirt half way up her thigh as she told Sam what she had learned about The Code. Together, Sam and Lenore had built a financial firm from a small ma and pa operation into a big money maker—Whitney Simenson Associates. WSA had become a big success. Total assets ran at several hundred million. Whenever Lenore spoke, Sam listened. But this time she sounded flaky as pie crust.

Sam sat ashen faced. He listened as Lenore told him the silliest thing he had ever heard. In the two decades he had known her, she had been the most sensible member of their financial investment firm. In fact, at one time early on, a loose romantic relationship had developed between them. For a couple of months, it had burned hotter than hell's chimney, then quickly fizzled out. Each of them later got married and had children that today were grown and through college and into jobs.

Now divorced and single, Sam and Lenore looked as though they belonged together. Both always took good care of themselves. Sam was tall and handsome, with that perfect blend of salt and pepper hair. His chin was strong, his voice full, his eyes clear and deep and dark. Many times he had fantasized about Lenore, wondering what it would be like if they were to rekindle the relationship? When they were talking business, going over investments, out for a drink, he would find himself asking her to repeat what she had just said, her words having slipped past him as he watched her distractedly. Lenore, too, had her own similar guilty moments.

Sam sat motionless. "Lenore, what are you talking about," he said, as she described what she had discovered. "Sounds like real weak tea to me."

"I know what you're thinking Sam; that's what I thought at first, too. But I went over it again and again, researched it to the max, studied it from every angle."

"It's preposterous," Sam said, quickly and dismissively. He leaned back in his chair and tapped his fingertips together. "Code? Code? You got it out of an old book written eons ago by…by who was it?"

Lenore shook her head. "I read about it in the Graebner library up in the Velvet Room, up where the rare book collection is. There I was, sitting, paging though a couple of old books, first editions of some great classics. I'm sort of a book nut, you know that Sam. So, for kicks last weekend I decided to go up to the Graebner and dig through some of the old books. I've done this before lots of times, especially when the weather sucks like the last couple of days. So, there I was and suddenly, for no reason, my eyes landed on a couple of books about Graebner. I pulled them off the shelf and started reading. And I'm paging though them, you know reading here and there, when I came across this section that described some really bizarre shit that took place at the old Schulenmeister Seminary before it was Graebner College. A bunch of the faculty were involved in a thing called a Code. It was an occult ritual...."

Sam leaned quickly forward, hands perched on his knees. "*Occult! Did you say occult?*"

"Keep your drawers on, Sammy boy, hang on...yes, an occult ritual conducted in the basement somewhere down below the library, the same building that's there today, I think. So, with this Code thing, they were able to, well, to predict the future from what I can gather. Get a glimpse of it at least."

Sam rocked back in his chair again, sending a blast of laughter into the room. "Predict the future!" he said as though he hadn't quite heard her the first time.

"That's right. Predict the future. There were these meetings, these Codes things, rituals of some kind. I wasn't able to get all the details, but we won't worry about that for now."

"Christ almighty, Lenore, what have you been smoking?"

"I don't smoke, Sam; you know that. Not weed, not cigarettes. Haven't had a puff of either in years. Listen to me now, Sam, will you? It could be, it just could be that this

Code thing is real. That it truly can predict the future to some degree or other. A lot of what I read in the books suggested it's possible. *Think* about it."

"It's a bunch of gibberish, Lenore. Even if we could do it, what then? Become the local weatherman or something?" He laughed like hell.

"Cut it out, Sam. Come on. What do we do for a living?"

Okay, play along to get along, he thought. "Invest, sweetie…we take money, we buy stocks, we make a few bucks in the process. We try to anyway." Then it hit. A long silence settled over the room. Sam's eyes looked slowly back and forth across his desk; he looked up and locked onto Lenore's emerald green. "You're not…you're not saying. Surely—"

"Well, I don't know what I'm saying, exactly. But what if, just image what it would be like if we could…if there were some actual way to predict where markets are going, for example."

Sam's mind flashed instantly through the possibilities. He muttered something inaudibly, shaking his head as if to clear his mind of the absurdity of what he had just heard.

"You sit there at that big mahogany desk of yours trying to figure out which stocks will be heading up, which ones will be going down. But you don't know. I don't know. Nobody really knows. Imagine if we could…well, just think about it."

Loquacious Sam was without a word.

9

Lenore learns more about The Code

Digging deeper, Lenore learned as much as she could about The Code. At first not much came up. All she managed to do was piece together fragments of information from several different sources. The details remained sketchy.

A few books alluded to Bérenger Saunière, a poor country priest from the late nineteenth century who lived in the village of Rennes-le-Château in southern France. People believed that he used a system like The Code called the Convocation of Venus to acquire extraordinary wealth, although there was no hard evidence to support that claim. It was suggested that he used powers gained from a sacred pentagram to see into the future.

But pentagrams have been used by scores of cultures for millennia. Religious ceremonies and mystic rituals are full of them. Wiccans use pentagrams. So do Mormons and Freemasons. It's part of the Seal of Solomon, the African

Serer Religion, the national flags of Morocco and Ethiopia, all of which have no relationship to The Code.

Then Lenore hit on a vivid link to something tangible. She started connecting dots. Sitting in the Velvet Room, she figured that if The Code was in anyway real, if it had true power, it might be revealed in ancient mystical writings. The Department of Philosophy and Religion had been major contributors to that area, having deposited a slew of ancient books over the years.

For one entire weekend, Lenore plowed through dozens of books. It was a long and tedious task that seemed to be futile. She was ready to give up when, lo, there it was, the needle in the haystack: an ancient medieval text that had been translated from Latin to English in the sixteenth century.

Almost everything she wanted to know about The Code—its underlying beliefs, its rituals, its practices—was there. At last she had a solid description. If what she read was to be believed, it was indeed a form of alchemy. But unlike alchemy where common elements such as lead are transmuted into gold, this form gave the practitioners glimpses of the future into any area they wanted.

Exactly how this occurred and where the power came from was not readily evident. Perhaps its origins were seated somewhere deep in the universe in some essential network in which time was sorted into the past, the present, and the future. By using The Code, it was possible to dissociate those in such a way that the future could be separated out and viewed from the present.

Simply put, it was this: we know that the past and the present are easily understood. We live with knowledge of the past, knowledge of our own past at least, and we witness the present each day, moment by moment. According to what Lenore learned, the future exists but is kept separate from the past and present. It is impossible to experience the future in the present. The reason is simple. If highly intelligent creatures could perceive the future, it would thrust their lives into perpetual chaos. Every choice, every movement, every decision would be calculated according to the pending inevitable outcome. They would become paralyzed in their choices, unable to move forward. But with The Code, it was possible to catch brief glimpses of the future, if just the right techniques were applied.

The Code required a minimum of two persons but could involve as many as ten. Long black robes were to be worn. One person acting as high priest would lead The Code. Thirteen candles were to be lit in the room, the first nine Stations of the Cross were to be attached to the walls. The high priest would lead the group past Stations of the Cross, starting with the ninth and going backwards to the first. One person, always a female, would lie naked on a marble slab onto which a black silk sheet had been spread. The priest would chant the sacred words of The Code in a ritualistic monotone. The woman on the table would drink a potion from a gold chalice. She would slip into a trance. The ritual must take place underground in a room with a five-pointed star on the floor, creating a pentacle, a connection between the Earth and other planets of the solar system and the universe. There were only two nights a month—the nights of the quarter moons—when The Code could be conducted.

All in all, the information left Lenore with a good feeling. She felt that she had cracked part of The Code puzzle. It was a good beginning, but it was far from complete. What was in the potion? How did they make it? Was it some weird ancient concoction that could not be replicated? What were the words that were to be chanted? Lacking those basic components of The Code, how could they conduct it?

And most importantly, how much of this was nothing but pure hocus-pocus? Medieval texts are jam-packed with nonsense, even Lenore knew this. She sat in a chair in the Velvet Room and looked up at the ceiling, thinking, wondering. She was not a person who bought into silliness. She liked her world to be predictable. Predictable and as surprise-free as possible. She never read horoscopes, never went to fortune tellers, never used tarot cards. She would laugh—almost mockingly—when her own sister partook in those things.

But...but let's just imagine there is a glimmer of truth to The Code, she thought. The quiet, undisturbed peacefulness of the Velvet Room allowed her to follow that thought for a long while. Would it be possible for her, Sam and her, to use it for financial gain? How perfect! When you came down to it, that's all Lenore cared about anyway. Manipulating money had been her passion for her entire adult life. She had no desire to be an artist, a scientist, a lawyer, a doctor, a butcher, a baker, a candlestick maker. Well, candlestick maker maybe. But it was financial management that thrilled her.

She picked the book up again and read on. There it was. The description of the potion—a simple uncomplicated mixture consisting of a tiny amount of dry chicken bone ground to a powder with a mortar and pestle, some Italian dolcetto wine, and a drop of blood from the woman's finger. All mixed together, the woman would drink it and spread out, naked, on the silk sheet. The thirteen candles were extinguished one by one until only a single candle was left burning. Warm wax was taken from the candle and rubbed across the palms and the top of the feet of the woman on the altar. The potion and the chanting caused her to go into a trance. While in the trance, a black cross was passed over the table. If all went well, if The Code worked correctly, short convulsive surges would shoot through her and she would gradually awaken. The chanting by the priest would begin again and the woman on the altar would recover from the trance, sit up, climb off the altar, and dress in her black robe.

Nothing unusual would happen to her until several days later when a short vision of the future would appear to the woman.

Lenore made a quick outline of what was needed for The Code, stuffed it in her purse, and placed the book back on the shelf.

10

Lenore convinces Sam that The Code is worth a try

Now Lenore had enough information to bring it to Sam without appearing to have lost all of her marbles—a few maybe, but not all of them. It would still be tricky though. Her longtime friend was even more practical than she was. He was not superstitious, not a gambler, never bet on sports, the horses, or the greyhounds. Though he was not averse to taking a calculated risk on an investment, he wanted to make every possible assessment of it before he dove in—chance or luck had nothing to do with it. His view was that if an investment went south, it was from poor planning, something that had slipped past them, occasionally from circumstances beyond their control, whether natural or man-made. A sudden skirmish in the Middle East that blasted the price of oil into the stratosphere, for example.

"Ah, we're back to this again, I see," Sam said as Lenore sat across from him and described the details of The Code.

Lenore ignored Sam's grumbling. "I think I have it figured out. I got all the important details."

What Lenore didn't know, what she hadn't yet learned, was that there was a downside to The Code. And a big downside it was. Ho boy, was there ever! If it didn't go as planned, if it was botched in even the simplest way, something very dark and very dangerous would happen. Something that would be hard, perhaps impossible, to correct.

"I'm wondering if there's some way we could try this out," Lenore proposed.

Sam leaned on his elbows. "Good God, you're really serious, aren't you?"

Lenore shrugged and nodded, trying to sustain Sam's interest.

"So where would we do this Code thing of yours?"

"I'm not sure exactly. There are certain conditions that must be meet. We'd need a special room, and there are other details too." She didn't want to dole out all the specifics just yet. She was still selling the concept to Sam. She knew better than anyone how to do that. Let him nibble a little, like a bass testing the bait to see if it's real or not before going for it hook and all.

Sam listened as Lenore unraveled her idea. It *was* cockamamie, to be sure. It made about as much sense as calling tuna fish chicken of the sea.

The major impediment would be finding an appropriate place to conduct The Code. They could create a place, build an underground room to the right specs. That wouldn't be a problem, but it didn't seem to fit the bill.

Then came a suggestion that surprised even Sam himself; he suggested to Lenore that they consider using Graebner. He had heard years before from Clara Parker about an old passage and staircase in the library. Parker knew little about it. It had been closed long before she took the helm at the school and there had been no reason for her to reopen it.

Lenore's jaw dropped. It sounded perfect. Still, someone was needed to approach Parker for permission to poke around below the library, and that someone could only be Sam. Only Sam had the kind of relationship that would permit him to float an idea as bizarre as this past Parker.

Lenore came up with a strategy. "Don't tell her what it's for. The less she knows the better. What you do is say: 'Clara, I need a favor. Sort of a screwy favor but a favor nonetheless.' Tell her we'll do all the work and that we just need her approval to let us do a little snooping and excavating in the library."

"Good God, Lenore. I can't do that!"

"Why not?"

"Because she's gonna ask why I want to do it, that's why, and then what do I say? 'Well, Clara dear, it's none of your damn business.'" Sam tapped his fingers anxiously on his desk.

For a moment Lenore was without an answer. She was thinking fast, not wanting the air to fizzle out of this balloon just when it was beginning to float. But Sam was right, what *would* he say? "She owes you a favor, doesn't she?" Lenore tried.

"She owes me a lot of favors, but she's not the type of person you try to bamboozle. There has to be a reason. Something legitimate, something besides we're trying to predict the future and make a ton of money and we thought—"

"That's it then, tell her there's a lot of good stuff in it for her. Parker's all about money, isn't she? No need to give her details, not now anyway—not ever probably."

Sam sat quietly and gave Lenore a 'you really expect me to go in and do that' look.

"Saaam—" Lenore said.

He held the palm of his hand toward her. "Just a minute, my dear, this is going to require some time. A *lot* of time to think it through."

11

Sam gets permission from Clara Parker to explore the depths of the old library

Sam did indeed think about it. For weeks, he did. Crazy as it was, he found himself wondering if Lenore's idea had some merit. Logically, they had nothing to lose as he saw it. It sounded harmless, almost like playing *Dungeons and Dragons* or some other adolescent game his kids once messed with. Of course, normally he wouldn't waste a minute on that crap, but he found himself becoming sucked into the whole concept the way great scientific minds in the middle ages had been lured to the idea of changing base elements into gold.

Then one day the opportunity arrived to pass Lenore's request to Clara Parker. Parker had contacted Sam's office and had set up time for a visit. Sam knew damn well what was on Parker's mind. She needed money—a lot of money—to finish the new stadium, a project that had come to a standstill due to cost overruns.

The Graebner Board of Trustees was on Parker's ass to get it finished. It was a good time for Sam to come to Parker's aid for many reasons, not the least of which was that Sam needed help on taxes for WSA and a hefty donation to the college would fit the bill perfectly. One hand does indeed wash the other!

Sam met with Parker and listened sympathetically to her pitch. For about seven million, they could wrap the stadium project up, Parker told him. It would be finished as planned, and Parker was even willing to slap the Whitney name on it.

"Just think about it: The Sam Whitney Stadium. Or The Sam Whitney Colosseum. That's even more impressive. Has a ring to it, doesn't it?" Parker said. Sam rejected this outright. First off, it wasn't all Sam's money they were talking about. Second, any more brick and mortar with the Whitney name on it and they'd have to change the school to Whitney College.

Sam knew he could get the money for Parker in short order, so he took the chance to drop his favor of a small 'archeological dig' below the Graebner Library. Sam and his group would do all the work; there was no need to trouble Clara Parker with any of it.

To Sam's surprise, Parker agreed freely. "Just make sure you don't blow the place up or something," she said. "We're trying to erect buildings here, not demolish them," she added, happy to have a commitment of money from Sam.

Lenore was surprised when Sam told her about his meeting with Parker. "She didn't ask why you wanted to do it?" Lenore said, befuddled.

"Not a word."

"Why not?"

"Clara was a happy camper; she got the bucks she needed. You could tell a heavy load had been lifted off her. I don't think she gave a tinker's what we're planning to do. I'm not sure she even heard much of what I said. Cripes, at that point I could have said, 'Clara, old girl, screw the stadium, what this school needs right now is a real first-class flop house out there in the student union.'"

"Now we just need to do a little searching, that's all," Lenore said. "Somewhere in the library there must be—"

"A good architect will know in second, assuming there's anything there at all there in the library. And I know *just* the person to do it," Sam said. "Leave it to me, honey. Frank Cusimano, a friend of mine, is an architect."

12

Frank Cusimano finds the old entrance and the hidden stairs

Sam, Lenore, and Frank Cusimano stood outside the Graebner Library. "Wow, this here place is a real gem," he said, looking fondly at the gray and blue granite building as though it were his firstborn child. "It's stuff like this that gets me going in the morning." He walked to the cornerstone. "Eighteen hundred and four. Yep, this is the original structure from when they built it." He rubbed his hand across the date as he spoke. "We don't erect buildings like this anymore. Look at the garbage we build now. How much of it do you think will be around in a hundred years, let alone two hundred years?"

The trio walked around the perimeter of the building, Frank took notes as they went. When they got to the northwest corner, Frank stopped, looked closely at the wall, then backed off and viewed it from twenty feet. "If I had to bet, I'd say that spot there was once an entrance." He pointed out the difference in the stones—the older original ones and the newer ones.

"Could have fooled me," Sam remarked.

"We'll know in a minute," Frank said.

They went around to the north end and entered the building and started up the staircase to the second floor.

Halfway up the stairs Frank stopped and said, "This is a no-brainer. These stairs were put in after the building went up. A hundred years or so after. Definitely not from day one, that's for sure. That you can tell immediately. But not bad actually, nice solid stairs. They did a good job. And nice wrought-iron railing too. Pretty...real pretty, but not original motif. But pretty just the same. It's the kind of thing they used at the turn of the century. Along about nineteen hundred or so. That's how you know these are not original."

Frank walked down the second-floor corridor sizing it up. "There we go, see that there, that there's the dead space I was talking about." He pointed to the northwest corner. "If you weren't looking for it, you'd never know, would you?"

"If you weren't an architect, you'd never know," Lenore said.

"Right smack where the old entrance had been. The one we saw outside the building."

They climbed the stairs to the third floor. Frank headed directly to the reading room—the only room on the northwest corner of the building. The room was empty of students and faculty. Frank walked along the wall, tapping a knuckle on the wood panels and bookcases. When he arrived at the corner, the sound changed. It was obvious to everyone. "There she be," he said proudly. "Nothing behind this panel but a whole lotta dusty air."

"No way!" Sam exclaimed.

"Way," Frank replied. "Nickel ninety-eight says that's where the old stairs are. They closed them off and slapped a nice sheet of real pretty mahogany up, same as the rest of the walls here, and put in new set of stairs out there in the hall."

"Why the heck would they do that?" Lenore asked.

"Million reasons. The stairs might have been unsafe maybe. Or maybe they were too narrow for the library once the school grew and more students started using them. Not all that strange, really. Show me a building on this campus that hasn't been fiddled with somehow. Schools grow and change, buildings grow and change." He looked around the reading room. "Just be glad they didn't decide to tear the whole place down and start over," he said, shuddering. "Imagine what that would look like. Let me guess, lots of tinny metal bookshelves, flagstone on the outside. Pretty gross, huh?"

With Clara Parker's permission, Sam and Lenore had the wood panel removed and reattached with a set of hinges and a latch. Clara was informed of their success but quickly lost interest in the details. All she knew was that Sam and Lenore were planning to use the passage periodically, and that it was tied into The Code thing that Sam had mentioned to her. The less she knew, the happier she was.

Only once did she go with Sam to see what they had found. He opened the panel. Parker stepped halfway inside, looked around, and said, "It's all yours, guys," then promptly turned and left. As far as Clara was concerned, Sam was a businessman *par excellence*. So long as a large bolus of his money periodically flowed over to Graebner, a happy camper she was indeed.

Part II

Perfect Alignment

1

Sam and Lenore perform the first Code

Whether Sam Whitney had as much faith in The Code as Lenore did didn't matter, for the moment he was committed to the whole scheme. But, of course, proof of the pudding is in the eating. If The Code worked, they would know soon enough.

Shortly after the panel door had been attached, Sam and Lenore made their first visit inside. Just as Nick and Katy subsequently found, Sam and Lenore came upon a series of long dark passages with candle holders attached to the walls, an altar chamber with arcane words inscribed above the door, a marble altar slab, and bizarre Stations of the Cross and an upside-down cross hanging lifelessly over the altar. Everything exactly as it had been left from the days of Schulenmeister Seminary a century and a half before.

There was a certain validation for Lenore standing in the altar chamber, even though they had yet to perform a single Code ceremony. Everything in the room fit the bill from what she had learned about it so far, from the various books she had read. In the days of Schulenmeister—whatever The Code had yielded back then, for better or worse—must have come from this one dark and mysterious place.

As they stood in the room, barely bigger than a good-sized mausoleum and feeling much like one, Sam and Lenore discussed The Code. It would be conducted with just the two of them, the absolute minimum needed. No point in trying to hunt up others—a difficult task at best, though it could be done using a few diehard friends Lenore had going back to her college days. The kinds of friends that would do anything for her no matter how weird or bizarre.

The last piece of the puzzle came when Lenore discovered the words of the sacred chant. After numerous visits to the Velvet Room, paging through dozens of books, she came across a detailed description. The Latin words read:

Ex sol solis quod luna
Mus adveho vox
Video vidi visum plurimus videlicet
Tunc muto quis ero nuto

Translated, they said:

From the Sun and the Moon
Will come the power
To see the most it is clear
And then to change what will be known

Lenore scribbled them onto a piece of paper.

The night before the quarter moon, Sam and Lenore held a pow wow in his office to go over the ceremony. Lenore would bring the robes, the dolcetto wine, a needle for the pin prick for the blood, a dry chicken bone, and the mortar and pestle for grinding the bone.

"The library will be vacant at one o'clock tomorrow night. You know how to turn the alarm off and then reset it when we leave, right?" she asked.

"How long will this take?"

Lenore shrugged. "Not sure. No details in the books on that. If I were to guess, an hour or so."

The Code was now real. Something more than idle talk. Something more than a foolish half-baked joke.

At precisely two a.m., Sam unlocked the main gate to the library, opened the door, and quickly deactivated the alarm. They went up the stairs to the reading room. Sam opened the panel door. They proceeded down into the altar chamber, lighting a few candles along the way as they went. The flickering of the flames sent shimmering light across the walls and ceiling. They moved slowly along, Sam in front, Lenore behind. In the chamber, Lenore stripped and pulled the black robe over her. Sam covered himself with a robe and lit thirteen candles—the light cut sparingly through the gray-mustard darkness.

Sam removed the black cross from the hook over the altar. Probably the same cross that had been used more than a hundred years ago in the days of Schulenmeister. They passed by the nine Stations of the Cross, stopping briefly at each. In the Catholic Church, the first nine narrate the condemnation of Jesus and the events up to the time he meets the women of Jerusalem. The remaining five stations, the omitted ones, describe the crucifixion and death of Christ, his removal from the cross, and the placement of his body in the tomb. The Code participants were required to pass in front of each station counterclockwise, as if retracing the events leading up to the crucifixion in reverse order.

Sam filled the chalice with a small amount of dolcetto wine. He took a piece of bone and ground it into a fine powder with a mortar and pestle and added a pinch of it to the wine. Lenore passed a clean needle across a flame and pricked her fingertip, allowing a drop of blood to drip into the chalice. She gave the concoction a small swirl, removed her robe, and stood naked in front of the altar, looking much as Sam remembered her from years past.

She spread her robe over the altar. Sam handed her the chalice. Holding it gently in front of her for a second, she carefully drank the potion and climbed onto the altar. Sam extinguished all the candles but one. Wax from the remaining candle was rubbed across her palms and the top of her feet. Holding the black cross over her, Sam began chanting in a slow rhythmic monotone, repeating the sacred verse over and over.

Almost immediately—uncontrollably and peacefully—Lenore's eyes slipped shut. An odd presence fell over the room, as though someone, something, had entered. Presently, Lenore began to tremble, slightly at first, then intensely. Her head tilted far back. Her shoulders arched out. Her legs stiffened. Suddenly, her body went into a series of short convulsive seizures. Ten seconds, fifteen seconds, thirty seconds. The seizures stopped. Five minutes passed.

She slowly opened her eyes and stared at the ceiling above her, naked and motionless on the stone altar, almost immobilized. Her hand moved deliberately to her forehead and across her hair. She let out a soft murmur and sat up. She swung her feet slowly over the altar facing him, then climbed into the robe and let it fall to her ankles. She was exhausted, drained, and invigorated. As though coming out of an intense dream.

In the sheer silence of the room, there was no way of knowing what they might have accomplished. It was any fool's guess. The paraphernalia—the chalice, the wine, and the bone—were gathered and carefully returned to the basket she had brought with her. Lenore got dressed and they worked their way up the stairs, extinguishing candles along the way. By three-thirty, they were out of the building.

2

What the first Code reveals

The next evening, Sam and Lenore were in THE CEO, an upscale martini bar in downtown Covington where company execs and top business people collected. They sat at a corner table, each with a single malt served neat.

"While we're it," Lenore said, speaking low. Sam pulled closer to the table. "Last night, you know when I was in the trance thing. Something strange happened. I had this weird surreal vision. Well, not really a vision, just a couple of words actually, as if they were written in front of me in red letters on a black canvas. They said, Red Rover, Red Rover. And then after a second I heard this voice repeating the words. A deep voice, creepy voice. It repeated the words several times: Red Rover, Red Rover. I remember this vividly. And then…then that's when I woke up. Like coming out of anesthesia after surgery or something."

Sam wrapped his hand around his glass and tapped a finger slowly on the side and thought for a second. "Well, personally, I wouldn't make much of it." He shrugged and said, "What's it mean? Nothing, far as I'm concerned."

Lenore looked around to see who was nearby. The room was quiet, conversations were easily overheard. They made a visit to THE CEO at least once a week, new the whole crowd well. She leaned forward until she was almost nose to nose with Sam. "If nothing else, it tells me this whole Code thing is real, I men *real*." Lenore said. "Damn real. Not just a bunch of mumbo-jumbo that I came across in an old book stuffed away on the library shelf."

Sam was far from convinced. "Not so fast, my dear," he said. He pointed out that despite what happened, they had yet to make a nickel off their late-night adventure.

The next day, and for three days after, Sam and Lenore went systematically about their business. They kept to their routines and their appointments and their schedules without variation or change, not sure what to expect from The Code. Their goal, of course, was to find ways to buy and sell before the horde of gambling idiots, the traders—professional and amateur—who place spastically conceived bets that drive stock prices chaotically up and down. With the help of The Code, Sam and Lenore would do this safely and calmly before a specific investment tempest arrived. So they hoped.

The trick was to know when to make their move and on what. Where would the information come from? Not likely to have a FedEx letter delivered that said, "Hey Sammy boy, here are a couple of gems to pile into your stock portfolio. Or a couple of rotten eggs to get rid of immediately."

But, yes, the message did arrive. It came in the form of a dream that Lenore had early in the morning, just before dawn. A strange dream in which the words "Red Rover, Red Rover" were repeated again and again as the word "Buratec" was emblazoned in red gothic letters on a garishly bright white wall.

Lenore came ripping into Sam's office at nine thirty that morning. She snatched the yellow legal pad from his desk and scribbled the word Buratec across the page in huge letters.

Sam looked at it, then at her, then at the word again.
"What's that?" he said.
"A stock! Buy it!"

Sam punched the word into his computer. A brief description of the company came up. It was a small biotech situated outside San Jose, California. Sam read the details aloud. "Profile: cancer research, anti-inflammatory drugs, autoimmunity, bioengineering." He skipped down. "The company has a variety of proprietary drugs used for…uhm, uhm…vaccine delivery systems, whatever *that* is…cancer research, other stuff." He looked up at Lenore. "That's about all it says. Selling for $3.46 a share."

"Buy it. Buy a ton of it," Lenore raged.
Sam aimed an obsidian eye at her. "Buy how much?"
"How many shares, you mean? A half million."

"You are *not* serious!" He made a calculation on his computer. "That's one million seven hundred and twenty-five thousand dollars," he said, looking at Lenore again.

"Yes, yes...buy it!"

Sam sat, dumbfounded.

"Sam, for Christ's sake, buy it!" Lenore said, all but ordering him. She walked smartly across the room and back and said, "That was the plan, big boy. Wasn't it?"

Sam groaned. "The plan, my dear, was to try out this Code thing and—"

"And we did, Sam. We did and that's what we got." She aimed a finger at the computer screen.

"Where in the plan did it say to dump almost two million dollars on some totally obscure stock? Why can't we just try it out? Ten K, for example. Give that a try and see what happens?"

"I don't normally get my head sprinkled with the names of weird little stocks I've never heard of, Sam. There's only one explanation, and that explanation is that it came to me because of The Code. It had to."

Sam pondered this. "And so, exactly how did *we* get it, this information of yours?"

"In a dream."

Sam stood up and leaned on his desk. "You must be kidding. In a dream!"

"Yes, in a dream, so what?"

"Come on, Lenore. I have dreams all the time. Crazy dreams. Stupid dreams. The sky is falling, I'm being chased by pterodactyls, the world's coming to an end—"

"So do I. But those are different."

"Let's get this straight. You want us to spend a million and three-quarter bucks on a company like this? A company that we know nothing about? A company that—"

"The plan was to use the information from The Code and then to go with it. If you don't trust the information you get, then what's the point? That was the plan."

"*Au contraire*, my dear. The plan was to test out The Code and see what came of it."

"*We did*. And now we know."

Sam rubbed his hand through his hair. "Augh," he groaned, staring at the computer screen.

"Do it, Sam."

"Do it, Sam? I thought it's supposed to be, play it Sam."

"Sam, just do it," Lenore said impatiently.

The on-line stock purchase page stared at him as if waiting to be used. He looked up the stock number for Buratec, entered five hundred thousand shares, and made one last check with Lenore. She didn't flinch.

"Here goes, honey." He pushed the purchase button. Instantly, they now owned a half million shares of Buratec. For better or for worse. Sam watched the price of the stock on the screen. It didn't change a fraction.

"Time for an early lunch and a *real* dry martini to soothe my frazzled nerves," Sam said. He grabbed his suit coat and the black felt hat he wore in the winter. They headed for the door. "Let's go. I can't bear to watch this," he groused.

Lenore pulled her Lexus in front of The Colonial Inn, a B&B with a terrific restaurant. They had a simple light lunch. Sam nursed his nerves with a couple of martinis. It was a good two hours before they returned to the office.

Sam sat at his desk and opened the computer to the list of stocks. Lenore was heading over to her office when she heard Sam call her back. "Lenore, hang on...hang on. Come here."

She turned and looked at Sam. He signaled with a finger to take a look. The price of Buratec had soared to $19.78 a share. The value of their purchase had risen from a million and three quarters to just under ten million in a couple of hours—they had made nearly eight and a half million dollars.

"What happened?" Lenore said, barely able to speak.

Sam searched for details. There it was. Buratec, the small insignificant California biotech company, had just released the findings from its phase-three trial on their melanoma cancer treatment drug. It had a highly significant beneficial effect compared to the placebo group—a p-value of 0.0001—meaning that the difference between the treatment and the placebo group could be accounted for by random chance only once if the entire study were to be repeated ten thousand times. Next to impossible. The stock was going crazy, and Sam and Lenore owned a load of it.

They watched the price climb throughout the rest of the day until the exchange closed. It hit $21.34 a share for a final value of ten and a half million dollars from the half million shares they bought. The big question now was what to do? Sell or hold?

"We could dump it now and take home a barrel of money," Sam said. "That's for sure. According to our investment 'rules,'" he made a pair of air quotes with his fingers, "we never hang onto a stock that goes this high this quick. Never! We unload and cash in. Who knows, tomorrow it could be back at three and a half. We can put it up for sale now. It will get snapped up in a second for sure."

Lenore, by far the most conservative investor of the two, the one who would normally make a statement like that, argued against it. "Hang on to it," she said unwaveringly. "The Code got us this far."

"The Code told us to buy Buratec, it did not tell us when to sell it. That's up to us."

"Maybe, maybe not. I say we hold."

Sam moaned. "And piss away nearly ten million great big George Washingtons just like that?"

Lenore wasn't as sure as she pretended to be—a bird in the hand and all that jive. But this time something told her to hang on. It was the same ethereal feeling that made her trust the dream about buying Buratec in the first place. She had never even heard of Buratec. Who would have unless you putz around with small-cap biotech stocks?

Sam fumbled nervously with his hands. "Let's go. I need a scotch, a very good scotch…an Edradour."

They went to THE CEO and sat at the bar talking things out. Lenore looked great in the dimmed pub light that made everyone look a notch or two better than they did elsewhere. Her face was brown from her visits to the tanning booth. Her teeth had been cosmetically whitened chiclets as the dentists call them. *Why is it that some women get sexier as they get older whereas others fizzle?* Sam wondered.

Sam picked up his glass, breathed in the musty-clean richness of the scotch, and took a sip. "No way I can believe any of what happened today had to do with The Code," he said flatly. "No way. It's been fun up to now—a crazy adventure. And if in the beginning I had to tell Clara Parker everything we're up to, if she had pressed me on it, I'd have backed off instantly. I like old Clara and she likes me, and I want to keep it that way. Up until now we've helped each other out in a lot of ways. Fact is, the only reason we were able to do The Code at all was because of her."

Lenore picked up a cashew from a bowl on the table and popped it into her mouth. "I say we hold onto the stock at least till the end of tomorrow. That's my recommendation. I know we're not in the 'easy come easy go' business, but this has turned into an experiment. We need to follow up and know where—how—to use the info from The Code. Need to know how reliable it is. We need some parameters or we won't be able to come back and try again. My brother, Matt, the scientist, always says the key to any experiment is its reproducibility. If you can't repeat it, it's useless."

That's how it went for several hours. As time wore on, Sam found himself unwittingly buying into Lenore's position. She was good at slowly and gently chipping away until she got what she wanted. She was no slouch at it. Still, this time she could have been pushed back by Sam, had he persisted. But he hadn't.

They remained at the bar until late, one Edradour after another. It should have been a moment of celebration, but Sam was worried. How often do you stumble onto ten and a half million in one day? They headed home. Neither slept much. Morning couldn't come quick enough.

At eight o'clock, the computer screen in Sam's office was tracking the performance of Buratec. Together they watched it as it continued to climb gradually but persistently upward until it hit $36.19. The value of their stocks had just climbed to slightly over eighteen million. Then it began to fall.

"That's it, time to dump this baby," Sam said nervously.

"People are peddling, that's all. They're cashing in. It'll head back up, just wait. No reason to panic."

"No reason to panic? Watch eighteen million go south and don't panic? Ha, ha!"

Twenty minutes went by. The stock picked up and again began to rise. It passed $36, the old high-water mark, and continued its push upward. They watched the screen, minute-by-minute through the entire day, not stopping for lunch or a break or to have a cup of coffee. At the close of trading, Buratec settled in at a couple cents over $41 a share. If they were to sell now, they would have slightly over twenty million from their original investment. But they didn't sell.

The next day, Buratec continued its climbed to $50, $60, and then $70 a share, finally slowing as it reached $76.55. Sam was in no mood for another long discussion about the stock. He reached for the mouse, aimed the cursor at the sell button, and pushed it. The stock was snatched up quickly. They had a whopping $38,275,000 on an initial investment of $1,775,000. Not bad for three days' work. Hard to call it work really. Wait and watch. No heavy lifting. Didn't break a sweat. Whatever the real source of the money, whether it was linked to The Code or not, didn't much matter now. A celebration was in order and celebrate they did. Dinner at Covington's one and only French restaurant.

3

The second Code

Life went on normally for the next several days. If anything, Lenore was more shocked than Sam that The Code had worked as perfectly and smoothly as it had. That was probably because Sam had yet to buy into the whole notion of The Code.

Their incredible success could have been nothing more than a fluke. Pure coincidence. Consider that the odds of being struck by lightning in the U.S. are about one in three hundred thousand. On average it happens to about a thousand people each year. Consider also that there are some five thousand stocks on the U.S. stock exchange. Hence, you have a better chance of picking a winning stock randomly than getting hit by lightning. Yet, every year some dimwit gets hit by a bolt of lightning and it has nothing to do with anything but bad luck. Or stupidity: walking around the golf course with an umbrella and a nine iron in the middle of a thunderstorm.

So, as Sam viewed it, the pile of money dumped on them had little if anything to do with Lenore's dream. It was a miraculous stroke of good luck, that's all. A once in a lifetime event that would never again be repeated.

The time of the next quarter moon was closing in fast. Did it make sense to try again, or was that pushing the envelope too far too fast? But money speaks—uh wait, no…money screams. What did they have to lose? This time they knew exactly what to do and how to do it.

The night was dark but not without light. Sam and Lenore approached the library just as the clock in the tower on top of the building hit two o'clock. Almost simultaneously they stopped and glanced momentarily at the quarter moon. White vaporous clouds slipped thinly past it. A lone student shuffled quickly along the path, uninterested, not looking at them. Lenore carried the sack with the robes and the necessary accoutrements of The Code. Sam checked and double-checked to make sure no one was nearby, then unlocked the gate to the library, opened the door and deactivated the alarm.

In less than ten minutes they were next to the altar, candles lit, wine poured. Sam prepared the sacred drink: the wine, the bone, the drop of blood. They passed in front of the nine Stations of the Cross and returned to the altar. Lenore removed her robe, set it on the altar, drank from the chalice, and lay naked on the altar. Sam held the cross over her and began chanting in the dim light from a single candle. The Code came off without a hitch. Now there was nothing to do but wait.

This time a full ten days passed without so much as a suggestion, a glimpse, into what the future might hold. Lenore's dreams were as ordinary as Wheaties. Nothing unusual. The ones where you're being chased by Quasimodo and your feet are as heavy as lead and he's gaining on you, those and tons of other off-the-rack dreams.

Then finally, at last, it arrived. She awoke one morning and scribbled the name Trimenium on a piece of paper next to the bed. It was a company she was familiar with. A big company, telecommunication, well-known, solid as a rock, and WSA held a load of stock in it. She leaped out of bed, jumped in the shower, had a quick bowl of Wheaties, and was out the door.

By the time she arrived at the office, Sam, the early bird, was there checking stocks and scribbling numbers on his yellow pad. She came in nearly panting.

Sam looked at the panic in her face, said nothing, waited.

Lenore called, "Trimenium, sell, sell, sell."

"Sell? That's a blue-chip, honey," Sam said wryly. "Don't you mean buy, buy, buy?"

"No Sam, I mean exactly what I said. Sell the bugger as fast as you can. There's no time to waste."

Sam knew the stock very well. It had been growing like Jack's beanstalk. "We've made a barrel of money off Trimenium," he declared, "and it's continuing to rise." He watched Lenore, saw the urgency plastered all over her face.

"Dump it, Sam! Dump it! Get rid of it!"

"Another dream?" Sam asked.

"Oh, screw it, Sam. Forget about that, just sell the damn thing."

This time Sam was far more pliable. The success with The Code the first time around made him reluctant to intervene. He gasped low and slow then pulled the stock up on his computer.

"Sell how much?"

"Well, all of it for Christ's sake."

Sam stared at her. "Nnnooo…kay." The button was pushed. The stock went up for sale. In less than a minute it was gobbled up. They had made a nice chunk of money off it. Close to five million probably since they had acquired it not long ago. But as Sam saw it, it still had a great future and there was no reason to unload. Its prospectus was positive. The company was solid.

For thirty-five minutes he watched the stock on the computer, periodically giving Lenore a string of 'nice going, Dearie' looks. The stock sat there; nothing happened. *So much for the Code and Lenore's dreams!*

Sam got up and walked to the wall of windows of his twenty-second-story office, hands in his pockets, and looked distractedly over Covington's small downtown, the cluster of houses out beyond, the rolling hills and farmland in the far distance, brooding in complete silence. He returned to the computer. Immediately, his eyes locked onto the screen, his forehead wrinkled. "What…the…?" he uttered softly.

Lenore slouched in a chair across from Sam. She watched, saying nothing. Best to let the news—the good, the bad, whatever it was—come from him. *Let me guess,* she thought, *the stock just soared. Yes, soared through the damn roof or something: eight, ten, twenty points in just a few minutes. Something like that.* The look on Sam's face revealed nothing. *Nice trick you played on us, dear Code, nice trick,* Lenore thought.

Sam leaned back in his kid-leather executive chair. "*Holy moly*," he muttered with a baffled look directed at Lenore. "Sucker just took a *huge* nose-dive. Five points just like that. No warning, nothing." Sam searched the internet to see what had happened. There it was, Trimenium had had a bad—no, make that disastrous—third quarter. The stock tumbled. Had Sam and Lenore held on to it, they would have lost a pretty hefty chunk of money; everything they had gained from it in the past several months, close to five million dollars, would have vanished. Not that WSA couldn't weather a storm like that, but it was a real crash landing for what seemed like a darn good stock.

Did Sam trust The Code now? Probably. Did Lenore? Probably too. Hard to fight with success. For some reason, the second success from The Code was even more convincing than the first, despite the lower cash-value of the reward. Selling stocks, figuring out when to, can be a huge dilemma, especially when everything is going along fine.

4

Another Code and some troubling information

Now the question was: should they continue with The Code at every opportunity, which of course meant every two weeks? They talked it over. Picked apart the reasons for, the reasons against. There weren't many against. Nothing had gone wrong and there was no expectation that it would. The worst that could happen would be a total misfire in which nothing turned up—shooting blanks and ending up buying a stock that was a dud.

They conducted The Code exactly as before. Afterwards, Lenore waited for the fateful dream. But this time it never arrived. Instead, the vision came in the form of a short but clear image that burst onto her thoughts in the middle of the day as she worked quietly and diligently at her desk. When it arrived, she shook her head as if to erase the strangeness of it from her thoughts. But the image flashed a second time.

She closed her eyes and pressed her thumbs and fingertips to her forehead. The hazy picture in her mind sharpened. A car. Her sister Jessica. Another car. A dreaded chill whipped through Lenore's body. She reached for the phone on her desk and called Jessica.

"Jessie, it's Lennie. Are you okay? Is everything all right?

Jessica laughed. It was instantly clear to Lenore that all was fine.

Lenore gasped and leaned back in her chair. "Oh, thank you, thank you, thank you."

"I'm fine, Lennie. Why, what's going on?" Jessica said.

Lenore had no intention of mentioning The Code. Besides, if Lenore was worried that something had happened to Jessica, she would almost have known instantly. They were two years apart in age and had been peas in a pod their whole life. For one to pick up on the other's feelings was not the least bit unusual. From the time they were children, they could sense each other's fears and worries.

They talked and laughed for half an hour. Lenore asked how Jessica's kids were, how Howard, her husband, was. Jessica probed briefly into Lenore's occasionally racy life, which Lenore never advertised, though a detail or two leaked out when the two of them were talking privately. They both harbored inner jealousies of the other. Lenore for Jessica's seemingly perfect marriage. Jessica for Lenore's heady professional life, money galore, the way she buzzed off to vacations on St. Bart's and other exotic destinations. Her flirtatious character. A personality that teemed with quiet sensuality.

After the phone call, Lenore sat alone in her office. Was she paying too much attention to The Code, waiting for something to happen? Lots needed to be clarified if they were to continue with it. That she believed firmly. Perhaps they had gotten lucky twice. More to the point, there was no guarantee that the revelations would be focused on *their* goal: money making. Maybe it would have to do with a tsunami heading for Indonesia, a tornado in Oklahoma, pending FDA recalls of aflatoxin tainted peanut butter. So what! Could she stop a tsunami or a tornado? She detested peanut butter. She didn't know much about the National Weather Service, but you could bet they had their share of crank calls from the end-time crowd claiming the sky is falling.

Sam had left at mid-morning for an overnight trip to New York. He would be back the next day. Lenore plodded lackadaisically through a block of investment portfolios for several hours until she had had enough. She would leave early, stop at THE CEO by herself, and who knows, maybe strike up a conversation with some hunk. Her last serious relationship had been several years ago.

She shut down her computer and headed for the door just as the phone on her desk rang. *Tomorrow, tomorrow*, she thought. *Leave a damn message, I'll get it tomorrow. Augh! All right, all right, all right, take it easy, I'm coming.* She went over and put the receiver to her ear. "Lenore Simenson," she said.

"Lennie, Howard here," came a fast reply. "It's Jessie. Her car got T-boned this afternoon. Some asshole ran a light."

"Oh my God!" Lenore moaned. "Is she…is she—"

"Yes, yes, yes, she's okay. He did a job on her left arm though. They took her to the OR to fix it. Doc says all in all it will probably be fine. She'll need some time to heal and then some therapy too. I'm calling from the hospital here in Tucson. They're keeping her overnight."

"Should I come?"

"No, no point. I mean, she's gonna to be okay. By the time you got here from Vermont and all it'd be—"

Lenore rested her forehead on her hand. "Did she tell you I talked to her today?"

"She mentioned it when I saw her in the ER before they took her up to set her arm. Crazy, huh. Crazy coincidence."

Lenore didn't reply at first, then softly said, "Uh-huh, crazy."

"Everything's fine, I think," Howard said. "I just needed to let you know, of course."

"Oh, of course, of course. I mean, my God!" Lenore exhaled deeply. "Thanks, Howard. Well, you know how to reach me. I'll talk with Jessie first thing in the morning."

5

The change

Lenore Simenson needed a drink now more than ever. A martini as dry as the whole Sahara. She would go to THE CEO and try to sort things out. She left the office, climbed into her silver Lexus LS, and headed for the bar.

The fancy up-scale room was dimly lit by pale indirect lighting. It was Monday and the bar was nearly empty, a few early birds scattered about.

"How's it going?" Lenore asked Charlie, the bartender.

Charlie stood behind the bar, white shirt, black pants, black vest, black bowtie—somewhat of a penguin. "I'm at work," he replied, his eternal joke for his well-known patrons.

"Martini, extra, extra, extra dry."

"Coming right up, love. One of those days, huh?"

Lenore merely groaned.

Charlie pulled a bottle of Grey Goose off the shelf, poured a long stream into a cocktail mixer, added a drop of Vermouth, cubes, gave it a ten second stir, filtered it into a martini glass and added an olive. "Enjoy," he said.

Lenore gave Charlie a wink, then drew in a slow sip of the ice-cold vodka. "Aaah…good Lord," she droned. She sat quietly, contemplating the events of the day: her sister, The Code. A whole lot about it needed to be tweaked. They were flying blindfolded. True, each time—Buratec, Trimenium, and now her sister Jessie—The Code had yielded a clear vision. There was no doubt about that. She stared into the glass in front of her. The light from the room reflected off the clear liquid like off a crystal ball. She took another sip.

A young couple, vivacious and pretty, entered and sat a few chairs to her left. They ordered red wine and talked in a brisk happy voice. The clanging of their glasses in celebration of something rang gingerly through the room.

Before she knew it, Lenore had all but finished her drink.

"Hey, love…another one?" Charlie asked politely.
Lenore sighed. "Sure, Charlie. Why not?"

"Coming your way." He set the drink in front of her, shuffled through a stack of CDs, and slipped Bob Mamet into the player.

A surgical foursome in gray scrubs rolled in after a shift at a nearby hospital. Lenore knew them all; she managed their portfolios. Billy Chang, the Porsche-driving anesthesiologist with the PASN GAS vanities on the front and back of his Carrera, puttered over.

"Lenooore, so good to seeee you," he said with one of his happy-go-lucky laughs. He gave a hug and a kiss. "Whaa? No Sammy tuh-nigh?"

Lenore shook her head and said, "No Sammy tonight, Billy."

"Well, you have fun anyways," he said, sparking a big grin and a wide smile as he headed to his group at a table by the window.

She continued to think about The Code. Was it really a great idea? What if they learned something they didn't want to know? Not about tsunamis or tornadoes or peanut butter recalls, but that something truly nasty was about to happen to *themselves*. Sam and Lenore hadn't considered that, had they? The situation with Jessie was too close for comfort. It harked to that old question: if we could find out when and how we were going to die, would we want to know? Of course, everyday people all over the world are delivered such information—perhaps told they have cancer, given a timeline of what to expect. Told to prepare the bucket list. But if we were to find out that, in the near future, maybe next week, maybe the week after, the end was coming, then what? What do we do with such devastating information? Suppose nothing could be done to stop it. It was a morbid thought, and it was beginning to wear on Lenore as she sipped her martini.

She needed to clear the thoughts from her mind, someone to talk to would help. She glanced furtively around the bar. It didn't look promising.

Just then, three gregarious young men in their late twenties or early thirties entered THE CEO. They sat at the bar next to Lenore. The one closest to her gave a smile and a nod. Lenore returned the gesture, projecting coy indifference.

Bet I look like garbage, she thought. If what had been running through her head for the past thirty minutes was any reflection of how she appeared…*pa-leez!* She took her purse and strolled casually to the lady's room and held her face close to the mirror. The harsh light did her no favors, but all in all it was not a total disaster, not by a long shot. *Still pretty good for forty-four,* she thought. A few crow's feet fanned out from the ends of her eyes. Her chin and neck were tight, and all without going under the knife. None of that shrink-wrap stuff for her. Her dress was just right for THE CEO. Black, above the knees. Perfectly fitted at the hips. Soft and silky looking. She combed her hair, fluffed it, and touched up her lipstick.

When she returned to the bar, another ice-cold Grey Goose was waiting for her. Charlie shrugged. He gave his head a tilt to the side indicating that it was a gift from her neighbor to the right.

"Wes," the man said. He raised his glass an inch off the bar. "*À votre santé.*"

"*À votre santé,*" Lenore replied, raising her glass.

"I think I've seen you here before," Wes said.

Boy was that a sad version of a stale old line, or what? But it worked and it fetched a friendly smile from Lenore. "I don't know…maybe." *This is Covington, Vermont, for Pete's sake, not mid-town Manhattan. Yes, he probably has seen me here before.*

They talked, the usual blather it takes to get a conversation going. Where are you from? What do you do? Lenore had no desire to reveal much to a total stranger. The better part of an hour went by. Wes's friends wanted to head out, to get into someplace where the odds were better, where something good might happen. Wes stayed, hoping his odds were good where he was. Lenore was beginning to feel better.

The surgeons were laughing and talking shop. Bones and blood.

.

6

Lenore expresses concern about The Code

It was mid-morning when Lenore strolled into work. She had spent forty-five minutes talking to her sister from home. Everything was going to be all right. The bone in her arm had been repaired with minimal manipulation.

Sam had just returned from his trip to New York when Lenore walked into his office. "How's it going?" he asked rhetorically, reaching into his briefcase and pulling out files.

"Sam, I think it's time we called a halt to The Code for a while," Lenore said.

Sam quit shuffling papers and looked up. "The Code. What's wrong with The Code? Seemed to be working swimmingly to me."

That was a phrase she hadn't heard in a long time. "Yeah, swimmingly indeed. Maybe *too* swimmingly." She went into the details of what had happened with her sister.

Sam sat in his chair, listening carefully. He got up and went to the windows and stared out for quite a while, pondering, as he always did when he needed a moment to think. He chewed on his lower lip. A habit he had picked up after he quit smoking. He did it to buy time the same as when he would pull a pack of butts from his breast pocket and light one up.

He turned and looked at Lenore. "You don't really know it had to do with The Code. You and Jessie are like this." He held his hand up with two fingers wrapped together. "You told me that a thousand times."

"This is different, Sam. It wasn't some vague premonition or hunch. I had a vision. A vivid vision. I saw all of it. And it wasn't in a hazy dream in the middle of the night. It flashed into my mind in the middle of the day. Right there in my office down the hall."

Sam said nothing.

"I spent a lot of time thinking about this yesterday. There's so much about The Code we know nothing about. I'm worried. *Real* worried."

"It paid off well so far. Damn well!" Sam was no longer the doubter.

"Twice…just twice, Sam. What's missing is that we don't know how to focus this Code thing. How to get it to do what *we* want. We need more details."

"And exactly how do you expect to get more details? Everything you learned so far came from some ancient book in the library over at Graebner. Now what?"

Lenore had no cogent answer. "So I go back and find out what else there is. If I could just get info about how to aim it, to direct it, I'd feel a helluva lot better. A *helluva* lot better."

This was not what Sam wanted to hear. Another Code night was fast arriving, and his plans were to go full speed ahead with it no matter how many icebergs lay ahead. At this point he didn't want any opportunities slipping away. Money screams.

Lenore said, "Why don't we hold off this time around. I'll see what I can find and—"

"And why don't we just go with it. Research as much as you like, but no point in missing opportunities. The next chance for a Code is four nights from now. Are you ready to let a train-load of money slip away?"

Was it a reasonable compromise to go forward? Lenore wasn't so sure. She gasped softly and reluctantly agreed.

Part III

The Change

1

Out of desperation, a change is made to The Code

Lenore and Sam stood next to the altar. A darkly shimmering glow of shadows from the flickering candles danced off the walls and ceiling. Lenore pulled everything that was needed from her bag. She handed Sam his robe, then stripped and pulled her robe over herself. The chalice was set out, the dolcetto wine, a clean needle wrapped in sterile gauze.

"Oh, do not tell me," Lenore said, rummaging through the bag.

"Now what?"

"No bone."

"No what?"

"Bone…no piece of chicken bone." She removed the mortar and pestle and hunted through the bag and turned it over, shaking it out, then tossed the bag in disgust on the altar and stared at Sam. "We need the bone; it's essential for The Code."

"We go without it."

"It's part of the ceremony, Sam," she said, hunting again in the bag and looking on the floor below them. "Will it work without it? I mean, I don't know. I don't know what's necessary, what's not. I assume it's *all* necessary."

Little by little the purpose of each part of The Code had become clear to Lenore. The Stations of the Cross from the ninth to the first signified the movement away from danger. The blood represented life. The wine had obvious religious overtones, though exactly in what way was unclear. The bone. Did it represent the core of life? Or was it death itself, that which is left when the body decays, when all hope is lost, when the body has been stripped of flesh? They were messing with the occult, and they had managed to get it to work for them. Never in her wildest dreams had she believed it would work, but it did.

Sam was a man not easily deterred. A man of resource and solutions. "Easy," he simply said. "You want bone?" He left the room, retrieved a skull from outside the door and returned with it under his arm looking sickly demented.

Lenore's eyes widened. "That's a skull, Sam. A human skull," she wretched. "We can't use that."

"What's it matter?"

"You want to grind up a piece of human skull? Grind it up and put it into the wine and have me drink it. Is that what you're saying?"

"Well not grind it up exactly. We just shave a tiny little bit off just like we did with the chicken bones. Not much, just enough to mix into...."

This did not sound at all good to Lenore. The chicken bone was bad enough. But powder from human skulls? It sounded cannibalistic. It *was* cannibalistic when you came right down to it. And anyway, the skull was old—who knows how old. It had been sitting in a decrepit underground passage collecting dust for decades, maybe centuries. Covered in cobwebs and the minutia of dead dust mites and God knows what else.

"Would *you* drink something made with that thing?" Lenore aimed an arm toward the skull in Sam's hand.

"If I had to," Sam replied in a voice not at all convincing. Then he backed his words up, saying, "Look, it's just a tiny little bit, that's all. Almost nothing. I really don't see how it can hurt."

"This is no place to have this discussion, Sam. We need to let The Code go for now, scrap it, and do it when everything is right."

"But everything *is* right. Let's *not* get all twisted over this."

Lenore groaned and circled the room.

Sam wiped a patch along the base of the skull with a Steriwipe that they always brought with them. He let it air dry a moment, removed a small emery board from the bag, and filed tiny specks into the mortar and proceeded to grind it into fine powder. He added a pinch to the wine, emphasizing all the while that it was just the tiniest amount. A drop of blood and, *voilà*, they were ready.

Glaring at Sam, Lenore pulled off her robe and stared at him for a moment, then climbed begrudgingly onto the altar. Each time she did it, it felt less like an altar and more like an operating table. And maybe it was—a mental operating table.

The Code came off flawlessly but for the unexpected initial delay at the beginning. They had become adept at the ritual. Everything went like clockwork. In little more than an hour, they were done and standing outside the library while Sam locked up.

Then, like two boats crossing in the night, Nick Sanchez scuttled past the library as he returned from a late rendezvous at Katy's. He stopped for half a second and watched Sam attach the lock to the gate. *Strange*, he thought. *Who's coming out of the library at this hour?* A blitz of crazy thoughts ran wildly through his head. Seconds later he was off down the path into the dark night.

"Did you see that?" Lenore said, waiting for Sam to finish. "Kid saw us."

"Forget him," Sam said, yanking several times on the padlock to make sure it was firmly attached. "He's heading back to the dorm after a night of swilling beer or something. Kid won't remember diddly when morning comes. Let's go."

2

Something is different, very different

The headaches. They didn't seem so bad at first. But they persisted, and that was perhaps the most worrisome part. That and the fact that they moved around in her head like something was crawling inside. A couple of hours up front just above the hairline. A half day back along the base of the skull. Then on the sides near the temples.

Of all the small infirmities people suffer from, headaches had never been a problem for Lenore. She'd never been plagued by migraines, coffee headaches, headaches from eye strain. Now, for a full week, they were a regular part of her life. Then, suddenly, just when she was set to pay a visit to dear old Doc Steinman, her internist, the headaches left—vanished and flew off as fast as they had arrived.

Once again, The Code paid off in spades. This time, it was a huge windfall from a small do-nothing oil stock that hit a big vein of black gold in west Texas. The stock soared through the roof moments after Sam and Lenore bought a bucket load of it. Another fantastic victory for The Code. Who could doubt it now? Everything was going along swimmingly, and Sam had no intention of abandoning it any time soon.

There were no celebrations that night. Instead, on the way home, Lenore stopped at the Market Basket. She picked up a piece of fish, Brussel sprouts, a bottle of good wine. Her celebration would be alone. This didn't bother her. She knew how to make the most of it. A meal, some classical music—Bach, Tchaikovsky—a soft chair, lights down low, wine.

She stood in the check-out line. Three more people in front of her and she'd be on her way. Suddenly, she heard, *Stupid old lady, she's buying enough food for a church picnic. Come on, come on, honey, move it! I want to get my butt out of here before Christmas.*

Good grief, where did that come from? Lenore turned and looked around. Certainly not from the blue hair with the Mother Teresa look behind her who had a couple of Swanson's and a Greek yogurt and some blueberries in her basket. It was from the guy in front of her. Had to be. But he hadn't uttered a word. Lenore knew this for sure because she had glanced at him moments before she heard the words. He turned, looked at Lenore, raised a palm impatiently into the air and shook his head in disgust, peeved by the hold up in the line in front of him. Lenore gave him a tiny smile.

So…had he grumbled it? Was that what happened? Or had Lenore merely imagined it? Or…or had he thought it and Lenore had heard…no, not possible! But for a moment, for just a second, she wondered if she had actually picked up on what he was thinking. Or was it her own thoughts rumbling loosely through her head while she too stood numbly in line. Of course, of course, that's what it was. Had to be.

At home, Lenore fixed dinner and settled restlessly in a chair in the living room. Her mind flitted back again and again to the voice in the Market Basket. The music and the wine were of no help. She couldn't stop thinking about what had happened at the Market Basket. "When you start hearing voices…yeah, right, we all know what that means," she mumbled.

She slipped into a pair of snug jeans and a loose beige sweater. She needed to be out, but not to THE CEO. Too many people like her. The choices in Covington weren't great, but there was always Jake's, the Graebner College hangout a block from the school. Mostly college kids, and a handful of townies who came in for the fried clams and burgers and French fries, the onion rings.

It was still early: eight-fifteen. The happy-hour crowd was thinning out, the evening partiers were ambling in—coeds in skintight jeans and snug tops.

Lenore sat at a table on the edge of the room. A young coed-looking waitress came over to take her order.

"What kind of wine do you have?" Lenore asked.

"Red, white, and pink."

Huhm, this is Jake's, after all. "Okay…pink, I suppose."

A college kid half her age swaggered coolly over and asked if he could join her. She gave him the once over, more cute than handsome. Anyway, too much like her twenty-year-old nephew. She delivered a kindly wink and sent him on his way.

While Lenore scrolled through the messages, texts, and tweets on her phone, Nick and Katy walked into the bar. They sat at a table far across the room, a good twenty-five feet from Lenore, and ordered a pitcher of beer. Lenore looked up. She didn't recognize Nick and he didn't recognize her. During their encounter outside the library, Nick's face had been obscured by the dark shadows from the maples and elms. Lenore had turned to him only briefly and then swiveling quickly away, hiding her face.

Music and laughter, raucous conversation, blurched throughout the room. At last Lenore was feeling better, glad she had come to Jake's, college dive that it was. She was no more out of place than the few remaining townies who worked on their beers and clams.

So, I don't know what was going on. All I can say is someone, two people, were coming out of the library. It was late, three o'clock probably, when I was heading back to the dorm.

Lenore listened, hand on her glass of pink. "Well, screw me, will you," she said just below her breath. She scanned the room, trying to find out where the words were coming from.

…I stood there and watched. Dude was locking the gate. Woman was waiting next to him. They had been in the library. Like I said, it was dark and I couldn't see much.

So who were they?

I'm not sure. Too dark to tell.
Musta been Kojak?
Nah. You can spot that shiny globe a mile away. Anyhow, why would Kojak be coming out so late, and with a woman?
Linkley?
Didn't look like Linkley either.

Lenore was flummoxed. Was it a nearby conversation or was it being piped right straight into her head? She tried to locate its source. It wasn't the jabber from a table next to her, thick with heavy laughter and raunchy jokes. They were keyed onto a couple of co-eds standing at the bar. "Sorority," one of the jocks said.

No, what Lenore heard was very different from this. The words came from inside her, like listening to music with a set of Bose headphones, hearing it inside your head, on the left side, the right side, the center…in perfect stereo.

She cupped her hands tightly over her ears, closing out the cacophony of noise in the bar, and still she could hear every word clearly. Her eyes landed on Nick and Katy sitting across the room. They were deep in conversation. She watched the movement of Nick's lips like HAL lip-reading Dave in *2001: A Space Odyssey*. The words in Lenore's head filled in what Nick was saying down to the last syllable.

So that's who was outside the library when Sam was locking up, she concluded. Lenore watched Nick and Katy carefully. Students for sure. Graebner for sure. They had that clean yet tattered look, that student look.

"Snoopy little millie!" Lenore grumbled. Her term for the millennials that packed the corridors and walkways of Grabner College. Now she'll tell someone else, who'll probably tell someone else, then another, on and on endlessly. That's how this stuff gets started. How it perpetuates, mindless as it is. Lenore picked up her phone and snapped a picture, brightened it, enlarged it, and saved it.

They were down in that chamber below the library, betchya anything. Why else would they be coming out at that hour? And I remember one of them had a large bag of some kind, the woman. But it was dark, hard to tell much else.

This was worrisome. Lenore decided to run an experiment. She got up and crossed the bar in the direction of the restroom, passing by Nick and Katy in the process. She glanced down long enough to catch Nick's attention. He looked up, blinked several times, a classic subconscious neuronal response the brain sends out when it thinks it has made facial recognition but isn't sure. On the way back, she passed the table again. When she was several feet away, she turned and looked behind her. Nick was watching her as she crossed the room. She returned passively to her table and sat, hand resting on the stem of the wine glass, thinking.

It had been just over six days since the last Code—a week filled with blasting headaches, voices, whole entire conversations that rolled through her head coming from the thoughts or words of others.

She watched Nick and Katy like a predatory cat tracking a pair of robins. Suddenly, the words were gone. The Bose speakers had been shut off. In a sense, that was the testiest part of the whole experience because there was no logical explanation for when it started, when it stopped. In the Market Basket, what did she care what the ticked off dude thought? But this was different. Lenore cared a whole lot about what the two millies across from her were saying. She wanted to hear every word of it.

A growing dislike for Nick was blooming inside her yet he meant nothing to her at all. He had seen her and Sam outside the library, so what? She knew something like that would happen sooner or later. College campuses buzz with activity even in the middle of the night. Even so, it left Lenore with the feeling that The Code no longer belonged to her and Sam. That its secret mystery had been trampled on. Worse still, it was clear to Lenore from what she had just heard that these two, whoever they were, had been down in the deepest part of the library's underground. What else did they know? The Code perhaps?

Nick looked passively around the bar, delivering an occasional nod to a friend or two. His eyes landed on Lenore sitting by the far wall. *He knows me for sure*, Lenore thought. She glanced away, feigning indifference.

Now more than ever she wished she could hear what he was telling the person he was with. But the voices were gone. Perhaps their conversation had drifted on to something else. There was no more leaning over the table tight and close. Maybe that's how this thing in her head worked—on a need to know basis. Nick topped off their pint glasses with beer from the pitcher.

"Nutha wine, hon?"

Lenore looked at the waitress standing over her. *Hon…how cute*, she thought. "Nutha pink, I suppose."

Maybe it *was* time for a visit to her internist, even though the headaches were now gone. Or possibly a visit to Martin Leidy, her psychiatrist. She hadn't seen Leidy in quite a while. Not since she had slipped out of a pretty good relationship, or so she'd thought, and slipped into a bout of depression. Even Sam had encouraged her to get help. Leidy had tried Zoloft at first and then moved her onto Wellbutrin. It worked superbly. She still took it. Even so, try telling a shrink you hear voices and that you can read people's minds. *Ha, ha, ha, go try that that out for size and see what happens. Good luck!*

It was ten o'clock. Lenore had been at Jake's for almost two hours. The place seethed with people. A table with frat boys was playing a game: hit on the MILF sitting alone in the corner of the room and see who would be first to score. It was getting tiresome. *Time to go*, Lenore thought.

She got up, grabbed her purse, and started for the door just as Nick and Katy were leaving. Pretending to be searching for something in her purse, she waited for a second, then followed them out.

Nick turned and looked at Lenore. He put his arm on Katy's shoulder as they headed toward campus.

3

Lenore is worried

There was no chance of finding anything about The Code on the internet. What little was there had nothing to do with the occult. The only connection so far came from the books in the Velvet Room at Graebner. As Lenore saw it, The Code was a jigsaw with too many missing pieces. She needed to learn more about it before going on. She had managed to put future ceremonies on hold, for now anyway, and had convinced Sam to wait. He'd reluctantly agreed. He could do little else. Without her there *was* no Code. She held all the face cards.

Truth be said, he was not at all happy about the decision. Money does scream. More to the point, the good old days of investing seemed unexciting and tedious, not to mention unfruitful. Worse yet, by skipping a Code, a big investment had probably gone south on them due to no fault of his. *You win some, you lose some. Remember how it used to be,*

Sam old buddy, he told himself, staring out his office windows. *Remember?*

Lenore took the day off and paid a visit to Doc Steinman, her internist. She had a nasty headache that flared up and then left almost as soon as it arrived. She called and told Sam she would be in later in the day.

Steinman took her blood pressure, listened to her heart, chest and lungs, checked her ears, did an EKG, and ordered an MRI "just to be safe."

Lenore hadn't said a word to Sam about the headaches or the voices. Sam was her business partner, not her father, not her brother, not her shrink. Though at times he acted like he was all of them. She was not opposed to sharing some of her most private thoughts together. But she knew how to maintain her privacy when needed.

Little by little, Sam continued to push for a Code. He walked casually into Lenore's office as though he was just passing by. "So, anything new from the books over at Graebner...about The Code?"

Lenore shrugged. She had spent one entire weekend in the Velvet Room. The jumbled disorganized nature of the place made finding anything over there a real game of chance. For that matter, there was no reason to believe information of the type she wanted even existed there. The Velvet Room was a repository of fine and expensive first editions and rare books, not a trove of accurate historical information.

"We're at an impasse I think," Lenore said.

Sam sat in a chair in front of her as he had done a thousand times before. But now, Lenore could hear everything that he was thinking.

"Well, just keep at it and see what you can find," he said. "We need a Code…soon. A lotta bucks are slipping away, big bucks. We're not peddling popsicles on the street corner or something, you know. We need to cash in again."

"I've got it marked on the calendar," Sam said.

"So, when?" Lenore asked.

"When what?"

"The Code, Sam, The Code."

"Oh yeah, The Code. This Wednesday."

Now Lenore was unequivocally convinced that these ESP moments were connected to the last Code they had performed. And that alone was enough to deter her from another one. But what had caused the change? What had been different? Every aspect of it had been done exactly as the other ceremonies. Well, almost every aspect. All but for the piece of the human skull that Sam had ground and mixed in with the wine and the blood. But why should that make a difference? *As Sam said, bone is bone. Right? Chicken bone, human bone…funny bone, so what?*

4

Not quite your standard Code

Wednesday arrived. To say The Code went differently this time would be an understatement. The Code itself went according to Hoyle, and Lenore made sure she brought a piece of chicken bone. No more human skull wine coolers for her.

This time, on their way into the library, Sam checked and double-checked, making sure the coast was clear before he opened the gate.

In the final moments of The Code, drew dizzy and almost fell from the altar. Sam reached and pulled her back. "Whoa girl, easy now," he said.

She sat woozy headed for a moment, then climbed off the altar.

⚰

Days passed, weeks passed, nothing happened. No truck load of greenbacks came sailing their way. They had a couple of wins, but nothing more than would happen on any given day. Nothing that couldn't be chalked up to fluctuations in the market.

Perhaps there would be no more goodies from The Code. Perhaps The Code had run its course. Perhaps they had sucked out all the alchemy they were going to get from it. Sam worried. Lenore worried. They waited.

5

Menacing thoughts

Saturday afternoon, Lenore found herself walking through Graebner campus. Something had sent her there, a vague urge from inside that told her to go.

She sat alone at a bench on the edge of one of the paths, feeling like an upscale bag lady.

"Cripes," she mumbled, glancing distractedly about as she pulled a book from her purse and started reading *Missing Person* by Patrick Modiano. Not Lenore's cup of tea normally, but the more she read, the more she liked it. Her tastes went in the direction of Sue Grafton. Now and then Stephen King and Dean Koontz. Her sister Jessie, the English major of the family, had insisted she read Modiano.

She removed her business card from inside the book. Modiano was taking Guy Roland on yet another excursion into an amnestic past. Twenty minutes went by quickly. She stopped and wondered, Roland-like, why she was there, what she was doing on the Graebner campus. *Never mind, it doesn't matter.*

The day was cool. The late afternoon November sun burned through the chilly still air. All in all, it was pleasant. A gaggle of students played Frisbee on the grass across from her. She stopped reading and looked down the leaf-strewn path. Coming toward her were Nick and Katy. They walked past her and sat on a bench across from her.

Can't go Sunday, got a test on Monday. But I think we need to try one more time if we're going to finish what we started.

But just one more time and that's it.

Lenore put on a pair of sunglasses and turned away, pretending to be reading.

Nick had no desire to make another trip into the belly of the library. He was too close to graduating, and that's all he cared about. But for Katy it was like plowing through a differential equation—you keep plugging in unknowns until you finally get an answer. In moments like this, it was usually Katy who won out. When she looked at him with her alluring blue eyes, it was impossible for Nick to refuse.

What we're going to do is check out the hallway that goes back behind the operating room, find out where it goes.

Lenore growled softly. "Little buggers do know about the panel door and the passage and the altar. They could have easily seen us." This ticked her off in spades. She wanted to stop them. Sam and Lenore would be doing another Code probably. The last one hadn't paid off yet. They need a repeat performance. But what if it went bad? It was a concern that had worried Lenore.

Little millies are playing a risky game, Lenore thought, *messing with old Sammy.* There was a 'don't mess with me' side of Sam Whitney that Lenore knew well. She liked it in fact. It had been the juice that had driven their small financial firm to new heights even without The Code.

Nick and Katy got up. The afternoon was rapidly chilling down under a steely sky that had settled in. The wind had a snap to it. Thin, slow-moving clouds collected and coalesced until the sun was nothing more than a white glow sinking weakly onto the horizon.

Lenore would find out who they were. *I'll follow them and then…no I'll hold off until later and then…and then what?* She wasn't sure. She shoved Modiano into her purse and tacked along behind them at a safe distance until they arrived at the student union. She turned and headed for her car.

6

Nick and Katy discover another passage

Lenore Simenson walked along the wall of the reading room, pretending to be searching for a book. Gustav Becker said it was a couple of minutes short of eleven. Exactly as Lenore predicted would happen, Nick and Katy entered the room just as eleven melodious chimes rang out.

Nick and Katy sat at a table and spread several books in front of them. Katy furtively watched Lenore. This could screw with their plans for the night. Rarely was anyone still around at this hour. Linkley sometimes, but only sometimes.

"Who's the woman?" Nick said, ticked.

"I have no idea. Doesn't quite look faculty, does she?"

"Not really. She looks vaguely familiar though." He flipped open a book and pretended to be reading. "But I can't place her. I might have seen her somewhere on campus. Could be faculty, I suppose."

"She's leaving. We'll give her fifteen," Katy said. "If she's not back by then, we go in."

In no time Nick and Katy were at the door to the entrance of the fifty-foot 'Green Mile' as Nick called it, the corridor to the operating room, he had dubbed the 'Sick Room'. The place where the stack of trepanned skulls rested in a disgusting pile.

From the Sick Room was a long and narrow tunnel covered with more green tiles and a dirty hardwood floor. Nick flipped a switch that lit a line of fluorescent lights along the length of the tunnel. They proceeded, going straight for no less than a hundred yards, eventually dead ending at a set of stone stairs on the top of which was yet another panel door with a latch. Nick gave the latch a turn. Unlike the well-oiled door in the library, this one swiveled belligerently open on tight and rusty hinges.

They found themselves in a dark closet. Standing there, it was easy to see how the door and passage might have gone undiscovered for decades, probably even to the present. Just as in the library, the panel door blended perfectly with the rest of the wall.

The closet was filled with a dozen identical locked metal file cabinets in a perfect row, each about shoulder high. Each had a printed label: A-D, E-H, and so on. The first letter of last names, no doubt. Some cabinets were dated with a sticker in the upper right corner.

Exiting the closet, Nick and Katy found themselves in a grand and elegant office, beautifully furnished with a large executive desk and leather chair, a leather sofa, a coffee table, and original artwork on the walls.

"Ha, ha, ha, know where we are?" Nick said.

Katy glanced out the window. "Parker's office...the Prez," she replied. "You mean that ratty tunnel from the library we just came through leads to this place? No alarms, no security, and here we are standing in the office of the president of the university?"

"Wanna bet not a person alive today knows a passage is there...not *even* Parker herself? Probably doesn't even know there's a door there. Look at it. It's just another plain wooden panel like all the others in the closet. The hinges are stiff as a rusty gate. Uh-uh, no way, no one's been down there in a long time. It's all part of the ancient layout of the ancient school that's been long forgotten."

The president's office was in one of the oldest buildings on campus, second only to the library itself, designed in the same beautiful Oxford style. One entire wall of the office was filled with the books in the genre of Parker's scholarship—twentieth century Russian politics. But it was a rich collection of hundreds of other works as well, new and old. Nick pulled a book from the shelf, paging here and there through it as though prying into the inner mind of Parker. The more he looked, the more he was happy to be a biology major.

He picked up a strange-looking book that had nothing to do with Russia or biology. It was old and worn and had a cover as thick as old cardboard and a curious title: *The Code*. He read a couple of pages and set it on Parker's desk.

"Have you ever been in this place?" Katy asked.

"Here...in this office, you mean? No way! And I hope never to be again. I'm trying to get out of this joint, reputation intact." Even so, Nick couldn't resist sitting in Parker's chair. He propped his feet up on her grand old desk. He looked at the time on his phone. "We gotta roll...like now, like immediately!" At the last second on their way out, Nick grabbed *The Code* from the desk. "Just borrowing it," he told Katy. "Think of it as a loaner."

They left. Nick pulled the panel in the closet until it clicked. Hurrying to get back, Katy forgot to lock the door that led from the altar chamber to the Green Mile and the Sick Room with her skeleton key. They hustled quickly up to the reading room. Nick snapped the latch. The door opened but no more than an inch. He leaned into it with his shoulder until there was enough space to pass through. Someone had wedged several of the heavy library chairs against the door. This was no accident; they certainly didn't get there all by themselves.

Katy stared at Nick, clearly worried. The room was empty, but the lights on the tables were on. Gustav Becker's hands pointed to twelve-thirty, too early for the library to close, much too early for Kojak to slip by and shut the place down.

"I know who did this," Nick said pushing the chairs back to the desk. "It was that floozy who was wandering around in here earlier. She wasn't looking for a book, no way. And now I remember where I saw her. It was when we were sitting on the bench outside a couple of days ago, remember? Did you see her?"

Katy shook her head. "No."

"Well I did. I'm certain it's her. I remember thinking she was checking us out." Nick stuck the book about The

Code in his backpack. They left the library and walked over to The Rat, where they bought a pitcher of beer.

Nick filled two pints glasses, watching as the head rose to the top. He took a big swig that left a frothy white mustache on his upper lip, then swiped it clean with his forearm.

"It's time to forget that place ever existed," Nick emphatically said. "Whatever's going on, it has nothing to do with us."

"The school's into it. Parker must be too. How could she not know?" Katy said.

"Good for her, I hope she gets what she wants. And I hope I get what I want, which is to buzz out of this place in a couple of months and fly straight into medical school."

When it came to matters like this, Nick and Katy were of a different ilk, formed from different experiences. Nick was far too practical to let such inconsequential diversions get in the way of his long-range goals. If nothing else, his father had pounded that notion into his cabeza time and time again because it was a notion that had been pounded into Nick's father's cabeza by *his* own father. In the bean fields, if the person next to you wasn't family, you could show little sympathy for their plight. You had your own plight to deal with. If immigration came by and rounded up a pack of workers on your left and a pack on your right, you never so much as looked up from the rusty soil and crops below you.

There was none of that kind of history embedded in Katy's DNA. For generations, the family was well-educated. Every problem was dealt with adroitly. If some issue surfaced, her father could fix it. It was the difference between growing up as a have or a have not.

But all said, Katy was content to have Nick declare that enough was enough and that they were done with it. She needed someone to flip that circuit breaker and drop the issue. Nick did it.

7

Lenore pays a visit to Nick's apartment

Getting into Nick Sanchez' apartment was a snap. The door was unlocked. Lenore walked right in. "Stupid dolt doesn't have the sense to keep his place locked," she mumbled. What monastery was he brought up in? She merely entered the building, walked up a flight of stairs, went down the hall until she arrived at apartment 24.

It was a student apartment building. Lenore hardly fit the bill, yet no one noticed. Not that it really mattered. She could have been a friend, a relative, a mother, who knows? Anyway, everyone she passed—four in all—were crunched over cell phones. She could have walked along stark naked. Could have passed them covered in blood, carrying a meat ax.

Apartment 24 was the right place. She had checked the mailbox in the hall. She walked inside and took a mental inventory of the rooms, opened the closets, rummaged through the shirts on the hangers, the piles of socks and clothes on the floor, the dresser drawers, the kitchen shelves and cabinets, the bathroom, the refrigerator—empty mostly: milk, cold-cuts, beer.

She plopped down in a soft overstuffed armchair, something Nick had copped at a garage sale no doubt. Strictly student decor.

There she was, in Nick's room—Nick of Nick and Katy fame. This would be a snap. She had figured it out, plotted and planned everything, thought it through. If nothing else, these days her thoughts were clearer than ever. More so each day.

She slumped in the chair, feet up on a mismatched vinyl ottoman and closed her eyes. *Things aren't going all that well,* she thought. *Cripes, is that an understatement or what?* The money kept rolling in over at WSA. For Lenore, that was about all that was doing well. Almost everything else had suddenly turned sour. The headaches came and went, she heard voices now and then when she was near Nick and Katy and Sam.

Lenore got up and checked her watch. Nick would be gone for at least another hour—plenty of time. She scrounged through a stack of papers and a set of books on his desk. Textbooks, a couple of novels, magazines, all the usual suspects. She pushed them aside. Unfortunately, she failed to see the most important book of all: *The Code*. She walked into the kitchen and pulled a bowl from the shelf, a box of cornflakes from the cabinet, milk from the refrigerator and had a bowl of cereal sitting at Nick's desk, above which a photo of him and Katy was pinned to the wall.

On the desk was a scatter of bills, all addressed to Nick Sanchez. "Right…just as I thought. That's the dork's name," she mumbled, crunching flakes. She stared at the photo: *Latino-ish*, she thought. *Part Latino at least. Not one hundred percent. Anglo in there probably. Good looking cat just the same.* Katy was pure co-ed through and through. Walk across Graebner and you'd see hundreds like her: same blonde hair, same perfect teeth, same cute smile, same eyes that revealed nothing, that delivered nothing up to the world. Even in the selfie taken by Nick, she made sure the eyes spoke not a syllable.

Next to this was another photo, also snagged on Nick's iPhone no doubt, this one from his bedroom. Katy was lying in bed, plain white sheet just above her breasts, head resting on her arm. Eyes that said, 'what are you waiting for?' Even Lenore, not the most analytical person in the world when it came to such things, noticed it immediately.

She set the bowl in the sink next to an empty glass and a plate. *Okay, time to leave.* She looked around the room one last time, left the apartment, and walked down the hall and out the building, passing two students, phones in front of them, barely moving to the side as they all but collided head on.

8

Nick learns about The Code

Two hours later Nick returned from his molecular biology study group and sat at the kitchen table sorting through the day's mail. Junk and bills and, *Drat*, nary a one from a medical school.

Afternoon winter sun trickled in from the window of his second-story apartment. He dug through the potpourri of stuff on his desk then picked up *The Code*, forgotten and buried under his papers.

Plopping into the armchair, he immediately sensed the smell of perfume, women's cologne, hairspray—something. Where did this come from, he wondered? The whole chair was lightly bathed in it. It surely wasn't something from Katy, and it surely wasn't something from him. None of that junk on either of them. Super odd. Could have been a lingering scent from a member of the study group. He put his feet up and started reading.

As was his habit, he went to the first couple of pages looking for the publisher, the dates, other basic info. Provenance always said a lot. But little there was. By all accounts it had been self-published by a certain Malcolm Slater in Boston, Massachusetts in 1954. There was no bio describing this Slater fellow, nothing about his background or credentials. Why was it even in Parker's personal library?

Nick read for an hour or more. The origins of The Code were not known. The first detailed accounting was linked to a group of rogue monks who practiced it in an isolated mountain-top monastery in southern France in the twelfth century.

The purpose was simple: alchemy. The rules were precise and explicit. It must be performed underground (a connection with the earth). It was done on a slab of marble (metamorphosed limestone or dolomite that results from recrystallization of the original rock, thus signifying a change in the composition of stone, one of nature's most durable creations). Nine Stations of the Cross (not fourteen) beginning with the ninth and going in reverse to the first, signify the undoing of the crucifixion and the movement of time backwards, a theme further signified by an upside-down cross over the altar. A person, always a woman, must lie on the altar, naked, and be cast into a spell by drinking wine mixed with her own blood and ground chicken bone (to signify the cock that crowed at the time of Simon Peter's betrayal) during the sacred chanting.

Nick set the book on his lap and contemplated what he had read. The fact that the whole scene fit perfectly with what he and Katy had found in the chamber below the library hadn't escaped him. Nor had the fact that he'd witnessed Sam and Lenore coming out of the library in the middle of the night. Were they performing an ancient occult practice right there in the caverns below the library?

A handful of monks, it said, had succeeded in the alchemy they sought. They had turned lead into gold. Their sudden wealth became hard to conceal. Monks sworn to a vow of poverty had vast stores of gold. Their downfall came in several forms. First, it was not easy keeping their discovery secret. The abbot, having quickly learned of this, wanted to be cut in on the bounty.

Ingots of gold made their way into the local markets and it was no secret where it had come from. What were those fat little monks on the hill doing, mining gold in and around the monastery? Soon the entire monastery was involved—all but for two old and pious friars who refused to take part.

The second problem came from the ceremony itself. It required a woman, the key obligating factor of The Code without which there *was* no Code. No such person existed in the monastery, of course. Women were forbidden to set so much as a foot on the grounds. Hence, a young peasant girl from the surrounding hamlet had been recruited. But that too had turned out badly. In return for a few slivers of gold, she submitted her body to the monks. It had become an orgy of the worst kind. They had violated the second of their sacred vows—chastity.

Then the monks refused to abandon The Code when ordered by the two pious friars of the community. There you have it. They had violated the last of the sacred vows—obedience.

It didn't take long for the Papal Inquisition to learn of the beleaguered group of heretics holed up on a mountain peak, stacking up roomfuls of gold bars. The rest, as they say, is history. Forty-three monks were rounded up, tried, tortured, and burned at the stake for their heresy.

Crazy story, Nick thought. But according to Slater, The Code was as real as could be. He cited numerous times since then when it had been used to accrue great wealth or great power. And each time it had ended in great disaster. Even Hitler had used The Code in his early days of conquest. But the dark side of The Code was always there and always impossible to control when it surfaced.

Nick stopped reading, slumped further in the chair, and again thought about the chamber below the library. He couldn't clear his head of the coincidences. He was now seventy pages into the book and here is what came out: violations of The Code led to unforgivable horrors. Two violations, in particular, guaranteed this. The first was the use of a bone other than chicken bone—human bone was strictly forbidden. The second was contamination of the ceremony through any form of the sexual act, as the monks had done.

And indeed, look what they had done, these sacrilegious monks. Through the occult they had violated their own beliefs and their own commitment to their religion. They had turned the cross of Jesus upside down and had reversed the Stations of the Cross. They had made a harlot out of the Virgin Mary. They had consumed their own blood, not the blood of Christ. And worse yet, they had taken—in the name of all of this—one of God's most base elements and turned it into the most rare and precious. The entire act of creation had been violated. And all of this came from none other than Satan himself. So, when all was said and done, The Code was the work of the Devil. Work so beautifully tempting, conscripting, and alluring that it was impossible to resist.

9

*Nick hunts for information about Graebner in the books
in the Velvet Room*

The following week, Katy flew to Chicago to attend a wedding and squeeze in a Blackhawks game with her father: the Hawks and the Rangers, two Original Six teams. Somehow that always made the game more fun—more interesting, historical. The Hawks won 3-2. Cory Crawford played a good game. Henrik Lundqvist, The King, played a better game yet chalked up the loss on a top-shelfer in the shoot-out by Jonathan Toews, Captain Serious.

Nick used the time to chip away at his studies. On Saturday, while most of the school was at the Graebner football game, he went to the Velvet Room in the library, claiming he was writing a paper on early medical practices. He was interested in any original books on the topic.

The librarian who managed the collection pointed Nick in the direction of the old medical texts, telling him to be very, very careful as they were extremely old and fragile. In fact, though, what he wanted was anything he could find about the history of Graebner College and as much as possible about The Code.

But to make his visit appear to be legitimate, he paged methodically through several medical books. One, published in 1637 in London, described the brain as consisting of "a softe vitreous humore that likens the perception." *Whatever that means.* Another had the nerves of the eyes connected to the nerves of the ears so that "when one saw something, it sent a symbole to the mind for the purposes of conjuring." Nick gave an enlightened laugh—*they're making this crap up.* Leonardo da Vinci had a far better understanding of human anatomy than that.

He set the books on the shelf and wandered along the stacks. For a long while, nothing hopeful appeared. Distractions were many. It was hard to resist picking up a first edition of Herman Melville's *Moby Dick*, or a copy of the 1865 novel *Alice's Adventure in Wonderland* signed in the hand of Charles Lutwidge Dodgson, the author who published the book under the pseudonym of Lewis Carroll.

Finally, he hit on a run of several books about Graebner. He took three from the shelf, sat in one of velvet chairs, and began reading. Similar to what Lenore had found, the school had been founded in 1801 as Schulenmeister Theological Seminary by group of theologians— four emigrants from Germany, one from Vermont, one from Boston—who had dedicated the institution to the training of students in a "reformed protestant tradition to be intentionally disconnected from the Lutheran and

Calvinistic theologies, enlightened and specifically devoid of puritan and evangelical tendencies."

The first class at the school had had eighteen students, all from an area in and around Covington. The curriculum consisted of Latin, Greek, theology, mathematics, geography, German, and English. Classes were taught in German. The intention of the school was to produce bright, forward-thinking Christian ministers who would serve the people and the community.

The school had begun in a single building, the present-day library, which had been built between 1802 and 1804, the exact date on the cornerstone.

The student body grew slowly, peaking at a hundred and forty-three by the time of the Civil War. Four buildings with close proximity to the library and all with classic Oxford architecture had been added one by one. Then came the Civil War. The student population dwindled to twenty. The doors were closed once and for all.

In 1867 a group of academics bought the school and changed it into a private liberal arts school. Graebner College flourished. Its reputation grew until it ranked as one of the finest small colleges in the US.

Nick paged through a book dated 1871, titled *Schulenmeister Seminary—A Short History*, written by Professor Isaac Johansson at the newly formed Graebner College. The entire book, covered in leather, was no more than a half-inch thick. Unlike the other two books, this version had pictures, old daguerreotypes of buildings and classrooms and students standing stiff and straight, some with long mustaches that angled down or turned up at the end. Nick began paging through the book, reading sections here and there. In all, the book consisted of six chapters. The first three were historical accounts of the theological seminary, similar to what he had already learned from the previous two books.

He arrived at Chapter Four. The paragraphs flew by. Nick became locked onto the words. Once, he looked around the room as if someone might come up, snatch the book from his lap, and say, "Give me that thing, buster!" But he was the only one in the room sitting comfortably in a deep, soft, velvet chair that resembled something out of an English country house. "Holy shit, Batman," he uttered softly as he read. It was 1846. Schulenmeister was in its heyday.

> It was in that year, that the unthinkable happened at Schulenmeister. It is believed to have begun simply enough, with a certain innocence that was never intended to grow to such horrific proportions that would lead to the demise and eventual deaths of six of the school's most respected faculty scholars. No one had expected it until one day…

Nick flipped the page only to find that the next six pages had been carefully removed. Dissected out. Cut close to the binding as if with a razor. Six pages later, the story picked up:

> all six members of the Schulenmeister faculty had been tried, convicted, and hanged for

their hideous activities. Three students were sentenced to long prison terms.

Nick paged back and forth through the book but found nothing more on the subject. He set the book on the table and stared blindly straight ahead. If what he had read was to be believed, something very bad had happened at Schulenmeister.

Nick would not be able to make copies of this. The librarian had told him so when he came in. He could not even take a picture with his phone, which had to be deposited at the desk with the librarian while he was there. If he wanted information, he could write it down. He recorded some of the details of what he had found. It amounted to little, barely filled half of a page, and then most of the information was a rather useless description of the original school. But clearly something of monumental proportions had happened, and clearly someone wanted it omitted from the record. *Dumb way to do it*, he thought. *Just take the stupid book off the shelf all together. No need to keep them there at all given the scant, irrelevant information they parted.* He went out to the librarian who was sitting at a fine old desk.

"Excuse me," he said. "I'm curious. Would there be any books on the history of the old college, the school that was here before Graebner? Since I'm up here…well, I've always had an interest in local history. Sort of a hobby, I guess."

The librarian looked kindly at Nick. "Did you find what you were after from the medical books," she said, getting up.

"Oh, yeah."

They walked into the room that Nick had just come from. "We might have a few. Not too many, but a few. We can look." They passed along the wall where Nick had found the books on Schulenmeister. "They would be here somewhere," she said, waving a hand vaguely across the shelf. "Mixed in with the old history books. The books up here are not laid out or categorized very well," she added somewhat apologetically, as though she had been remiss in the task.

"Most people who come here aren't looking for anything special. It's more like a repository of special old books than a library reference room, you see. Professor Hartman from the English department, the provost now, built this collection practically from nothing. It's his baby. The school allows him a smart budget for this, let me tell you." She rattled on as though she couldn't wait to say something, anything, to whomever would listen. Like a Carthusian monk granted five minutes of unrestricted speech to out any word that came across his mind. "And he's well-connected, Dr. Hartman is. That's how we ended up with the Gutenberg. Him and President Parker, that is. One of only forty-eight known to exist in the world. A businessman, an alum, a wealthy banker from Wall Street, he snatched it up instantly when it came up at auction and gave it to the school. Got to have buckets of money to do that. Probably has his own island…plane too." She stopped talking, glanced over at Nick, looking confused. "Where were we now?"

"Something about the college. Graebner, its history, and—"

"Yes, yes. This is it. If there's any to be found, and I doubt that there is much. But if there is, here's where it will be."

"Nothing else?" Nick said.

"Other than this? No. When you're up here day after day like I am, you get to know the place pretty well. You know the lay of the land, I guess you could say."

"Actually, I found a few books on the subject," Nick said.

"Oh, you did?"

"Oh, yes. A couple."

"Well, that's probably it then."

"So, nothing anywhere else then?"

"Oh, no, no. The collection is all right here in Rooms A and B. Except for the extremely rare books. They're in Room C. A and B are like this. C is for the rarest—the very special ones. Someone would need an awful good reason to go in there."

"No photocopying. Is that right?"

"That's correct. We don't even have a copier up here, so there's no temptation. And the books are not allowed out. And let me tell you, this place is as secure as Fort Knox. You'd have a better chance of holding up a Brinks truck than getting something out of this place. There are silent alarms everywhere. Even if someone tried to break into the library down on the first floor, after hours let's say, the alarms would go off." She pursed her lips together and gave a big nod. "Video cameras, too. They can make those things tiny as a bug these days, you know."

Nick's mind flashed to the night Katy and he were trapped inside the library. Good thing they didn't make an attempt to get out. He wondered—worriedly—how they had failed to be spotted. "So, this is a big deal up here, huh," he said.

"The books, you mean? Oooh, yes. Very big deal. All in all, there's some twenty thousand books here. Doesn't seem like it but there are. Most worth several thousand dollars. Some, tens of thousands. A few even more. You can do the math. And that's *without* the Gutenberg."

"Funny, but I've never heard much about this part of the library."

"The school keeps it that way. Of course, it is part of the library and so it's open to anyone who has a legitimate reason to be here. Like yourself, for example."

"Crazy," Nick said. He checked the time, thanked the librarian, and left.

10

Back to the Velvet Room

The following day, Sunday, Nick returned to the Velvet Room. The same librarian was on duty. She gave the same kindly smile.

"Back again?" she said.

"Yeah. Another look at the medical texts, I think."

"Were they helpful?"

"Oh, for sure. Very." He set his backpack next to the librarian's desk, took a notebook and pen, and entered Room B, where the medical books and the books on Schulenmeister were. This time, he was not alone. Another person, a man in his fifties, was there. He wore khaki pants and a rather uneventful plaid shirt. He was trying too hard to look casual, like when Nixon was walking down the sandy beach at San Clemente wearing wingtips. This person seemed to track Nick's every move.

Nick pulled a medical text from the shelf and set it on the table and continued to peruse the shelves for the books on Schulenmeister he had found the day before. Odd—the books were gone. This was the right place, the right room. There was no doubt about it, but there was a space on the shelf where the books had once sat. Nick was beginning to feel uncomfortable, sensing as though he was being watched. He went out to the librarian. She looked up.

"Excuse me, but remember yesterday we discussed some books about the old Schulenmeister school?"

"Yesterday...hmm."

"That's right. Yesterday when we were in room—" He turned and looked at the entrance. "In B over there."

"The librarian tilted her head, eyes up toward Nick. "No, I don't think I remember."

"We were in there and—"

"Don't think I remember. Now I do remember you asking about the medical books. Yes, I remember that. You said you wanted them for—"

"But then I asked—"

"Nope, must have been downstairs at the main circulation desk," she replied with a shrug.

This was going nowhere. "Okay," Nick said. He picked up his bag and left.

11

Just as Lenore suspected

Lenore watched as Katy left the math and physics building. *Little millie seems in good spirits. Way too happy,* Lenore thought cattily. *Must have aced a test.*

Lenore had come to campus on her lunch hour. She'd originally set out for a stop at Macy's—shoes, a purse maybe. This time it would be a clean visit. No more polishing one off in the dressing room. Besides, she had already cranked it out in her office at ten-thirty that morning. Sam was in a meeting. Her door had been closed, mostly. *Yikes, enough, stop it already!* There would be no more of that in the department store at least, that she vowed. *They have cameras in those places, don't they?*

She watched Katy. The network of paths that criss-crossed campus became a clot of students as they burbled out of the buildings after the eleven o'clock classes. Lenore, dressed as she was, could easily pass as faculty—English lit, maybe art history. It didn't much matter though, college campuses are a mishmash of people of all kinds. Always some of the forty-to-fifty clan returning to college for the degree they never got. You might as well be in a train station or an airport.

It was easy to follow Katy. When she stopped to chat with a friend, Lenore pulled her phone out, pretending to be checking a message. No one on a college campus would ever consider they were being tracked in the middle of the afternoon unless they knew something wasn't right. Katy had no reason to believe that.

She kept walking until she arrived at The Whit, the student union. There, she stopped and waited. Minutes later, Nick showed up. They went inside and ordered hamburgers, fries, and soda. They sat at a table. Lenore pulled up a chair at a nearby table, back to them. She pulled a bottle of Fiji from her purse.

"The whole thing was weird," Nick said. "I think she figured out what I was really there for, and for some reason she pulled the books from the shelf. They were there Saturday, gone Sunday. Stupid little books. Not much information when you come right down to it."

Nick explained the missing pages. "Why would someone deposit books in the library with missing pages? Totally illogical. If you don't want anyone finding it, just leave it off the shelf if it's so important. No one will find what's not there."

"One of the books described what happened at the old seminary, Schulenmeister it was called, before it became Graebner. They were messing around with the occult."

Christ, they do know, Lenore thought.

"You know I don't really give a rat's about what happened a hundred years ago. I'm more concerned about right now, like my test in two days. But the crazy thing was that when I came back on Sunday, the librarian pretended she knew nothing about the books. But I know she did. She's the one who pulled them off the shelf! Her or that creep who was sitting in the room when I got there. Strange guy. Didn't seem to belong there. I got the feeling he was watching me the whole time. Like he was the CIA or something."

Lenore listened and watched.

"But anyway, according to the librarian, that place, the library I mean, is a virtual fortress. Alarms, cameras, you name it. The works. It's all because of what's on the fourth floor in the Velvet Room. Those books are worth a fortune—irreplaceable. And from what she described, it's a miracle they didn't find out about us when we were trapped inside. The cameras these days are tiny. You don't even know they're there. And they can record in dim light, almost no light at all."

Katy thought about that. "So maybe they did know we were there. Now what??"

"Yeah, great! And then what if Kojak or someone slaps it on the internet for the whole bloody world to see?"

"It goes viral and we're famous," Katy said. "I don't think I'd worry. Kojak doesn't strike me as the sharpest knife in the drawer."

"Well, if it goes viral, my goose is cooked. Not quite the promo I want for my entry into medical school," Nick gasped.

Medical school, huh? Thinks he's headed for medical school. We'll see about that.

"Forget it, that's up on the fourth floor. I doubt that they'd put any of that in the reading room. I mean, what's the point? Videos of Professor Linkley? You can't be serious. It also could be that very few people, not even security, know about the underground chamber. If I had to bet, I'd say the reading room isn't even on the security list."

That did it, Lenore had heard enough. She twisted the cap onto her bottle of Fiji and left.

12

Lenore discovers the passage to Parker's office and takes some liberties

Lenore loitered in her office, waiting for Sam to depart for his daily visit to the gym—forty-five minutes on the treadmill and rowing machines. She looked down on the parking lot and watched as Sam climbed into his SLR McLaren Mercedes-Benz and sped off. If nothing else, Sam was a creature of habit. Lenore knew he kept the key to the library in the top drawer of his desk. And from their multiple trips into the library, Lenore knew exactly how to unlock the door and turn off the alarm. She also knew that he would never miss the key since they had no plans for a library visit any time soon.

Evening came. Lenore read a little, fell asleep in a living room chair for a while, read a little more. Finally, it was one-thirty. By the time she drove the three-quarters of a mile to campus, parked her car, and walked to the library, it would be well after two a.m.

A flash of snow had made a terse appearance earlier in the evening, then ended just as fast as it had arrived. Cold wind blew down the brick paths as Lenore moved through campus. She arrived at the library, looked around several times—checked, double checked, and triple checked to make sure no one was nearby. There were the ever-present campus police. These dudes weren't your Barney Fife of days gone by. What with all the hostile intruder attacks at schools, campus police were outright swat teams, pure and simple. Blue-black shirt and pants. Combat boots. A couple of Sig Sauer p229.40 S&W automatic pistols strapped onto the side. Kevlar vests. They were prepared. One false move is all it would take, especially in the middle of a dark night.

Lenore pulled the key from her purse, unlocked the door, and adroitly turned off the alarm. She waited for a minute in the shadow before going in, making sure everything was copasetic. So far, no blazing sirens.

It was damn creepy being in the library all alone—no Sam, just her. The place seemed spookier than during any of her previous trips with Sam, as though all the characters in all the books were about to suddenly leap to life in a massive Walt Disney animation and come charging at her, dancing through the halls and downstairs. My, how our mind returns to that of a child's at moments like this.

Up the stairs and across the reading room. She pulled a twelve-inch flashlight powered by four D batteries from her purse and started down the bleak passages that led to the altar chamber. Carefully and cautiously she went. The last thing she needed was to take a nosedive into oblivion and land face first on a hard stone step.

Standing in the altar chamber, everything seemed vaguely different. First off, she was totally alone—she hoped. The smells were different. The staleness of the old plaster walls seemed to be filled with decay. The room, too, looked different, the crazy way our mind toys with us when we've altered the circumstances of something we're used to. The light from her industrial-strength flashlight added to this: cold hard light unlike the flickering glimmer of the candles. Spooky though the light from the candles was, it imparted a feeling of gentle comfort, nonetheless.

Lenore leaned against the altar suddenly wondering why she was there. She had no earthly idea. It was somehow because of the conversation she had picked up on while sitting at The Whit listening to Nick and Katy. Lenore felt sure they wouldn't be making an appearance down in the chamber. But for a couple of minutes her mind imagined they were right there: Lenore, Nick, and Katy. Katy was tied and strapped, horrifyingly, to the marble slab. Nick was bound up in the corner. She was holding a sharp...*all right now, forget it, Lenore! Forget it!* She shook her head, cleared her thoughts, and flashed light around the room. As the beam passed along the back wall of the chamber, she noticed that the narrow wooden door was open a crack. Whenever she and Sam were down there, they had never opened the door, though Lenore had wondered what was behind it. Wondered where it led. She pulled the door slowly back, finding herself greeted by the Green Mile. She thought for a second. Did it make sense to go in? What if the door swung closed behind her and she was trapped inside? Who would find her? How would she get out?

But she ventured in nonetheless, soon arriving at the Sick Room, where she was confronted, just as Nick and Katy had been, by the pile of skulls, the gurney with the leather straps, the old tin cabinets. "Good grief!" she uttered, gasping.

The long corridor that led further on from the Sick Room was next. Climbing the stone stairs at the end, she emerged in Parker's closet and then in her office. She had no idea where she was other than it was the office of someone important. Then it hit. She was standing in the middle of Clara Parker's office. Lenore knew Parker only casually, having accompanied Sam to a couple of black-tie ordeals hosted by Parker. Sam hated to go alone. Though he and Lenore never pretended to be husband and wife, it at least saved Sam from being one of the few single persons at the event. Lenore didn't mind. The food was good, the alcohol excellent, the people were okay—mostly.

From the window, she watched the wind work the branches. A silvery moon hid behind leaf-bare trees, peaking in and out of translucent cirrus clouds. *Now this is what I call an office!* Lenore thought. Windows deep set in stone sills. None of that plain-as-pablum office-park stuff that housed WSA.

It was clear why Sam liked hobnobbing with Parker, what with Sam's penchant for moving in top circles. He liked money, he liked power, he liked influence. But the big deal was Sam was up to something. It involved Parker, for sure, and Lenore wanted to know what it was. That's why Lenore had been dragged through this little excursion that landed her right straight in Parker's office, or so she believed anyway. *Yeah, they're using me, all right,* she realized. Little by little she had become convinced of this. True, Lenore's expedition that night came from the conversation between the twits, the millies, she had eavesdropped on at The Whit. "The Twits at The Whit," she chortled softly to herself. "The Twits at The Whit...ha, funny! But cripes, my own pal, Sam...geez!" Her partner for years. What was going on?

Even in her rather muddled mental state of recent days, she wondered if she was over-reacting. Then, too, she couldn't totally rule out that Sammy and dear old Clara Parker were up to no good, and that somehow Lenore was the focal point of it all. Okay, maybe she was acting a *leeetle* paranoid, just a tad. But what about the voices she periodically heard? *If the voices were bogus, would she be able to tie them to somethings that was really happening?* she wondered. *Not if they're bogus. But if you connect them to something that is real, something that really happened, something that is happening....*

And what about the predictions that had come from The Code? They were as real as a heart attack. Sam and Lenore had the bucks to prove it. What's more real than a big gigantic pile of money? And another thing, Sam could vouch for every penny of the money and where it had come from—how they got it. Two people don't go nuts together, do they? They don't think and experience the exact same things, do they? Come on, even Chang and Eng couldn't do that. And let's face it, we are all a *little* paranoid. It's only a matter of degrees between those who are on Thorazine and those who are not.

Lenore laughed vacuously at each suggestion, as if they were being proposed by an invisible shrink seated there in the office.

Suddenly, she heard someone shuffling in the hallway outside the door. She listened for a second, holding as motionless as a cat. "A guard," she uttered as she raced to the door to the closet and fled down the stone stairs just as Parker's door opened.

13

Say it's not true

Lenore had a good handle on Nick's routine. Within a week, she knew everything about it. Students operate on a regular schedule. The good students probably even better than the rest. It's that small dose of OCD that gives them the edge. On Wednesday nights, Nick had a two-hour evening class in immunology, one of his last biology courses needed to wrap up his major. Occasionally, afterwards, he would stop at the Rat for a pitcher of beer with Katy, but his early history class the next morning, a NoDoz event by any measure, meant that the evening never ran very late.

By nine-thirty, Lenore was in Nick's apartment. *Jeepers creepers, doesn't this guy ever lock his place!* Lenore mumbled. Even with the lights out, there was enough light from the windows to move about easily. She found his apartment almost exactly as before: books lying on the floor, piles of papers on the kitchen table. Plates, glasses, and silverware in the sink. She sat for a second in his over-stuffed chair, got up, and went to the window and looked out from behind the curtain. She knew exactly which direction Nick would be coming from. There was only one thing to do now: wait. That and one other thing. She went into the kitchen and opened a drawer—tableware, forks, knives. She opened another: potholders. Another: knives. She poked around the knives and found what she was after. A long sharp one, a twelve incher, a real gem. Something you would carve a ham or a turkey with. For some reason, she couldn't imagine Nick doing any serious cooking. Hot dogs and hamburgers, tuna sandwiches, PB&J, the diet of a student she figured. In all likelihood, the knife had never been used. From her jeans' pocket, she pulled out a white cotton glove, slipped it on her right hand, and carefully picked up the knife from the drawer. It had a good even balance to it, sturdy and solid. She touched the blade with the tip of her finger—oh, yes.

Sitting by the window, time moved heavily along. She looked at her phone. Ten-fifteen now. *Pretty soon he'll...okay, there he is.* Lenore got up and watched as he approached. She shifted her weight nervously from one foot to the other the closer he got. She heard the door to the front of his apartment building open. *This is it.* She went to the hall closet and buried herself behind a stack of coats, clothing, shoes, boxes, other debris.

Nick trudged into the apartment, tossed his backpack on the chair, pulled a bottle of Mountain Valley from the fridge, and paced through the apartment, shuffling around slow and tired. Lenore listened carefully. The footsteps faded off—into the bathroom or bedroom perhaps. Then he was back again. The flat screen came on. He scrolled through a dozen channels and flicked it off. All activity stopped for ten, fifteen, twenty minutes. Had he fallen asleep in the chair? Ugh! That was not part of the plan. As she waited in the cramped closet, her legs began to knot up. She stretched as best she could.

She hadn't heard a peep in a long time. Pushing the closet door open just a bit, she was able to see most of the living room. It was empty. The sound of water came from the bathroom. Soon, he passed through the living room and went into the bedroom. After five minutes, the light in the bedroom went off. She waited another ten minutes, then emerged ever-so carefully from the closet, knife in hand. She stopped for a moment and double checked to make sure her phone had been muted. The last thing she needed now was the ping of a text or the ring of her phone.

Her hand grasped the handle of the knife tightly as she moved toward the bedroom. The door was open several inches. Nick was asleep, turned on his side away from her. She grasped the edge of the door and opened it softly. Standing motionless for several seconds, she began to move toward the bed. Barely a foot away, she stumbled over a shoe on the floor. It was enough to cause Nick to stir. He looked up toward the ceiling, turned and looked over his shoulder. Lenore started for him, holding the knife up high. He leaned back, holding his arm out, expecting the knife to come down. He was wide awake. If the sight of someone coming at you with a carving knife doesn't wake you up, nothing will. Lenore froze in mid-motion, afraid she would not be able to overcome him if a battle ensued. In an instant, she turned and tore out of the room, stabbing the knife point-down on the kitchen table.

Lenore fled out of the apartment. Nick ran after her, but by the time he got to the apartment door, Lenore was already through the hallway and halfway down the stairs. He could see almost nothing of her in the thin hall light. From the window of his apartment, he watched as she raced to her car, leaped in, and drove off at break-neck speed. She turned onto the street, tires spinning, headlights off.

14

Lenore takes a break

Sam pushed hard for another Code. Lenore pushed back. Spread The Codes out, she told him. This annoyed Sam. Having skipped the last opportunity for no good reasons, they were overdue. Sam's face was flushed—fifty shades of red. He was generally good at hiding his emotions, all but for this one biophysiological response that he could not control, try as he might. He said, "The time's right again next week…the moon and all." His right knee jiggered up and down, an obvious giveaway of inner anxiety.

But Lenore knew everything was far from right with her—the voices, the paranoia that filled her thoughts belied one who's mind was usually settled and collected. But what to do? That was the question. Reluctantly, she paid a visit to Martin Leidy, her psychiatrist. She gave him a general account of all she was contending without fully divulging the scope of the problem to him. She never mentioned, for example, the afternoon she spent poking around in Nick's apartment. There was no way she could broach that without having to explain what she was doing there. Likewise with the aborted attack on Nick in his apartment. The problem was, anyway, she herself remembered only portions of what had happened. She wasn't even sure any of it was real, that it had happened in real time. Try as she might, all she could recall was a series of fuzzy dislocated events, dreamlike inchoate events that rippled through her thoughts. She was suddenly in his apartment. How she got there, she wasn't sure. She had no recollection of driving over, parking her car, going inside. None of that. Her only memory was of walking around submerged in half-darkness, knife in hand, and later standing in Nick's bedroom ready to attack. The rest of the details were missing. It didn't matter, she had no plans to tear open that bailiwick no matter what.

"Next week," Sam proposed again. "What about then."

"The Code you mean. No can do, won't be here. Five days in St. Bart's on the beach—fun, sun, and mai tais."

"Oh, really. *When* did you decide *that*?"

"Cut it out, Sam. It's been on my calendar for weeks.... I told you." Lenore got up and looked out the twenty-second-story window. Snow buried the landscape below, the houses, the trees, the streets. It had arrived early in the morning, this time depositing a full six inches of soft powder. Lenore watched as a plow chewed a white layer off the street in a thick sheath.

"St. Bart's, huh?" Sam murmured. "Don't remember but, well, whatever."

"I need a little R and R, that's all. By the way, what's Parker know about The Code?"

"Say what?"

"Parker. What's she know about The Code?"

"Parkie? Clara you mean? Not a thing, why?"

"I don't know. You talk to her, I don't. I was just wondering if the topic ever came up."

"What is this? Of course, it didn't. Parker never asked. Woman has a lot on her plate, whole lotta fish to fry without poking around in our lives. You might think her job is no big deal, but let me tell you, I wouldn't do it for all the oil in Arabia. It's one big fat kiss-ass job when you come right down to it. Always got her hand in someone's back pocket. That's what they pay her to do. That Gutenberg Bible over there in the library, it was her doing. Do you know what that means having that baby there? Know how important it is to the school?"

"So, you're saying she has no idea what's down below the library?"

"How would she?"

Lenore knew from her excursion into Parker's office that she must know, whether Sam realized it or not. Unless she knew nothing about the tunnel from the closet—it's possible she didn't, being as well covered as it was. Just a dark closet with file cabinets that were probably never visited except once or twice a year by a secretary to fetch a student file.

"So, no Code next week then?"

"Sammy, you really do need a vacation. Do like I'm doing. Find a nice secluded island somewhere. You'll come back a new person."

Sam breathed tightly. She was right and he knew it. Yet, as he saw it, so long as the freight loads of money kept rolling in, he was on the vacation of a lifetime. "When are you leaving?"

"Saturday. Back on Friday."

The date for the next Code was Tuesday. "Fine, we'll do it when you get back," he replied, pretending it didn't matter.

15

Sam proceeds without Lenore

Lenore stretched out on a lounge chair under a warm Caribbean sun—beach hat, sunblock, black bikini.

Back in Covington, Sam sat at his desk looking over his day planner. It was Monday. The shape of a quarter moon on the calendar was marked with a note indicating that the next day they could perform a Code. He was determined not to let it slip by. He paced nervously across the room, looked out the window at the layer of snow that covered the town. A dirtier and less appealing snow now than when it arrived five days ago. He returned to his desk, picked up the phone and placed a call to Clara Parker. In less than an hour, he was in Parker's office.

Though Sam had told Lenore that Parker knew nothing about The Code, in fact she knew a lot about it. He felt compelled to let her in on it. What she heard troubled her, but it was a worry she was willing to live with. She trusted Sam. That was her rationalization.

Sitting on the gray leather sofa in Clara Parker's office, Sam was uncharacteristically nervous. He had come for some sage advice on a prickly issue. "I'm desperate to conduct a Code," he explained in a voice ringing with urgency. "But my dear old buddy Lenore decided to shuffle off to St. Bart's, thank you, and left me high and dry. In the past couple of weeks, we had a few investments spin off—lost a pretty hefty chunk of money." To Sam, losing money was a root canal without Novocain. "So, here's what I'm thinking. I don't need Lenore for The Code, not really. Anyone will do, but it needs to be a woman and—"

"Who do you have in mind?"

"No one yet. That's why I'm here. If I could get a worthy candidate, someone we can trust, I can move ahead without Lenore. If Lenore finds out though, watch out. You're going to hear a thousand-amp fuse explode. You can bet on that! We need some discretion in the matter."

Parker tossed out a few names. Most of them Sam had already considered and rejected for one reason or another. Too much to expect to plop an idea like The Code in the lap of a loose acquaintance and expect them to instantly buy into it. It had to be a person Sam knew well. Someone he could trust and someone who trusted him. Parker looked at her appointment schedule. "Augh...faculty senate meeting in twenty." She rose from her desk. "I'll see what I can do, Sam. Give me an hour or so,"

Driving back through Covington's slushy streets, Sam suddenly hit on the right candidate. Ira Pavlovich. Of course, he should have known all along. What better choice could there be? Born in the U.S. from Russian parents, she had a vivacious smile and cerulean eyes and waves of natural blonde hair. She held a master's degree in finance from Princeton and was imbued with an old-world work ethic that pushed her to succeed in a culture where personal effort made a difference. For better or for worse, a high-pitched competition had bloomed between Ira and Lenore almost from Ira's first day on the job. It came as no surprise to Sam; he knew all about Lenore's strident unyielding type-A personality and the way it frequently put her at odds with everyone in her path—male or female. No matter what, Lenore was going to be top dog. The edginess between Lenore and Ira surfaced perpetually at staff meetings. It always brought a lurid smile to Sam's face. A little push-back for Lenore didn't hurt a bit as he saw it.

But…but could Sam convince Ira to go along with his wacky scheme? All he could do was try. All he could do was explain it plain and simple and hope she was adventurous enough to give it a whirl. There was a big risk though. Once she knew about The Code, the toothpaste was out of the tube. No chance to get it back in. How flaky would she think her boss was, messing around with the occult? What kind of company was Ira working for? What sort of pig-in-a-poke was Sam trying to peddle to her?

Ira sat stone-faced as Sam prattled on. He watched her reaction with every word he spoke but got few cues. He wanted to be able to maneuver away if need be. When he was done, Ira laughed gaily. "Sure," she said, never balking for a second. Ira had grown up with stories of gypsies, spells and potions, witchcraft and black masses. The tales were mysterious, foreign and distant to her. Sam's crazy request evoked thoughts of a time she had never known.

⊥

Tuesday Night. Did The Code go well? Ira was the perfect participant, uninhibited, compliant, willing. "Wow," she moaned as she woke up from the trance. She climbed off the altar, light from the candle shaking and shimmering off her body. Pulling the robe over her, she strolled around the altar chamber. "This is a crazy, crazy place," she said. "How in the world did you find it?"

"Long story."

Ira opened the door that Lenore had left unlocked on her recent visit, the one that led into the Green Mile. Down the corridor Ira went, Sam behind her, wondering where they were going. They arrived at the Sick Room. "Yikes," Sam uttered as he gawked at the pile of skulls, the gurney, the cheap metal cabinet, the operating table light on the ceiling. "Yikes!"

"Someone performing operations down here?" Ira asked.

"At one time, maybe. Not exactly the place I'd have a triple bypass."

Ira climbed onto the gurney and rested her head in the leather straps. She looked up at Sam for a second, then climbed down and walked down the long corridor. At the end of the corridor, they climbed the stone stairs and ended up in Parker's office. A moment of awareness came over Sam. *Parker must know about The Code. Has she ever made her way into the chamber from this end?* he wondered. *Spying on us?*

16

Sam and Ira cash in

Thirteen million in six hours. That's how much the take was this time. A cheesy little company named Widget World had raked in tons of money from TV infomercials about all kinds of stupid kitchen gadgets. People were buying them up like doomsday was just around the corner and these were the only means of escape. *The garbage people will spend their money on*, Sam thought, looking at Widget World's website. New and improved Pocket Popeils, instant French fry potato slicers, cabbage shredders, onion dicers, vegetable scrubbers. Sam laughed. "Go for it, buy, buy, buy," he groused as he scrolled down the company website.

This time, unlike in the past, Sam didn't hesitate before he bought. It didn't matter that he had plopped down almost a million big ones on it. Widget World could have been selling buckets of warm manure; Sam would have scarfed up as many buckets as he could. The Code had led him to it, and by now he knew the rules. Buy or sell. Since they owned none of Widget World. The choice was easy.

And buy he did, with great glee, but this time with a new twist. None of the money came from WSA. One hundred percent came straight out of Sam's pocket. A million bucks, in fact. All of it from him. Two reasons drove him to do it. First, were he to purchase the equities with WSA money, Lenore would know immediately. She would know that Sam was flying solo, performing a Code without her. Off would go that thousand-amp fuse, loud enough for the whole world to hear. The second reason was more practical—greed, pure greed. A nice satchel of thirteen million had been tucked away in Sam's personal bank account. *How sweet it is!*

One little troubling detail remained. Ira Pavlovich now knew all about what Sam was up to. It was she, after all, who had been delivered the name Widget World in a dream, exactly as had happened to Lenore in the past. When Ira gave Sam the name, he'd been cool, feigning indifference. But Ira was no idiot. All afternoon she'd watched on her computer in her office as the stock had climbed, minute by minute, hour by hour. When Sam had first left the idea of The Code with Ira, she'd taken it with a very large grain of salt, never believing her pinstriped boss was deep into the occult. Now she believed, and it didn't take long for her to realize the power The Code had. She stared motionless at the computer screen, watching, thinking, thinking, wheels spinning at warp speed. *Money, big money*, were the words rolling through her head. The question was obvious: could she get Sam to let her cash in on it in the future?

⚜

Lenore returned on Friday with a dark, movie-star tan. She was rested and lively and sparked with energy. "Yeah, Sammy my boy, get your ass out of this place and off to an island, that's my advice."

Sam smiled gratuitously.

"So, what did I miss? Any grand windfalls?" she asked.

"Not here. You win some, you lose some. You know how it was in the good old days. We make money the old-fashioned way—we *earn* it," he spoke like John Houseman in a Smith Barney commercial.

"We need to roll into a Code then."

"I somehow remember saying that last week," Sam retorted.

Meanwhile, Ira Pavlovich made up her mind. She would approach Sam with the idea of partaking in The Code with the hope of tapping into a big pile of money of her own. From her limited experience with the ritual, she knew it was complex and that it had to be performed precisely and that she knew almost nothing about the actual ceremony itself, but it was clear this was not some Harry Potter scheme Sam had dreamed up. She had hard proof of that. And it was easy to realize that Sam had approached her because he needed a female partner if it were to work at all. Lenore was Sam's usual choice. Ira pieced that much together.

Ira Pavlovich waited for the right moment to approach Sam. A day when he was in a good mood. These came and went sporadically, given his manic-depression tendencies. Ira's sharp perception had given her a good read on Sam's moods. Dark blue suit meant manic and probably happy. Gray and especially black meant dour and depressed. Then, too, there was the issue of when to approach Sam. That was equally critical. It bugged Lenore to see Ira talking to Sam in his office. When that happened, Lenore's neuroses dripped over in the paranoid direction. Not what you would call psychotic but edging in that direction in Ira's eyes at least. In fact, it was Ira more than anyone who thought Lenore had slipped deeper into a state of paranoia in recent months.

Two days later, everything was right. Sam was jovial and joking and wearing a blue suit. Ira watched as Lenore left for lunch, then gave a soft but firm tap on Sam's door. Sam looked up; he had a good suspicion of what was on Ira's mind. He nodded for her to have a seat in a chair in front of him.

"Mr. Whitney—"

"Cut the crap...the name is Sam."

"Yes, yes...Sam, I just want you to know I'm willing to help you out anyway I can." Ira's voice was serious and purposeful, though she never mentioned The Code. Sam had already been moving in that direction. Doing a Code now and then for the company was good, but tucking a wad of money into his pocket was even better. Sam had once touched on the issue of doing this with Lenore, who promptly rejected it. For all her faults, she was without question the most loyal of all of them to the company. Whatever money they made or lost was for the company. Now Sam saw a chance to head out on his own without Lenore ever knowing it.

Some finessing would be needed, however. Sam would have to find a way to cancel a Code with Lenore when the time came and make it convincing enough that it would not draw suspicion from her. Lenore knew nothing about Sam and Ira, or so he thought. Nor did Lenore know about Sam's big win at The Code roulette wheel.

After Ira left, Sam studied his day planner. There were two possible Code dates coming up in December. One he could do with Lenore. That should be enough to pacify her for a while, anyway. The second he could do with Ira just a couple of days before Christmas. It would be easy to tell Lenore he had a prior commitment at that time. He made notations on his calendar.

17

Lenore catches Sam and Ira in the act

Lenore's trip to St. Bart's had been a blessing in more ways than one. A chance to unwind, but she also learned that the voices happened only in and around Covington. On St. Bart's, she felt like the old Lenore. The one she knew and trusted and preferred.

Sam planned a Code with Lenore for mid-December. A wave of Sam's thoughts flitted through Lenore's head as they talked about it. He managed to keep Ira Pavlovich out of his mental radar, almost as if he suspected that Lenore could pick up on it, though he knew nothing whatsoever of that.

The Code was performed. All went well. They hit a huge vein of money, bigger than any so far: fifty-four million. It was a risky white-knuckle venture from top to bottom because they piled almost three and a half million WSA dollars into it. But they stuck greedily to the plan until eventually even Lenore said it was time to click the sell button and cash in.

As the days moved toward Christmas, work at WSA slowed. There was the annual Christmas party, this year complete with a flash of pithy and snide remarks by Lenore—glassy-eyed from too much punch—that were directed at Ira Pavlovich, whom Lenore found to be far too provocative in a tight slinky dress. Sam pulled Lenore aside and told her to cool it lest she ruin the party. Then, while the party was still going on, he stuffed her into a taxi and sent her on her wobbly way, directing the cabbie to see that she got safely into her condominium.

The next Code was scheduled to take place two days before Christmas. Sam begged off, telling Lenore he needed to make a short quick visit to his brother's place in Boston where the family had planned a holiday party. "Can't get out of it," he told her.

Lenore knew immediately something was up. Whether she had tapped into his thoughts or she was merely suspicious of his motives was unclear. Either way she knew something was cooking. But there would be an easy way to find out.

The night was dark and blistering cold. The Graebner campus was all but deserted—none of the occasional students buzzing across campus. The whole place was like an empty train station, like a town abandoned due to an impending hurricane. Lenore dressed in black from head to foot. She huddled behind a tall bush fifty feet from the library entrance, checking her watch frequently. One o'clock, one-fifteen, one-thirty. She scanned the paths for activity.

Not a soul in sight. With a soft moan, she pulled her goose-down parka to her chin. Then, far down the walk, she saw two people approaching. They swept briskly through the shadows of the elms and maples and oaks. Lenore pulled down into the bush and watched.

Closer and closer they came until they arrived at the steps of the library. Lenore saw Sam's face in the dim light above the entrance. He looked around. Ira stood next to Sam.

"Damn," Lenore growled beneath her breath. Sure enough, it was Sam. *Sam and that wench Ira Pavlovich right there with him.*

Lenore watched as Sam unlocked the gate. They slid quickly into the library, Ira carrying the bag with all the goodies for The Code. Lenore was livid. "That little tramp, Ira," she kept repeating. She climbed from behind the bush and paced anxiously up and down the walk, unfazed by the stiff cold wind that blew past her. Her plans were forming already.

An hour later, Sam and Ira snuck out of the library. Lenore had moved on.

↟

The Monday after Christmas, WSA Investments was back in full swing. Lenore watched every movement of Ira like a cat spying a dove. She seethed with anger every time Ira passed her in the hall, the two barely acknowledging each other's presence. Lenore knew from a party Ira once hosted where she lived. She also knew that Ira lived alone. Lenore had it all figured out.

A full staff meeting had been set for the next day at ten in the morning. It would take several hours. It would be a full slate of business. Lenore told Sam to proceed without her, claiming she had a doctor's appointment. Fifteen minutes into the meeting, Lenore ventured surreptitiously into Ira's office. Pulling her phone from her purse, she snapped a picture of the keys to make sure she knew exactly how to replace them on the desk. In ten minutes, she was at the local Home Depot making copies of every key. Twenty-seven minutes later (she timed it), the keys were back on Ira's desk, set precisely as they had been according to the picture on Lenore's phone.

For a week, Lenore stalked Ira, sometimes parking down the street, sometimes watching from the corner or walking carefully past her house. She knew Ira's routine perfectly. We all live according to a routine, though we may not think so. We come home about the same time each day after work, go to the supermarket about the same time. If we go shopping in the evening, we leave the house at about the same time, return about the same time. Same for going out to a party or a movie in the evening. Lenore recorded Ira's every movement in a small notebook down to the hour and the minute.

Part IV
Lenore Strikes

1

Take that, Ira

The day arrived. Lenore left work at four o'clock, went straight to Ira's house, and let herself in. She had parked up the street around the corner. Working with the keys she had copied, she tried each until she found the correct one. A big concern now was the house alarm, if it existed. What if it went off? What if it was a silent alarm that sent a message to the security office? Not much to do but wait…and hope.

She sat in the living room, checking her watch frequently. It would be easy to know when Ira arrived; the driveway was directly adjacent to the house. She could see it from the living room window. Still, everything had to work perfectly now. The only hope was that Ira would come home alone. If not…well, that could screw things up royally. By all accounts, that was unlikely to happen. But stuff does indeed happen, and most of it happens when we least want it—Murphy taught us that.

Lenore waited a while, then got up and began snooping around the house. She pulled open drawers in the bedroom, but most important, she needed a place to hide. A closet was the obvious choice, just as she had done in Nick's apartment, not that she remembered much of that episode. What with most of it having been etch-a-sketched from her memory.

The center hall closet would be a good choice: roomy with easy access to the rest of the house. She stepped inside. It was big and spacious and scented with the fragrance of the cologne that Ira always wore. Fruity...mangos or something. Lenore hated it with a passion.

As she poked around inside the closet, she heard the front door open. She quietly pulled the closet door shut. *Voices!* Ira had a male companion with her. Lenore listened intently. She was unable to make out all the words, yet both voices were unmistakable—Ira and *Sam*. Lenore could identify his voice anywhere.

They were talking about The Code, how it had paid off with such grand success. Having plopped down ten million smackaroos of his own money on another unknown entity, Sam had pigged-out as never before. He'd ended up with an astronomical two hundred and sixty million, a quarter of a billion! Ira had scraped together every penny she had, and then some, a grand total of one hundred thousand dollars. The Code lottery had spun its wheel and delivered two million six hundred thousand to her. In all her thirty-three years on the planet, never had she stuffed that many ducats into her bank account in one fell swoop. She was heady just thinking about it.

Sam and Ira talked for a long time while Lenore was crunched up in the closet listening intently. She seethed hearing about it. Another Code was in the works. Lenore's name was mentioned; she was their main dilemma now—how to work around her and not let her know what they were up to. Lenore heard every word in her mind clear as can be.

She's going to be a problem no matter what. She won't let me do a Code without her, and she won't do one that won't benefit WSA. We're stuck.

The conversation suddenly dropped off. They couldn't possibly know Lenore was in the house, could they? True, her silver Lexus was parked down the street and it bore the license plates WSA2. Plates that Sam would recognize in a flash.

The closet was getting warm. Lenore was getting warm. Suddenly, she felt trapped by her own plan. But hearing Sam and Ira scheming fueled a new level of anger. The conversation picked up again. Several options were floated. Find a new place for Sam and Ira to conduct The Code. It seemed like the only solution. But even that had complications since The Code could be conducted only two nights a month. Hence, Sam would need to perform two in one night, one with Lenore and one with Ira, like a parish priest traveling from one church to another on Sunday to say mass. At that point the conversation abruptly broke off for good. The front door closed. Sam was gone.

Lenore heard Ira pacing through the house, high heels clicking as she passed across the hardwood floors. Time grew to a slow crawl. Eight forty-five on Lenore's watch.

Lenore's mind began to swim through a hurricane of wild thoughts. She thought she had this all planned out so perfectly. Now she wasn't sure. Could she abort the mission if need be, maybe wait for the right moment, then tear for the door with her coat over her head and get out unrecognized?

Ira's movements in the house slowed. She entered the bathroom; the door was part way open. Water flowed in the tub. Lenore wiped beads of perspiration from her forehead. The flow of water into the tub stopped. Ira came from the bathroom, went to the bedroom, and returned naked. She climbed into the tub, sinking down until just her head was above the water. Lenore waited five minutes, then emerged on cat's paws from the closet. She stood momentarily outside the bathroom, then blasted in.

Ira looked at Lenore in shock, recognizing her instantly. "What are you doing here?" she demanded, sitting part-way up in the tub.

Lenore held a leather belt she had taken from Ira's closet. She gave it a short spin over her head and slashed it down toward Ira like a wild west rodeo rider. Ira reached out. Turning her head, she was able to partly intercept the blow, but the buckle landed squarely by her left ear creating a deep gash. Lenore leaped for Ira. She pressed the belt across her throat trying to push her down into the tub. Ira grabbed Lenore tightly at the wrists. Ira was wiry and surprisingly strong. She pulled one foot from the water and pried it between her and Lenore.

"I know what you've been doing, you little…," Lenore screamed as she leaned down onto Ira. "You've been with

Sam, using The Code to make money." Lenore's voice was coarse and almost ghoulish.

Ira tried to speak. "What are you talking about...." But this was not the time for logic, not when you're about to be submerged in a tub of soapy water.

Lenore abandoned the belt and with a vicious burst of energy grabbed Ira by the neck and slammed her against the porcelain tub.

Ira felt a welt grow on the back of her head.

Lenore tried to position herself over Ira. With all her might, she jammed Ira's head below the water. Ira pushed back, pulling herself quickly out, having taken a throat-full of soapsuds-laced water in the process. She squeezed part way up, but Lenore pressed her thumbs into Ira's throat.

"There will be no more Codes with Sam!" Lenore growled.

Ira gasped and jammed the palm of her hand into one of Lenore's eyes and pushed with great urgency, sucking wind, pulling short breaths into her lungs, but it was too much for her on her back in the water. Lenore slammed Ira's head against the porcelain tub again and held it under the water. The gurgling stopped. No, there would be no more Codes from Ira and Sam.

Lenore stood up, wet and breathing fiercely. She wiped her hands dry on a towel, looked around the room, and delicately pulled a tube of red lipstick from the cabinet above the sink. In large ragged, red letters she scribbled Red Rover, Red Rover on the wall over the tub then slipped the lipstick into her pocket and walked nonchalantly out the front door. At the corner, she tossed the lipstick into the sewer and climbed into her car and drove off, whistling.

2

Ira goes missing

In the morning, Lenore woke up feeling cloudy-headed and carrying almost no memory of the night before. For thirty minutes she lay in bed. She wasn't hungover, hadn't stayed out late. But she couldn't recall a thing about where she had been. She got up slowly.

When Ira Pavlovich failed to show up at work the next day, no one was overly surprised. When she didn't show up for the second day, Sam became concerned. He decided to call the police. They arrived at Ira's place, rang the bell, went around to the back entrance and peered inside, then circled the house looking through the windows. Everything seemed fine. At the bathroom window, one of the officers propped the other up on his knees. "*Oh…geez!*" he uttered. "*Oh, geez!*"

A call was put in for an ambulance. The police pried open the back door with a crowbar. There in the bathtub, floated Ira—lips the color of a purple crayon, skin gray and puffy. No EMS crew could reverse that. The whole event was studied and photographed and recorded. An hour later Ira's body was in the morgue.

A Covington detective arrived at the suite of WSA Investments. A secretary led him into Sam's office. He introduced himself with the flash of a wallet badge—Detective William Blum. It was Sam who had put the original call into the police. Now it was immediately clear something bad had happened to Ira. Blum described what the police had found. "Drowned in the tub," he said in a drab voice, adroitly watching Sam's reaction.

A hard silence settled across the room. Sam sat motionless in his chair and turned toward the window for a long while, saying nothing.

"When did you see her last?" Blum asked.

"Who? Ira?" Sam looked at Blum. "Two days ago."

"Where was that?"

"Well, she works here."

"That was the last time you saw her...alive."

Sam resented the phrasing. "I saw her a couple of nights ago for a few minutes...over at her place."

"How many nights ago?

"How many? Two, I guess. The day before yesterday."

"The day she was killed," Blum said.

"I suppose...according to what you said."

"And so, what happened there?"

"Nothing happened there. We talked about some investments, that's all. The kind of thing I've done dozens of times with her."

"Over at her place?"

Sam groaned softly. "At her place, here, at a restaurant at lunch, just about anywhere...we're in the investment business."

Blum jotted notes in a small spiral notebook, Colombo-like. It would have been comical had the situation not been so real.

"Look, if you think *I*..."

"I don't think anything..."

Can say that again, Sam wanted to say.

"...I'm just gathering information."

"Who should tell the people here?" Sam asked.

"It'll be on the local news tonight and in the *Gazette* in the morning. If you mean, who should tell the people here at your place, I'll leave that up to you. We'll be talking to everyone in your group pretty soon."

Sam nodded.

Blum turned to leave. "Oh...by the way, what does Red Rover mean to you?"

Sam's eyes widened enough that any cop, rookie or veteran, would pick up on it. Ira had told Sam about the words when she'd described her dream of Widget World. Yet, in all the time Sam had performed a Code with Lenore, *she* had never mentioned the phrase.

Sam repeated Blum's question. "What does Red Rover mean?" He shook his head. "Nothing. Kid's game...why?"

Blum smiled curtly and left.

Sam was not yet ready to deliver the bad news to the office. He needed to tell Lenore before going to the group. He walked into her office just as she was arriving for work. Sam's face was blank and devoid of life. He looked at

Lenore, then merely turned and left. She followed. As they entered his office, he closed the door. "Have a seat," he said, walking to the windows.

Lenore watched Sam. Something was up and it wasn't good. She had that bad feeling you get when your boss is about to tell you you're being fired. Of course, she knew he couldn't do that. Sam and Lenore were co-owners of WSA. They were equal partners. She was as much the boss as he was.

"Something happened to Ira Pavlovich," Sam said in a meek voice, his back to Lenore.

Lenore said nothing. She sat uncomfortably in the chair.

"Ira's...Ira's dead."

Lenore pulled her hand to her mouth in utter shock.

Sam turned, walked to his desk, slumped in his chair, and rested his face in his hands. After a long silence, he said, "She was murdered."

"Oh...my...God. When?"

"Couple of nights ago. Someone got into her place." Sam's voice was jittery, the words were difficult to get out. He cleared his throat. "Drowned in the bathtub. I know nothing about the details. The cops were here a few minutes ago. They're coming back to talk to people."

A while later, Sam called everyone together and gave the bad news. He told them to go home and take as much time off as necessary.

3

Lenore reads of Ira's death

Lenore sat at the kitchen table reading the morning edition of *The Covington Gazette*. There on the front page was a picture of Ira Pavlovich with a big smile. *They always do that, don't they? Plaster a picture of some victim of a tragedy looking happy, chipper, and jovial.*

Lenore sipped coffee and read every word of the article intently. It described Ira and her job at WSA and gave plenty of details about the gruesome murder. No motive was given, not a hint of a reason. All in all, this was certainly not the kind of news Sam or Lenore would want for WSA. By tomorrow, similar articles would be out in the *Boston Globe*, *The Manchester Register*, *The Portland Reader* in Maine, stuck in the middle pages perhaps but there for all to see, nonetheless.

The article suggested the police had little to go by. One telltale event stood out. The words "Red Rover, Red Rover" that were splattered wildly on the wall in bright ten-inch red letters. When Lenore read this, panic flushed through her. She stared out the window of the breakfast nook, took a sip of coffee, and thought. Like the small events that trigger your memory the day after a dream, the words brought back flashes of her time with Ira on the night of the murder. Lenore was standing in the bathroom. Ira was low in the tub.

Lenore looked at her right arm, at the enigmatic scratch that started up by her elbow and ended near her wrist. She had no idea where it had come from or how she had gotten it, but now she was worried. The police hadn't talked to her, but they would. A good convincing story is what was needed.

She racked her brain trying to remember what she had worn that night, but her memory failed on that as well. In the bedroom, she began frantically tearing clothes off hangers, examining each piece one by one, tossing them on the bed. In the dresser, too, and the dirty clothes hamper. Something dark is what she would have worn. She took all her black slacks, the black jeans, the black blouses and dark shirts, and stuffed them into the fireplace. Packed paper under them and lit a fire.

When she was done, a significant amount of ash was left behind. She placed a couple of logs inside and watched as they burned, figuring the ashes from the wood would mix with the ashes from the clothes. A flash of panic moved through her as she watched the flames. How could she destroy evidence if she didn't know what evidence to destroy? How? And shoes? What about those? It was safe to assume she had worn a pair of tennis shoes or running shoes. But which ones? Of those, she had many. Besides, you don't exactly toss shoes in the fire without making the entire place smell like you're burning truck tires or something. But they, too, had to go. And she had way more than a few pairs of shoes. Lenore was a shopper. Not shop-till-you-drop perhaps, but a shopper just the same. It was one of her frequent indulgences—money was never an issue.

She went to the closet and fetched every pair of running shoes she had, packed them in a kitchen trash bag, and started out the building, suddenly realizing it wasn't such a great idea to be seen heading out with a bag of shoes. *Get with it Lenore, you've got to think of everything now! Get with it!* She went back inside and stuffed the shoes into a large gym bag, put them in the back seat of her car and drove through Covington. Practically every strip mall had a clothes donation container. This was Vermont; people were good at helping each other out.

Indeed, clothing dumpsters were everywhere. She stopped at one after another until each pair of shoes was gone. It took the better part of an hour and she had no idea that she wasn't merely handing the police murder evidence. Is that the first place they go…to dumpsters and drop-off containers? Could be, for all she knew. *What makes a cop's mind tick? If you believe all the crud on TV, they never leave a stone unturned. But what are my options? Dump the shoes in the river?* That sounded to be even worse. A dozen shoes, and damn good shoes at that, floating down Covington's only waterway couldn't be good. *Would the police check that also? Who knows?*

Lenore returned and double-checked her condominium to make sure she had dealt with all possible evidence.

When the ashes cooled, she swept them from her fireplace into a bag and tossed them in the building dumpster out back. It was her standard routine for this; surely that couldn't be mistaken as somethings sinister. On the way up in the elevator, she ran into old lady Grundy, the hag with the walker whose nose was in everybody's business.

"Some nut had a fire going in the fireplace this morning," Grundy told Lenore. "Smelt it burning when I went outside with the dog."

4

Nick puts two and two together—it doesn't look good

Nick Sanchez was as shocked as everyone to read the article in the morning *Gazette* about Ira Pavlovich's death. He sat in his soft chair, pages of the paper unfurled across his lap. He knew nothing about Ira Pavlovich, nothing about WSA Investments. Then he read the description explaining the words "Red Rover" on the wall. Where had he heard that recently? *Yes, of course, part of that crazy dream I had after the first time we went into the altar chamber.*

Loosely related chunks of the story began to come together: first, the altar chamber below the library, then the Red Rover dream, the two people he saw leaving the library late at night, and finally the book on The Code he lifted from Parker's office. And there was the night Lenore was ready to do open heart surgery on him with a carving knife in his own bed. It pointed in one very dark and morbid direction.

But what should he do? Go to the police and tell them what he knew, which wasn't all that much when you came right to it. *Is there any point in going to Parker? No effing way!* Nick was Mr. Low-Profile. He knew the best way to get on the good side of the administration was to stay as far away from it as possible. Remain invisible.

What was WSA Investments anyway? Nick turned on his computer and Googled the words. Up popped the WSA website. Lots of glitzy pictures of their services: financial planning, estate planning, tax-deferment systems, all the rest. And sure enough, there were pictures of Sam Whitney and Lenore Simenson smiling happily, looking like the kind of people you just might want to turn over your nest egg to.

Nick was sure they were the ones he had seen coming out of the library late at night. "Geez," he mumbled softly. Although he was unable to make little face recognition that night, what with dark shadows and the half moon, the faces on the computer screen convinced him of the connection. Yes, it was her, the same person he'd spotted eyeing him and Katy when they were in Jake's, and that time in the reading room when she was pretending to be hunting for a book but mostly stalking *them*.

Nick fidgeted. If she had something to do with the murder of Ira Pavlovich, why was she after Nick? The middle-aged woman with green eyes smiling ever so seductively in the picture on the website could not possibly be a cold-blooded killer...could she? A serial killer who stalked her victims along the quiet paths of Graebner College and closed in for the kill? Nick got up and checked the door. It was locked just as he had left it the night before. No more open-door policies for Nick. The news in *The Gazette* was one thing. The fact that he might be on some nut's list was something else altogether.

5

Clara Parker tries to warn Sam

The day *The Gazette* article appeared, Clara Parker called Sam. They met for an hour in Clara's office. Clara knew that Sam had performed a Code with Ira. Was there a connection to her death? Could there be? In what way? The very thought of it made Clara's palms sweaty—her normally steady hands trembled. Suppose there was a connection and the whole thing landed right smack in Clara's lap.

Clara told Sam there was something she needed to show him. She went to her bookshelf, filled with hundreds of scholarly books, and ran her finger across the row looking for a title, one shelf after the other. "Odd," she muttered. "Hmm, can't find it." She scanned the shelf three times then turned toward the window and stared at the white winter sky. Sam sat quietly, almost obediently. Clara told him she had retrieved a book from the Velvet Room shortly after coming on board at Graebner. She went into a diatribe about how the rich old battle-axes had been hounding her at fundraisers. It was always the little skinny ones with the frail bony hands that clutched you at the elbow as they spoke in a crackly voice, holding a glass of Chardonnay and pushing to see if you knew anything at all about Graebner or if you were nothing but a sop for the university board. Clara had done her homework—she had learned the names of every person who had sat in the big chair in the president's office since the school had started, all the way back to eighteen hundred.

"Did my research, I did," she told Sam. "I knew everything there was to know about this flophouse. That's when I came across the book on The Code and the nasty stuff that happened at Schulenmeister Seminary." Clara sat in her chair and rested her forehead on her palm. "Now where did that book go?" she said, thinking hard.

6

Blum presses Lenore hard on Ira's death

Lenore hoped all the incriminating evidence was now gone. But what about the words "Red Rover" scribbled on the wall? What had been used to do that? *Paint? A red pencil? …Blood? If so, doesn't that mean there will be fingerprints?*

She couldn't remember using the tube of Ira's lipstick to write on the wall. Never remembered tossing it in the sewer on her way down the street. In fact, she had no clear indication that she was the one who had killed Ira. Therein rested the problem. But she was convinced more than ever that if she had, it was a something bad that had come from The Code. After having been gobsmacked by physiological changes in her, the voices she was hearing, had she now been turned into a serial killer? A Jekyll and Hyde kind of serial killer? And then there was the revelation about Jessie's car accident. She was now convinced that The Code had done much more than merely allow her to foresee the accident, she believed it was responsible for it.

She sat at the kitchen table tapping her finger, mulling everything over. She was cornered, trapped in something over which she had no control. Did it make sense to do another trip to see Leidy, her psychiatrist? But even if she did, what would she tell him?

The buzzer for her door rang. "Who is it?" she said through the intercom.

"Blum, Lieutenant Blum, Covington Police."

Lenore pressed the buzzer that opened the front door of the condominium and waited for Blum to arrive. He flashed his badge and politely stepped inside. They sat in the living room. Lenore felt her pulse rise, her hands tighten.

Blum looked around the room. "Nice place." He pulled his notepad from his jacket pocket. "I guess you realize I'm here to talk about Ira Pavlovich. I have a couple of questions, if you don't mind."

Lenore nodded.

"How long did you know Ira?"

"We hired her about four years ago as I recall."

"Did you know her before that?"

"No, she had just finished grad school at Yale. We had an opening and she applied. She was a good employee."

"Did she have any enemies at your place?"

Lenore shook her head.

"That's a no, I take it."

"That's a no. She got along with everyone."

Blum jotted notes. He thought for a second, appearing to be formulating his words. "What about you? How well did you get along with her?"

"I got along fine, why?"

"Well, I talked to several others this morning. One person said there was friction between the two of you."

"Nonsense. Ira and I got along just fine."

"So, there was never—"

"Nope. Ira worked for me. For me and Sam. If I really had a problem with her, I would have just let her go, don't you think?"

Blum flipped the pages on his notebook. "There was some sort of incident at the recent Christmas party. Something between you and Ira. You got into a gutter fight, I heard."

"A what?"

"A squabble."

"Not that I recall."

"At least two people that I talked to mentioned it, saying Mr. Whitney had you put in a cab. Said you were tipsy to say the least."

"Tipsy maybe. So what? Too much punch I suppose. Isn't that what Christmas parties are for? For having fun. What's that got to do with this?"

"And there were words between you and Ira. That's what I heard."

Lenore tilted her head and rolled her eyes.

Blum reviewed his notes, taking a long time as he went back and forth through the pages. An old cop trick, no doubt: make the interviewee feel uncomfortable by spreading the questions out and watch their reaction, see what cryptic revelations are emoted.

"You probably read this morning in the paper the words Red Rover at the crime scene. Strange thing to put on the wall in my opinion. Does it mean anything to you?"

"Yes, I read it. No, it doesn't mean anything to me." Lenore delivered her best poker face. If the dumb-ass cops had left *that* out of the *Gazette* article, Blum's question would have landed totally sideways and caught her totally off guard. *So why did they allow it to get in the paper*, she wondered?

"When was the last time you saw Ms. Pavlovich?"

Lenore thought. "Three days ago, probably. The last time she was at work, I think."

"Did you see her that evening or the next morning maybe?"

"I was at work the next morning. I wasn't paying attention until Sam told me and then broke the news to the office staff. I don't, didn't, work all that much with Ira. Sam did now and then, but she had her own portfolios to manage. That's how it's done at our place."

"Where were you three nights ago…in the evening?"

"Oh, cripes, I'd have to think." Lenore leaned back for a couple of seconds. "Here at home…uhm, uh, I was here all evening. I remember watching that sitcom. The stupid one about the guy who owns a bakery and can't—"

Blum nodded and smiled slightly. "See you had a fire burning this morning," he said, looking at the fireplace. "The woman downstairs commented to me, saying someone was burning a fire early this morning."

"That's Grundy, Millicent Grundy. She doesn't have anything better to do than keep up with what's going on in the building."

"Good watchdog, huh."

"I don't know, I suppose," Lenore said, shaking her head. "I was saddened by the news about Ira, so I sat in here and built a fire in the fireplace. It helps sooth my nerves sometimes. I don't know why it does, but it does."

Blum paged through his notebook as if hunting for an entry.

"Do you have an idea who might have done this?" Lenore asked, knowing it was a ridiculous question and that Blum would never reveal what he knew.

"Not yet. We have some physical evidence that could be important." He gave no details. "That's it for now. Best if you hang around Covington for a while in the event something comes up."

Lenore agreed and showed Blum to the door.

A huge sense of concern passed through Lenore. What if they had found physical evidence leading to her? Could she be held accountable for something she had no recollection of? She was worried; she needed to talk to someone, someone she knew well. Sitting in the living room was only making her more nervous by the second. She gave Sam a call. They agreed to meet at a café in Covington.

Lenore had never seen Sam so forlorn. He was pale and shaken and depressed. She got straight to the point. It was time to abandon The Code, abandon it totally. Not merely a moratorium but an all-out shutdown. Sam was confused. He fussed with his chin, chewed on his lip, looked around the room. He had been thinking about the tragedy of Ira's death, not about The Code. He hadn't put all the pieces of the puzzle together the way Lenore had.

Lenore couldn't remember if she had told Sam about Red Rover during her dreams. Probably not, but she wasn't sure. If she had, Sam would have been all over her about it, himself having been asked by Blum and having read the description in *The Gazette* that morning.

"Some guy from the Covington Police named Blum came by this morning," Lenore said.

"He's talking to everyone." *Could it be that Lenore did this? That she killed Ira? Geez, I hope not. There were problems between her and Ira, yes, but I can't believe Lenore would even consider something like this. She's not the killer type.*

"You don't think *I* did this, do you, Sam?"

"Cut it out, Lenore, of course not." *If it wasn't for Red Rover, I wouldn't...but—*

Hah! He knows about Red Rover. How? Did I tell him? I know how he found out. It was from the time he and Ira snuck out and did The Code. She must have mentioned it to him. Now he's piecing everything together. Who else would have put those words on the wall? Who? Who would even think to? If someone wanted Ira gone, why slap those words on the wall? This was hugely troublesome for Lenore, knowing that she herself had indeed killed Ira. Drowned her in her own bubble bath.

Sam said, "You're really ready to give up the big bucks from The Code, is that it?"

"Totally. Lots has happened that I can't explain."

"Such as?"

"I'm not going into it, Sam. Take my word. It's not been pretty."

"Stuff with you?"

"Stuff, just stuff, Sam. Okay?"

Sam groaned. "It would be nice if I knew what you're getting at."

Lenore sat quietly, nervously, in front of Sam.

Sam had to ask. "Lenore, you didn't...I mean about Ira—"

Lenore's nostrils flared. "*No*, Sam, I didn't. Did *you?*"

"Did *I?* Why would *I?*"

"And why would *I?*"

"What about Red Rover?"

"What about it?"

"Is it connected to The Code?"

Lenore didn't flinch. "Not as far as I know. Why do you ask?" she said, defiantly. "Do you know more about The Code than I think you do? Why is that? Been messing around with it on your own perhaps? Maybe with Ira Pavlovich perhaps? Maybe it didn't go so well, The Code...perhaps. Is that it, Sam?"

Sam growled, "Who are you, Detective Blum?"

Lenore got up and stormed out of the café.

7

A drastic plan by Lenore to change the course of things

Desperate times call for desperate measures, and for Lenore these were desperate times. If all the darkness that came out of The Code had to do with ancient sorcery and the occult, then by all accounts the solution had to come from ancient sorcery and the occult. Indeed, if the evil that had settled in her brain was due to The Code, then there was but one solution. Trepanation. The humoral of evilness that was cursing through her body needed to be rooted out at its source. She was ready to take the plunge no matter how drastic.

For three straight days, Lenore, Sam, and their coworkers were the subject of frequent visits from Lieutenant Blum. It was getting tedious. Lenore knew she was a prime target of his investigation, not because of the questions he fired at her but because of the thoughts that rumbled through his mind, the unspoken questions from the unspoken conversations that she could pick up. Every visit from

Blum got worse. Why? Maybe he had her body language pegged. Cops do that, don't they? They read body language like a pro. The good ones are like Leidy, her shrink, who did more than listen to the answers to his questions. He would watch her carefully but inconspicuously during their sessions. Now she was sure Blum was doing it.

And she was right to be worried because Blum had a pretty good hunch that Lenore knew a whole lot more about the murder than she let on. Ask the same question a dozen times in a dozen different ways and see what bounces back, see how many times the answers match up. Or don't match up. Surely even a small-town cop like Blum would know that. He had learned it all coming up through the school of hard knocks as a cop. It was a technique as standard as the off-the-rack suits he wore, but it worked time and time again.

Is it really conceivable to be trepanned in this day and age? Who would do it? Where do you even begin to try to find someone, a trepanner, if that's what they're called? Are there specialists, physicians, who perform such things? Of course not, that would be sheer quackery! But anything in the world could be had these days. Anything. She could find all she needed to know on the internet. Maybe not who would do it, but surely how it was to be performed à la the twenty-first century. She checked and, sure enough, there was plenty of info there about it.

But that was not a solution to her problem. *The solution will only come once I've found a reliable and knowledgeable person to conduct the, the*…she had trouble saying the word, trouble even thinking the word…*the trepanning.* She needed someone with medical experience, and more than just a modicum of it. *No fish-oil peddlers, thank you. If you're going to have someone drill a hole into your skull, Christ almighty it better be done right!* Lenore thought long and hard. No names came to mind. Then, finally, yes—Allison McClure. A registered nurse and a good friend, and very bright if perhaps a little fringe in her thinking at times. Into holistic medicine. If anyone would know about this, surely it would be Allison. In fact, Lenore even remembered her talking about trepanation once not so long ago.

Lenore wasted no time getting in touch with Allison; they set up a meeting to discuss it at THE CEO. Even if Allison couldn't help her out with the trepanning, it would be a chance to catch up with an old friend, maybe stop thinking about Blum for a while.

Lenore arrived a full twenty minutes before their scheduled meeting. She needed time to arrange her thoughts and a couple of moments sitting alone with a martini to build her courage.

Charlie was off that night. Willie was on. She knew Willie, but nowhere near as well as her old friend Charlie. He did put together a whopping-good Grey Goose, however.

She thanked him, left a tip, and located a table on the edge of the room. It was early, just before seven, and THE CEO was not especially busy. But then, it was rarely all that busy. It was a high-end whiskey bar that made its profits off the jacked-up prices of expensive liquor from people who could afford it. For the price of a single ounce of any of the standard whiskeys and single malts, you could buy the whole bottle in a store. Or you could go nuts and get a Pappy Van Winkle's Family Reserve or a Hibiki, each of which would rip about a hundred and fifty bucks out of your wallet for one single little ounce.

Lenore settled in at the table. If nothing else, Willie had eclectic tastes in music. Tom Waits' *Chocolate Jesus*, it was. Allison McClure strolled in—a hug and she sat down and flagged the waitress, "One of whatever she's having."

The dim light made Allison's naturally ruddy skin appear tanned. Her blue-gray eyes, darker. And of course, any woman sitting next to Lenore looked better no matter what their age. It was an odd inexplicable gift bestowed on Lenore by the gods, something more than a few Hollywood movie stars would die for. It didn't take long before the conversation moved on to trepanation.

Lenore toyed with her martini glass, rubbing her finger nervously over the stem. "Tell me what you know about it."

Allison shrugged a shrug that said she knew a lot. "It's done more often than you think, that much I know."

"You've been there for these…the trepanations?"

Allison nodded. "But if I was sitting here talking to someone else, I'd lie my ass off. I am a registered nurse, you know." She took a small sip of the martini and said, "How many times? Oh, I don't know, a couple dozen probably. At least that many."

"Where are they done?"

"Just about anywhere, actually."

"Not in the OR. I gather."

Allison laughed. "Ha…no, *not* in the OR."

"Too bad, would be better, right?"

"Of course." Allison fetched the green olive from the bottom of her glass with a toothpick. "This is holistic medicine were talking about. The country isn't ready for it."

Lenore grimaced. "A bit far out on the holistic scale, don't you think?"

"Oh...depends," Allison said, unconvinced. "Look, I deal with conventional medicine every day. It's what pays the bills, and most of the time it works fine...let's just say that most of the time we're not *killing* people. And yes, true, we do a lot of good now and then."

Lenore listened intently. She wasn't fully committed to the idea. "The trepanation, does it *really* make a difference? You know me, Allison, I'm pretty much white bread all the way when it comes to these kinds of things."

"Does it? Sometimes, yes. Well, quite often, yes."

"You believe it then. I may not be a doc, but I do know it's possible to fool the hell out of yourself if you're not careful. Get yourself to believe something really happened when it didn't. The old placebo effect," Lenore said.

"If I thought there was no benefit to it, I'd never get involved."

"What kind of people have it done? What do they have it done for?"

"Lots of people for all kinds of reasons—housewives, top-tier execs like you, ditch-diggers, college kids. Take your pick. People of all ages, adults. No children."

"But for what? Why do they have it done?"

"The most common reasons are probably depression. Headaches too. The kind that won't go away...migraines et cetera, the ones the docs can't fix. Too, we also get some people, men mostly, who are looking for a cure for impotency. On the flip side, we even had a young woman, late twenties as I remember, who was about as close to being a true nymphomaniac as there is. I'm telling you that babe's engine was running all the time, red lining…autopilot and way out of control and she knew it. All the professional help was of no use. She was getting laid eight, ten times a night…couldn't get enough. Pretty remarkable." Allison's eyes ballooned up. "She stalked the bars every night. It was flat-out ruining her life."

"So did trepanation help?"

"Settled everything down perfectly. Exactly what she wanted. She was worried it might blow her over in the other direction. You know, turn her into a nun or something. But it didn't. Now you tell me if you've ever heard of a shrink performing that kind of magic. Oh sure, they'll say they have hundreds, thousands, of successes. Don't believe them though. I'm a nurse, not a neuroscientist, but I can tell you there's a lot going on in this noodle of ours that no one understands. A *heck* of a lot! And I can also say that if trepanation really didn't work, why would people have done it for thousands of years? Why?"

"Well, they also tried to make gold out of lead for thousands of years, and that didn't go so well," Lenore said, suddenly remembering her own successes with alchemy. In truth, alchemy worked great if you knew how to do it. Maybe with trepanation too…if you knew how to do it.

Willie sent the waitress over to check on the needs of Lenore and Allison. The bar began to fill up. It was moving on toward eight o'clock. A few happy-hour devotees remained, men dressed in their perfectly tailored suits, ties loosened, collars open. Women in expensive dresses looking as spiffy as the moment they arrived at work nearly a half day ago.

"You never said why you wanted to do this, Lenore," Allison asked. "Some issue, I suppose."

Lenore had prepared herself for the question. It was inevitable, she knew it was. She pulled an answer from the list Allison had laid out moments ago. "Headaches," was her first, which wasn't altogether untrue, though it was hardly the real reason. "Yes, a lotta headaches," she repeated. "But not just that, I've had a long spate of depression that I can't seem to shake. I've tried all the usual stuff, medication from my doctor, talk sessions with him my psychiatrist, the whole caboodle. I'm not at the end of my rope, nothing like *that*, but I need some relief and, well…well I thought—"

Allison smiled and nodded several times, she had heard it all before.

Lenore said, "But if I'm going to do this, I need to know *everything* about *everything*. I need to know the details ahead of time as much as possible. What's the downside, the risks?"

"About the same as any surgical procedure. Infection, but very rare. Less common than in the hospital. Those places are gigantic incubators of nasty bugs. Almost any procedure done outside the hospital, if done properly, is safer these days."

Yet Lenore knew there was more to be concerned about than she was getting from Allison. She knew it because she could hear Allison's unspoken words. Something about *Patrick Grayson...not quite a raving success...and Sybil....*

The sudden revelation of that worried Lenore.

"When you come right down to it, the procedure isn't all that invasive," Allison said.

This was beginning to worry her, too. Allison seemed to be pushing the technique a bit too hard, a little like an unscrupulous dentist telling a patient they needed a crown when in fact the tooth was fine.

"Where do you do it?" Lenore asked.

"We use several places, unless you have some place you prefer."

"We'll get to that in a sec," Lenore said.

For seventeen years, Allison McClure had worked as a surgical nurse in the operating room at CGH, Covington General Hospital. It positioned her well to have access to the autoclave for sterilizing the drill bits—shiny titanium bits, razor sharp but otherwise not unlike something you would use to put a hole through a two-by-four. On any given day as needed, she would take one of her bits (she had an entire set by now, all sizes, all types), wrap it in autoclave paper, run it through the sterilizer, then slip it into her purse on the way out at the end of the day. Smooth as silk, not a soul the wiser.

"And the actual procedure, what about that?"

Allison went into it in exquisite detail. No point in making it sound like they'll be baking brownies. Lenore listened to every syllable. The quiet light of the room added a bit of unnecessary tension that Lenore felt grinding away slowly in her belly as she heard the description.

It was an uncomfortable question, but Lenore had to ask, "Any deaths?"

"Deaths? Oh, no, absolutely not."

"Bleeding?"

"A little now and then," Allison declared. "I've been involved in a lot of these. Vic, Victor Boudreau, is the one who does the procedure. He's a surgical nurse too, works in the OR at CGH with me. Guy has terrific hands. Could have been a great surgeon if he had gone to medical school. I watch some of the procedures he helps with and I want to say, get that barber out of there and let Vic take over. I'm telling you, he's that good."

At that point Allison leaned toward Lenore and pulled her hair apart on the right side of the head. "See it? I had one done not so long ago. Best thing I ever did." Lenore stared numbly at a scar about half an inch across. "It's totally grown over, hair and all. Nice thing for women, they can pull their hair across the wound until it's healed."

"Did it help, the, uh...."

"Trepanation? Absolutely. Ask my husband. I was having problems with sex. It just wasn't there. Victor did the procedure and *wow* what a change! I've been going at it ever since like a rabbit tooting coke. Go ask Ralph, he knows."

Lenore had decided if it was to be done, it would happen in the altar chamber below the library, assuming it passed muster on Allison's part. They would use the old tiled room with the gurney and the operating table light. She gave Allison a few of the details and said she would bring her to see the room late at night after the library was closed. The procedure, if they were to do it at all, also would occur at night. Sam would be kept out of the loop on this.

There they left it for the moment.

"I heard about the bad news over at your place, the person who worked for you. I read it in *The Gazette*," Allison said. "Gave me the chills. I mean this is Covington, Vermont, for the love of Mike. When was the last time we had something like that happen here? Well, I can't remember. Most of us live here to get away from that kinda junk…those big city troubles we don't need."

"I know. Sam's beside himself over the whole thing. So am I." Lenore looked down at her martini glass as she spoke. "They're looking into it, the Covington Police, some guy named Blum, a detective. They may get the person yet, hope so anyway."

Allison took a sip of her drink and shook her head. She turned and looked to her left and her right. "You know what's most creepy about this? It could have been anyone here in this bar. Anyone. We could be sitting in the midst of the killer right now, *right here*. And that's the kind of world we live in these days and you can't get away from it either. Twenty-four-hour news cycles, cripes. And social media, you know Facebook, Instagram, and all. Sometimes I want to go out and live in a cabin in the woods far, far away. I've even said this to Ralph. No TV, no internet, block everything out, 'not there, not there' like the guy in the Stephen King movie *Rose Red* kept saying. Well, I hope they find the low-life and send his ass up the river for a good long time…a good long time."

"They will," Lenore said, practically choking on the words.

"I'm going to have to head out," Allison said. "I told Ralph I was doing a 'catch-up' with you…he's cool on that kind of thing."

"Just out of curiosity, does he know about the trepanations?" Lenore asked.

"Ralph? Sure, all of it. We're open about everything we do. Anyway, ever since he had that small bout with cancer, he's been a whole lot more into holistic medicine. Never had a trepanation himself, but he knows all about what Vic and I are doing." She checked her martini glass and caught the last sip. "Any-hoo, that's it." She opened her wallet to pay her bill but was waved off by Lenore.

"Let me know kiddo…K?" Allison said, and left.

Lenore stayed at bar thinking and listening to Lightnin' Hopkins' crackly voice, "Long Way from Texas." When the Pogues started singing "Dirty Old Town," and a wad of tipsy thirty-somethings joined in as though sitting in an Irish pub, belting out the chorus and pounding their fists on the table as they sang, it was time to leave.

Lenore accomplished little during the next three days. She sat blindly in her office, thoughts bouncing back and forth between her conversation with Allison and the trepanation. Was she going to do it? If it really worked, it was probably worth the risk…perhaps. And she did need relief. The voices were getting worse, and she *was* getting depressed, and Blum was now more of a pest than ever. He was a damn mosquito that she couldn't get rid of. The kind that buzzes your ear seemingly just to harass you. He was showing up perpetually, plowing through the same wretched questions.

8

Sam pays a visit to Clara Parker

Even Sam was ready to back off on The Code for a while. He moped around at work trying to smile, attempting to get the mood of the place back on track. Seeing the boss moving back to a state of normalcy seemed to help. The bigger problem was communicating with Lenore. After their blowout earlier in the week, everything was touchy. Sam gave a gentle knock on her office door and peered in. "Got a minute?"

She slipped him a cold nod.

"I've been thinking, maybe you were right about The Code. You know me, Mr. Correct…always have to be the decider. Who was it who used to say that?"

"Dubya. Remember him…Bush?"

"Oh yeah, him. So anyway, we'll let The Code go for a while. Sound all right?"

"Sounds all right."

They shook on it. A layer of tension lifted from the room. Lenore smiled. Sam smiled.

Lenore said, "Now if we can just get that piker Blum off our back. He's beginning to frighten the whole team here. Guy's ticking me off. If I were him, I'd be poking around good and hard to see what Ira's boyfriends were up to. Let's face it, she had droves of them."

"Blum's at a total loss, that's my take. He's rolling snake eyes so he's killing time here until he gets a better lead. I wouldn't worry about it. No one from our group was responsible for Ira," Sam said. He almost believed it. "Wouldn't surprise me one bit," Sam told Lenore, "what you said about one of Ira's boyfriends. Ira was hot, all right. Real eye candy." Sam's mind flashed to the nights the two of them had done a Code, Ira standing in the tenebrous flicker of candlelight in nothing but her birthday suit. "And I know she had an issue with some guy. I heard it from Melissa, the secretary, they were good friends. Ira told Melissa the guy was stalking her."

"Come on, get your act together, Blum," Lenore sparked as if Blum were right there in the room.

"He is, he's on it. Melissa told Blum everything."

Lenore sighed loudly.

Sam and Lenore went to lunch. They were like husband and wife after a spat, tartly happy again.

9

News about Detective Blum

It landed like a rock in an empty well. Detective Blum was dead.

Officer Mike Smith met with Sam and Lenore in Sam's office. Smith stared out the window for a long while, saying nothing, thinking, looking into the far horizon where the whiteness of the snow and sky fused. He turned, looking first at Sam then at Lenore. Clearing his throat several times, he rendered the grim details.

Detective Blum had been found in bed in a room in the Sleepy Hollow Motel at eleven-thirty that morning by the maid. He'd been knocked unconscious and suffocated with a pillow.

Lenore's gut tightened. *I was at work most of the morning, right?* She took off her glasses and rubbed her eyes. She couldn't remember for sure.

The room was filled with an uncomfortable silence. Finally, Smith said, "We thought you probably should be told since it was Bill, Detective Blum, who was on the Pavlovich case."

What Officer Smith left out of the discussion was that Blum had been at the motel that morning for a rendezvous, that he had had sex, and that whoever had been in bed with him may well have killed him. That, or there was one other equally realistic possibility.

Blum, good-looking and virile. He had chalked up more flings than even he could count. His wife knew about it all too well. So, too, did the people Blum worked with. He had been warned about it more than once by the chief. At the very moment Smith was talking to Sam and Lenore, the police were questioning Blum's wife. Perhaps she had had enough of his antics and this was where it all had finally ended, a crime of passion as common as any there was. Yet Smith revealed none of this to Sam and Lenore. *Ain't none of their freaking business as far as I'm concerned*, Smith thought. Nor did he mention the words "Red Rover" on the wall above the bed.

Thus, from the police's viewpoint, there were two possibilities. First, the same unknown person who had killed Ira had killed Blum. In this case, the assailant must have had a grudge against Ira, and maybe wanted Blum out of the picture for the obvious reason that he was investigating the murder. Second, Blum's wife had killed Ira because Blum had been balling Ira, and his wife also killed Blum because she found him in bed again with yet one more person.

But Lenore knew better because, as she figured it, as incomplete as much of this was in her mind, she was the one who had wiped out Ira, with a bit of encouragement from the demons of The Code, of course. But what about Blum? She had not so much as a whiff of a recollection of that, yet according to Smith it had happened no more than a couple of hours ago.

"I have little else to tell you. The investigation of the Pavlovich death has been passed over to another person at the station. Some leads are continuing to come in."

Sam thanked Smith for coming over in street clothes. The last thing they wanted at WSA these days were more cops showing up. Smith nodded and left.

Once Smith was well down the hall, Lenore said, "Guess that's the end of Blum harassing us."

"And, unfortunately, the end of the investigation into Ira's death. Would be a good thing for all of us if they could get to the bottom of it. Close it up and be done with it. My guess is the Covington police department doesn't have the resources to probe much further into the murder."

"Probably not," Lenore said, carefully hiding her immense glee.

Sam sat quietly for a moment, rubbing his temples, staring at his desk blotter. *This couldn't have anything to do with Lenore, could it? Oh, geez, let's hope not. No, not possible. Could it? She did come in late for work this morning though. What time...about eleven o'clock or so....*

Picking up on this, Lenore snapped from her chair. "Do you *still* believe someone from here killed Ira?"

"Never said I did. And besides, let's not revisit that, okay? It didn't go so well last time we tried."

Lenore agreed.

"We have bigger fish to fry right now. Don't forget, tomorrow the Blum thing is going to be in *The Gazette* for everyone to see. Yes, only a few people would know to connect it to Ira, but it's still another bizarre murder here in little old Covington, Vermont. It's going to scare the bejesus out of a lot of people."

Lenore got up. "It's out of our hands…completely," she told Sam in a quick and edgy voice.

10

Nick tells Katy what he knows and warns her about Lenore

A January snow fell heavy and wet, wrapping half of the state of Vermont under ten thick inches. Throughout Covington, the plows were out from early morning, sending white sheaths of snow onto the curbs and burying the cars along the roads that had failed to heed the call to vacate the streets. Katy shook off the snow as she entered Nick's apartment, rubbed her hands together, and gave him a hot kiss.

Nick had the article from the Covington *Gazette* spread out on his kitchen table. The death of Blum did indeed make its way into the paper, but not on the front page. This time, the murder drew nothing more than a small blurb in the interior of the paper in the obits section next to the police blotter report. No details were given about Blum's death. Nothing about the crime scene. Not a word about Red Rover or any other gruesome information. Nick did not draw a connection to the death of Ira Pavlovich that had appeared in the paper barely a week before.

Nick hadn't told Katy about the late night visit he'd had from Lenore. It had scared the pants off him, and he knew it would scare Katy half to death too. But he decided he needed to tell her anyway. His worried that, for some unknown reason, Katy was on Lenore's 'to do' list as well.

"Cripes, that's terrible!" Katy said. "You think you know who the person was?"

"Not sure," Nick replied equivocally. "But I saw the car as it sped out of the parking lot. Unfortunately, I didn't get the license, or the exact make of the car, but I'm fairly sure it was a Lexus."

"I think you need to report it to the campus police, don't you think?"

Nick didn't like the idea. The last thing he wanted was light shining on him, good or bad, now that he was four months from wrapping up his days at Graebner and moving on. "I'm going to keep it quiet. But you need to be careful— I mean it. Who knows what this witchy creep is up to?"

11

Lenore takes Allison McClure to the altar chamber

Lenore had no choice. The evilness inside her had to be stopped. She called Allison McClure. They spoke briefly, going over some of the details again, then Lenore coolly said, "I'm ready."

The first order of business was to select a place for the procedure. Although Allison offered several possibilities, Lenore was certain about where it should be done. They set up a time to go into the library at night on Thursday, two days later.

But before Allison and Lenore ventured down into the altar chamber, a few ducks needed to be lined up. On top of the list, was clearing out the pile of skulls in the Sick Room. This meant a trip down there by herself. She would need the library key for this, the one Sam kept in the top drawer of his desk. It wouldn't be a challenge to get the key. She had done it before. She waited until Sam was out for his afternoon trip to the gym, went to his office, and snatched the key from the back of his desk.

At two in the morning, Lenore was standing next to the gurney in the Sick Room. The skulls had to go. At the very least they would raise a lot of sanitation issues, not to mention the morbidity they implied. Lenore gathered armfuls of them and deposited them in a nice neat stack in the corridor that led to Parker's office. It was either that or cart them out of the building. Something she had no intention of doing.

On Thursday night, Lenore and Allison stood by the gates to the library. The night sky was bright from a full moon, unlike the half-lit sky of the quarter moon when The Code was performed. Lenore unlocked the gate, unlocked the door, and turned off the alarm. Up to the reading room they went and then down into the chamber. Lenore leading, Allison following.

When they arrived at the altar chamber, Allison looked about and gasped. "What the heck is this?" she said in utter amazement.

"Old room, that's all. Basement of the old library. No one uses it. I'm not sure anyone knows it's here." Lenore started into the corridor in the back of the chamber. "Here, follow me," she said.

"Good grief!" Allison gushed when they entered the Sick Room.

"I know, pretty bizarre, huh?"

Allison went straight to the gurney and examined the head straps on the table. "If I didn't know better, I'd swear this was used for trepanation." She looked at the walls, opened the old cabinet, and flipped the switch on the operating light over the gurney. "Works fine...amazing. Not the best I've ever seen but not the worst either."

"The room is all right then?" Lenore asked.

"Needs a real good cleaning. Walls, floor, this thing here." She pointed to the gurney. Looking at Lenore, she said, "You know, we could just as easily do this in your condo, and I know of at least one other place that would work fine."

"I'd prefer here," Lenore replied.

Allison continued to explore the room. "It'll work...I think."

Late the next night, Lenore did her cleaning duties. She scrubbed the walls, ceiling, floor, and gurney with Clorox and an assortment of other disinfectants. When all was done, the room looked better, smelled better. The tell-tale musty odor that had all but clogged the air was gone. At Allison's request, Lenore brought a small portable table for the surgical instruments and set it next to the gurney. Everything was set. They were ready for launch...T minus one week and counting.

12

Unexpected happenings

Lenore lay awake but motionless on the gurney. Victor Boudreau looked around the room, shuddered at what he saw. Pretty damn spooky.

He gave Lenore 10 mg of diazepam to help relax her. On the table next to the gurney, wrapped in autoclave paper, was a set of surgical instruments: a stack of sterile gauze, sutures, two surgical drills, sterile gloves, and a set of trephines, the drill bits used for the procedure. A sterile hospital drape was placed over the gurney. Another drape covered Lenore. Her head was gently wrapped in a lightweight cloth. Her face and the side of her head was exposed. Victor and Allison donned surgical gowns, gloves, masks.

"How are we feeling?" Victor asked in that first-person plural voice that hospital staff so annoying use. (Did we take a bath today? Did we have a bowel movement? No, nurse Ratched, *we* did not have a bowel movement, we did not have a bowel movement, but *I* did.)

"I'm okay," Lenore replied softly.

"Ready to go?"

She took a deep breath and stared at the shiny green tiles on the ceiling. "Yes, ready."

"Remember, you won't feel the drilling. I'll give a small injection of anesthetic into the skin around the area where I will make the incision with the scalpel."

Allison turned on a pair of battery-powered clippers and removed several locks of hair, shaved the area with a razor, cleaned it with surgical scrub, and waited for it to dry.

"Now I'm going to inject the anesthetic into the surface skin. You'll feel a couple of pricks," Victor said working to her side and toward the back of her head. He waited a few minutes and rubbed his finger on the skin. "Feel that?"

"No."

Victor picked up a scalpel and made a one-inch incision through the skin and reflected it to the side. He motioned for Allison to re-position the beam from the surgical lamp onto the incision and blot a drizzle of blood that ran from the cut.

"All okay there?" he asked Lenore again.

Lenore felt a numb trembling pass through her body. "A little tingly."

"That's to be expected…nerves. Everything's going fine."

Lenore lay quietly. Allison rested her hand on Lenore's shoulder and gave several reassuring nods.

Victor picked up the drill. "I'm going to use one of the battery-powered drills," he explained. "You'll feel some pressure when I push on it slightly." He tightened the trephine in the drill and positioned the tip on Lenore's skull and pulled on the trigger. The bit spun smooth and even, gradually boring into the bone, producing a fine powder that fell on the floor as he passed a millimeter at a time into the bone matrix. Victor leaned gently on the drill. Lenore felt the pressure increase. He stopped and waited for Allison to blot the blood that trickled from the cranial bone, being that it's heavily perfused with blood vessels. His conversation with Lenore dropped off as he concentrated quietly on the procedure at hand, with an occasional, "Almost there, just a little more."

Lenore listened to the drill grind on the bone. She looked up at the ceiling and imagined for a moment she was in a hospital OR. The recently scrubbed tiles could almost fool you: the beam from the light above her, the gowns, the instruments, Victor's gentle but firm and steady hands.

The pressure increased slightly as Victor Boudreau continued to drill. He backed off, then applied more pressure. "We're doing fine," he said.

Breaking gently through the cranium, he removed the trephine that held the plug of bone. A God-awful smell suddenly filled the room. A putrid smell as foul and sour as death itself.

"Whew! What's *that*," Lenore said, freaked.

Victor had no idea. Nor did Allison. They had never experienced anything like it before.

The smell settled onto the room as though it were more than a bad odor, as though it were a film of dense molecules that floated about the chamber and then sank down on everyone like a damp mist on a hot day.

Victor pulled in a breath, trying to determine the source of the malodorous smell until he realized it was coming from right in front of him. As if Lenore's brain were...as if it...as if it were filled with decay. As if it had rotted. Maybe not all of it but some portion, like a bad spot on a tomato that forces you to pull quickly away from where a worm had munched out a portion of its innards, chewed it up, and spat back sour juice.

"It's nothing," Victor replied, continuing with the procedure. Of course, he had not so much as a glimmer of an idea as to where it had come from. "Just the drilling. It happens sometimes," he said fraudulently, looking quickly at Allison.

He peered at the hole, at the dura and arachnoid layers, below which was the subarachnoid and pia and then the brain itself—the most sacred of all organs. He removed the bone plug from the bunnell and scraped a tiny chip of bone fragment. "We're done. Through the skull. Nothing to do now but put it back and close it up." He set the drill on the table. "Still okay there, Lenore?"

Lenore groaned almost inaudibly. She wanted this to be over as soon as possible. "So far."

"That's the worst of it. It won't take long now. Hardly any bleeding, barely any. One of the best I've seen. A good sign."

Lenore exhaled uncomfortably.

Victor took the bone plug and repositioned it in the skull as if replacing a carved-out eye from a pumpkin. He pressed bone putty softly along the edges of the plug and pulled the flaps of skin together. Allison handed him a needle holder with a needle and a fine silk suture.

Victor said, "I'm gonna give you a half dozen or so of these little fellas. It'll leave almost no scar and the hair will grow over just fine. We'll leave them in for a week." He sewed the flap together, spread antiseptic ointment over the wound, and taped a piece of gauze on top of it. They lifted the drapes off Lenore and swung her feet slowly on the side of the gurney.

"How do you feel?" Allison said.

"Not sure. Little woozy, I guess, but okay."

"Take your time," Victor said. "Just sit there a while." *Damn strange place all right*, he thought, having no real desire to hang out longer than necessary.

13

From bad to worse

Dr. Helen Coombs, the Covington medical examiner, made a long ventral incision across the chest and the abdomen of the body laid out on the metal table. The body had been rolled into the medical examiner's office by a fire department ambulance at ten that morning. A neighbor had detected a horrible odor coming from the apartment next to hers. On the toe of the cadaver was a tag with a number and a name: 44675, Victor Francois Boudreau.

Dr. Coombs looked carefully at the internal organs. She cut a piece from all the essential real estate—liver, pancreas, spleen, kidney, adrenals, small intestine, colon—and plopped each one into a jar of ten-percent neutral buffered formalin that her assistant, Walter Scott, labeled with a sharpie. Coombs cracked the chest. A rancid odor blew out. Good God almighty, the lungs were nothing but a bloody mass of pink and white flesh with a little gray blended in, having the consistency of runny snot. She didn't put that into her recorded comments, but it would have been the best description possible.

In her days, Helen Coombs had seen some badly rotted bodies. Like Sigmund Blackburn, ninety-four years old and still working his small farm until the day he collapsed in his barn. Dead for a full week. Fortunately, it was winter. It were as if he had been delivered straight into one of the morgue storage lockers not long after he hit the floor, all but for his face, which a handful of mice had joyously dined on, having chewed it nearly to the point of non-recognition.

But no, Helen had never seen anything quite like this. An almost perfectly preserved body except for the putrid lungs. For a split second, she wondered if perhaps she might be staring at the opening salvo of some outrageous new virus—influenza perhaps, some virulent pig or swine strain that was making its debut in Covington, Vermont. A new devastating strain. Or something worse. Something mankind had never seen before. Something that tore through the body, through parts of it at least, like a brush fire in west Texas that leaves a swath of destruction in its path.

Helen Coombs pulled a piece of the slimy flesh of the lung parenchyma, held it over a bottle of formalin, and dropped it in, saying nothing, merely looking at Walter Scott's blank and frightened face. One piece wasn't enough for something so delectable, seconds were indeed needed. She took several more samples from each lung, from all five lobes and from the top and the bottom and each side. She traced her way up along the trachea, what little there was—now porous and riddled with holes. Besides the formalin specimens, she took tissue pieces and placed them in a vial filled with liquid nitrogen that Walter Scott held at arm's length. They would be used for virus, bacterial, and fungal testing.

The cranium was opened and the brain was removed. Macroscopically, it looked fine—most of it did. Helen Coombs dictated. "Hemorrhage with possible contusion, left frontal cortex." She took a piece and placed some of it in formalin, some in nitrogen. Oh, yes, she was worried. Had this—whatever it was—traveled to the brain, or had it traveled from the brain to the lungs? She had never seen anything like it. *Ever.*

14

Again

Victor Boudreau had lived alone. If he had any close relatives, no one knew. He did have friends though. Allison McClure being one. She was the first to be informed of Victor's death. She promptly told her husband, Ralph, and then called Lenore. Thirty minutes later, she was sitting in Lenore's living room.

"It's scary," Allison said. "They don't know what caused it. Vic was fine the last time I saw him and that was just two days ago at work. He was his usual self, laughing, poking jokes at the doctors. He wasn't there yesterday though. I just assumed he had the day off. Then today I got the call telling me what happened."

Allison described it to Lenore as it had been described to her from Dr. Coombs, with the gory details omitted.

"Well, they must have *some* idea, don't you think?" Lenore said.

"A respiratory thing is what Dr. Coombs, the medical examiner, thinks. That's where the problem was…down in the lungs. And if so, it went fast. Damn fast." Allison stopped speaking and looked away. After a long while, she turned to Lenore and said, "Well anyway, you're looking good. Got your hair pulled across the wound, I see."

"It's a top secret. Ryan at Duvee's Spa gave it to me once when I was getting my hair done for a wedding. Never wore it…not until now, that is."

"Couple days and I'll take the stitches out."

Lenore did her best to appear calm, but she was desperately worried about the news of Victor. Did it have something to do with the trepanation? How? In what way? She wanted to ask Allison but didn't know how to broach the question.

If anything, Allison was twice as worried. She wished they hadn't done the trepanation down in the grisly room below the Graebner library. Was there something in the air—something bad and dangerous—that had infected Victor, and possibly Allison as well? The slight chest pain she had woken up with in the morning didn't help matters any. That was before she had heard of the news about Victor. *A winter cold coming on perhaps*, she had thought. *Stupid winter cold.* That's what she believed until she heard about Victor.

"Coombs said they're checking for a virus," Allison explained, looking colorless and drawn. She drew in a deep breath and exhaled. "Well…I need to see if I can locate Victor's family." She got up from the sofa and gave Lenore a long hug. "I'll be in touch. The stitches in a couple days, now don't forget. I'll get back to you."

Allison left. She drove through the snow-crusted streets of Covington across town to her house. All she wanted to do now was get home, see Ralph, forget the world. She pulled into the driveway and turned off the car. Gasping twice, drawing in two deep breaths, she died.

15

Helen Coombs is desperate

For a second time that day, Helen Coombs was removing stringy globs of gelatinous lung tissue from a corpse. For a second time, her fears drove her deep into the realm of the unknown. Halfway through the autopsy, she stopped and suited up in hazmat and had Walter Scott do the same. The gross pathological findings were identical to what she had seen hours before. Everything appeared fine—all but for the rotted lungs and the spots of black decay on the brain. This time, Coombs placed the entire lung in a large jar of formalin. She completed the autopsy, showered head to toe with antiseptic soap, went to her office, and placed a call to the Vermont Department of Public Health.

"Epidemiology please," she requested.

"Delworth here," came the eventual reply from Dr. Oscar Delworth, one of the state epidemiologists.

"Oscar? It's Helen Coombs over in Covington. I have something here you need to see."

"What is it, Helen?"

"Better you just come over and take a look, Oscar."

"That bad?"

"Yes, you need to see it."

"All right. Covington, right? Be there in forty give or take a few."

When Delworth arrived, Helen Coombs had everything ready for viewing. They both suited up in hazmat.

"Good grief, this *must* be bad," Delworth said as he fit himself into the suit.

"I don't know, but I'm not taking any chances."

They entered the autopsy room. The jar with the lungs sat on a table. Delworth picked it up and turned it around with fastidious care and handed it to Delworth. "Good God, what is this? Not much left, been dead for weeks, maybe longer."

"What if I told you two hours, at the most. She was alive this morning. Alive and moving about chipper as a squirrel, the picture of health so I'm told. She went to visit a friend, came home, and collapsed in the driver's seat of the car. Her husband found her when he returned a little while later. Name's Allison McClure. She's a nurse here in town. I know her, more or less. Met her a couple of times…small town, you know."

"Weshooie," Delworth uttered as he turned the bottle. "Hard to imagine anyone blowing air out of those bellows."

"Worse yet. This is the second in the same day. The first was a fella named Victor Boudreau. Turns out he was probably dead for a few days, but everything was the same as here. I'll show you."

They went to the coolers. Coombs slid out the drawer with Victor Boudreau's body and the one with Allison McClure's body.

Combs said, "Except for the lungs and the brains, everything else looks pretty much what you'd expect, macroscopically at least. These are not the bodies of people with lungs that rotted, and I've seen more than my share of dead bodies. But never any this strange."

Delworth had seen enough. The sooner he was out of the room and the hazmat, the better. They scrubbed down and went to Coombs' office. Delworth sat uncomfortably in a chair, brow furrowed. "Infection. At this point I'd have to bet on infection."

Helen Coombs shrugged dolefully. "That's where my money is, for now at least. I took fresh tissue for bacterial cultures and virus isolation. If it's bugs, they'll grow fast, a day or two probably. If virus, it'll take a while longer. Three, four, five days or so."

"I had better gather as much information as I can," Delworth said. "Who can I talk to?"

"Allison McClure's husband. Ralph." She wrote the address on a piece of paper.

Oscar Delworth caught up with Ralph McClure at his house. A handful of friends sat with him, consoling him, talking quietly.

Delworth introduced himself, asking if he could have a couple of minutes with Ralph. Epidemiologically, if Delworth was going to track down the cause of the deaths, it required making a detailed map of everyone and everything Allison had contacted in recent days. The list turned out to be long: Allison had a string of friends. Running down each of them would take time, something that he felt he did not have a lot of, given what he had seen at the morgue.

Ralph McClure provided what information he could. He told Delworth that Allison and Victor Boudreau worked together at the hospital and that they were in contact with each other in the OR. But Ralph also knew that they performed trepanations together, and that they had done one recently. He never divulged that factoid to Delworth. No way was Ralph going to pick up *The Gazette* and read something as shocking as that about his sweet dead wife. Nor, for that matter, did he know whom they had performed the recent trepanation on, or where it had been performed. Delworth was left with a deep dry hole from which no crude would be flowing when it came to information about Allison McClure.

16

Love you to death

Lenore was scared out of her shorts when she heard about Allison's death. Now she was convinced that there was a link between the deaths of Victor and Allison, and the trepanation. The tally of dead bodies in her wake—caused in whatever way—was growing fast: Ira Pavlovich, William Blum, Victor Boudreau, Allison McClure. Just being around Lenore was becoming an invitation to the Covington morgue.

The problem, too, was that the trepanation had done little to undo the problems Lenore had been having. Selective though they were, the voices remained. She worried that she had been *imagining* the voices the way psychotics hear voices. But then most shrinks will tell you that psychotic people aren't imagining the sounds and voices that float around in their head, the voices that no one else hears. Rather, the voices are quite real—real as a bee sting. It's all part of the dubious distinction between that which is in our mind and that which exists in the world around us. The drummed-up imaginary world versus the existential one. *This* was what worried Lenore to death.

Yes, the worrisome voices, but also the fact that the headaches were not gone either. True, now they flashed by more quickly, came and went more rapidly: an hour or two instead of a day or two. But they were indeed headaches. Does anyone ever question whether they have a headache or not? 'Hey, Bill, I *think* I have a headache. Think I might but not sure'. No, no one does *that*. You have a headache or you don't, pure and simple.

But there was a whole new twist to this. Something inside Lenore told her that she could control everything and everyone around her. That she had a power unlike anyone on the planet. And with this came an invincibility. Little by little she was beginning to believe it. She knew the Covington Police was shooting blanks when it came to Blum's death. His wife had checked out fine, the lie detector revealed no foul play on her part. You might think that Blum's leads about Ira's death, that little notebook of his that was chocked full of leads, had been passed over to the new investigator. But not so—here's why. Sitting in her living room, Lenore rested back in the Lazy Boy, tired, eyes closed. Little by little, the details of what happened to Blum appeared to her as if they were happening all over again.

⊥

He was checking her out on his many visits that were intended to gather information, but most of the time the only information he wanted was to find a way to get into her knickers. She knew this because, each time he showed up at her door he asked the same lame questions, pretending to be searching for information about Ira's death, Lenore could hear what he was really thinking. It was more than a cop game, he was planning his move.

On one of his morning visits, he said, "You're a darn good-looking woman...you know that, I'm sure."

Lenore didn't reply. She watched and listened as Blum poured it on. He knew the routine, had been through it before—many times before. And, to be sure, he was indeed a hunk. Six-one, about her age, physically fit, salt and pepper hair, a little more salt than pepper, gray-blue eyes, warm smile, cute dimple on his chin.

"I think we could have some fun together," he told Lenore as he sat in a chair in the living room.

Lenore listened but still said nothing.

"Well, that's it for now." He got up and started for the door. Turning, he said, "Room 18 at the place over on Highway 4, ten o'clock this morning. I'll be there."

Ten minutes after ten, Lenore swung her Lexus into the parking space next to Blum's. He paid for the room, came back with the key, and opened the door. A gritty room laden with flowery scents of cheap detergent and a heavy dose of Lysol from the bathroom greeted Lenore.

When Lenore came out of the bathroom, Blum was in bed with the sheet halfway up his bare chest. She stood next to the bed for a second and then pulled a rubber mallet from her purse and ferociously slammed it down onto the side of Blum's head. His eyes flickered then quickly went out. She crammed a pillow tight over his face. There was a momentary struggle as his body gasped reflexively for air.

She pushed hard for several minutes until his chest stopped moving. But she took no chances. She slowly lifted the pillow; Blum's pupils were fixed and dilated—wide black circles surrounded by a thin rim of light gray.

There was no evidence of breath. She watched as Blum lay motionless. She took his pulse. Negative. She took a pair of pruning shears from her purse and positioned it high on the third finger of Blum's left hand and pressed down with both of her hands. The bone cracked and snapped. She removed Blum's ring, wiped it clean, and set it on the table next to the bed. With the blood from his finger, she decorated the wall in large letters:

RED ROVER, RED ROVER, SEND BLUMIE-BOY OVER

Ah, but there was one last thing she needed. She recovered Blum's notebook from his jacket and slipped it into her purse and peeked through the curtains to the parking lot, everything looked fine. The lot was nearly empty, an occasional car.

A Hispanic maid parked a pushcart in front of a room on the other side of the drive and gathered an armload of sheets and towels and entered a room. Lenore slipped out the door and climbed casually into her Lexus where she sat for several minutes paging through Blum's notebook. Sure enough, there it was. She was his prime suspect in Ira's murder. Lenore read: 'Story doesn't jive. Said she didn't know Ira all that well. Said they were good friends. Contradicts herself a lot. Which is it?'

So why was he willing to ball me if he thought I killed Ira? Some weird fantasy of his? Sick game of ball the killer? Is that how he got his jollies? Well, well, well, no more jollies for this jolly giant. Or maybe he thought he could get an outright confession once he had gained my confidence, and this was the way to do it?

Lenore backed the Lexus out and drove down Highway 4 until she arrived at the west branch of the Saco River that runs through Covington. She parked the car and walked on her spiked high heels awkwardly on the balls of her feet through the low bushes and overgrowth until she arrived at the shore. She swung the hammer behind her and gave a mighty heave and sent it far out. It splashed into the dark water. She did the same with the pruning shears. All gone forever, she hoped.

⋏

Lenore opened her eyes—so that's how it all happened. She barely had any recollection until this very moment. How could she have done something like that and not remember a thing about it? This is what perplexed her. Perplexed her and worried her. Her body had been turned into a drone. Sent wherever to do whatever. But not just her body, her mind too. That was the most worrisome part of all. The Code had turned her into Dr. Jekyll, complete with her own warped version of Mr. Hyde.

17

Nick and Katy return to Clara Parker's office

Nick and Katy sat in the reading room. The last student had left. Only Byron Linkley remained. But this time he was doing more than merely mindfully reading, or perhaps preparing a lecture, or working on a paper, or occasionally straightening his bowtie—green and red and yellow striped tonight. He was furtively watching Nick and Katy from across the room, now and then pretending to be reading something on his iPhone. But Katy wasn't the least fooled. She was convinced he was snapping pictures of them like some inept CIA mole.

Nick and Katy were there to pay a visit to President Parker's office through the underground passage. Nick still had the book he had lifted from her office. He felt increasingly guilty having taken it and wanted it back on Parker's shelf.

"What in the world is Linkley up to?" Katy snapped in a barely audible tone. "Playing library monitor or some damn thing? Excuse me Professor Linkley, but we have a right to be here."

A current of fetid air spread throughout the reading room coming from Linkley's direction.

"Go home, Linkley," Katy firmly uttered. "Go home."

"He's keeping tabs. He knows something's up. I have no idea why…or maybe he's taking selfies of himself. This whole thing is making me totally paranoid."

Minutes later, Linkley gathered his things, aligned his green, red, and yellow bowtie between his collar, and left as though oblivious to the presence of Nick and Katy.

They waited. Gustav Becker ticked off the minutes, landing with a bing-bong on the half hour. Nick got up and walked into the hall—no sign of Linkley, no sign of anyone. He came back and quickly opened the panel door. They vanished inside.

Within minutes they were down in the altar chamber, through the Green Mile, and standing in the Sick Room. It looked different to Katy—cleaner, almost modern. "What's this? The skulls are gone." Katy pulled open the door to the corridor that led to Parker's office. There they were, the skulls, stacked in tiers exactly as Lenore had left them.

Through the narrow tunnel and up the stairs into the closet in Parker's office they went. Nick slipped the book in with the others on Parker's shelf. Katy walked to the window and looked out. The campus was dead and lifeless. An occasional lone student or a pair of students moved quickly down the walk. She looked in the other direction. Fifty feet down the path was Professor Linkley, looking up at the window to Parker's office. Katy pulled away from the window.

Part V

Clara Gets Involved

1

Sam and Clara Parker discuss mutual problems

"I'm in dire straits," Sam told Clara Parker, his voice full of urgency.

Clara didn't answer. She rose from her chair, walked across the room, and stood by the window. She had a sense of what was coming, but she had a serious problem of her own. She needed to tell Sam about it. Trouble had brewed, and Clara was on the hot seat. Looking out the window, watching the students pass along on the snow-cleared brick paths one floor below the administration building, she listened intently to Sam. A fire crackled in the large old fireplace, something Parker considered a worthy perk for the long hours she put in on bitter days like this.

"We took a big hit over at WSA and it knocked us flat on our ass."

What Sam was talking about was the sudden and unavoidable change in good fortune for their investments. Their collective portfolios had, within a span of one short week, plummeted badly. Sam had watched as each of their best stocks went south. The problem was, it had no connection to the movement of the markets. The markets were strong and solid, heading upward nicely. But for weeks Sam and Lenore had seen their key stocks drop, one after another. Sam never connected it to The Code; there was no logical reason to do that. As he saw it, The Code operated through a completely different set of simple rules: run a Code, wait for the dream, get the message from it, buy or sell quickly, watch the performance of the stock, dump it and rake in the money. Every time, that's how it happened. Now what was happening was a total aberration, and Sam was worried as never before.

Though Sam never tied the bad luck to The Code, Lenore knew better. Everything in her life was being ruled by The Code, it seemed. It was no surprise to her that The Code was taking on a life of its own.

"We had some real bad luck," Sam repeated. "It's not the first time this has happened to us at WSA. What I do for a living is nothing more than spin Fortuna's wheel. And every time something like this happens, I swear to myself it's time to get out. Time to cash in and sell my part of WSA, buy a beach house in Florida, and hang out with the geezers down in God's Waiting Room…you know, sit and stare at the ocean. Or maybe Maui, some place where I can watch the sun go down. Ice bucket. Single-malt scotch. Destroy my liver. Maybe write that novel I always said I would. But right now, my chances aren't looking good." Sam laughed in the most unfunny sort of way.

Clara Parker listened. She turned and walked quietly back to her chair and sat down. "The school endowment's in trouble, Sam" she finally said. "Big trouble." She pulled a cigar from the box on her desk and tossed it to Sam. She kept them handy for the fat cats who paid a visit now and then. Cigars, cognac, caviar—whatever was needed. Sam declined. Normally, Sam would have lit-up, but not under the pressing circumstances of the moment.

"Oh yeah, the endowment is in big trouble," Clara said again softly, worried. "We have, we *had*, just shy of one billion dollars. And like you, I had a plan, but mine was not to sit on the beach and drink scotch. My plan was to rocket the endowment into the stratosphere. Not just one billion, but two billion, four billion when all was said and done. It seemed easy. All I had to do was take some of the endowment money, pick good safe investments, and watch it grow instead of letting it sit in a bunch of fixed-bond accounts. The market's been going nuts for quite a while now. You know that better than I do."

Sam also knew that if that's all there was to investing, everyone would be millionaires…or billionaires.

"So last year I got a little crazy, I started leveraging the endowment. Not totally crazy, mind you. Went for the tried and true investments. The blue chips stuff…the banks, the oils. I never said a word about it to anyone, not to the board, not to the provost, not even to you, Sam. Probably should have, but didn't." Parker spoke in clear, round words like someone on the witness stand in court. "When I arrived at Graebner, the endowment sat at eight hundred million, just shy of a billion. Like I said, for a school of this size, an endowment like that's nearly unheard of. Enviable...damn enviable. The endowment is everything. You're an investment jock, Sam, you know what that means. If you have eight hundred million and pull in ten percent a year from it, you end up with eighty million in funny money for things like a new stadium, new bio labs, an auditorium, yada, yada. I figured if I could make the endowment grow, maybe even double it...look what we'd have then. That was going to be my legacy here. But then, I don't know what happened. Everything I bought flipped on me, turned sour. So, I threw more money at it. Like those dorks in Vegas who double-down on their bet again and again when they're in a hole. It did *not* go well." Parker stopped speaking. She got up and walked to the fireplace. "No, it did *not* go at all well," she said, her gaze lost in the flames.

"So...how much?" Sam asked politely, as if not really wanting to know.

There was a long and fateful pause. Parker turned to Sam. "Almost four hundred million."

Sam gasped.

"Four hundred million. Gone...poof. Burned up. I'm in a heap of trouble, Sam. That's the reason I needed the money from you folks a couple of months ago to finish the stadium. There weren't any cost overruns, nothing like that. I just couldn't suck any more from the endowment. The board doesn't follow the money very closely. That's how I got away with it. You'd think they'd watch every last nickel, every last penny, being the tight wad bastards they are. But they don't." Parker circled the room nervously, stopped at the window again, then paced around, saying nothing for a long while. "You know, I didn't do this for me," she said as if in a confessional hoping for a lighter penance. "Didn't pocket so much as a penny of it. It was for the school. All for the school. What I'm wondering is…well…about this Code thing of yours. You said you've been using it to make money—"

"So far, uh-huh. So far, anyway."

"What's the chance we…you and me…you and me and whoever you need, give it a try. All I want is one big hit. I'm not an investment jock. I just need to clean up what got out of control. I should never have messed with the endowment…should have left the damn thing alone. Tell me more about it…The Code."

Sam spent a half hour going through the details.

"You need a woman for this, I gather," Parker said.

"Right."

"Lenore?"

"No way," Sam replied, giving little explanation. Too busy, way too busy these days."

"All right. Any ideas then?"

And Sam sure would like to get back to it for his own sake. If they could come up with a candidate for The Code, it would be perfect in more ways than one.

"We need a plan to make this work. For example, after we do The Code, if all goes well and once we find out where to place the money, we'll need to have loads of money ready to go right away. Ready to dump on the stock. That's how it's done. How much can you come up with?" Sam asked.

"Meaning?"

"How much are you hoping to recover?"

Parker grimaced. "Four hundred million, that's what I lost."

Sam calculated. "You have what…four hundred million now? Is that right?"

Parker nodded.

"When the time comes, we take all of the four hundred million that's left and invest it through The Code and wait for it to double. You will have recovered the four hundred million you put in and get back another four hundred million. You'll be right back where you were before you started messing with…playing around with the endowment. That brings you back to eight hundred million. Right where you were before. If it triples, or quadruples, or goes totally crazy, no telling what you'll get. But we've never tried this with anywhere near this amount of money."

Parker's face tightened. "Oh, Christ." She placed her hands on her temples and aimed her eyes down on her desk. "And if it fails, I'm dead meat."

Sam said nothing.

"Has it ever failed yet?"

"Not yet. But I'm not here to sell you a notion, Clara. It's something you'll have to—"

Parker nodded slowly and held a palm toward Sam. "Just the same, if it fails, the school's out four hundred million and I would have pissed away the entire endowment. Every bit of it *like that*." She snapped her fingers.

Sam waited. His hands were sweaty, but he tried to appear calm.

Parker said, "I thought I had big decisions to make here, but this one takes the cake. If I blow this, I'll make Bernie Madoff look like a skiver."

"We both need to score," Sam added. "My quarterly report is coming due and right now it ain't looking good."

"Let's get it done soon. I have no wiggle room; I'm pinned to the wall." Parker said.

The last time Sam had approached Parker on conducting a Code, she'd been characteristically indifferent, offered little help finding someone for Sam. Now she vowed to find a woman for The Code.

Sam pulled out his day calendar. "The next opportunity is coming up fast, next week. Too soon to get someone?"

"Not a bit. Consider it done."

Clara Parker sat quietly, barely moving a muscle. The wheels were turning. She pressed her lips together. "We will take care of it Sam, old buddy. We *will* take care of it," she said almost boastfully—the old Clara Parker that Sam knew.

And take care of it she did. No need to recruit Lenore, or try to talk Phyllis, one of her secretaries, into participating, or seek the help of any of Clara's reliable old friends for The Code. *Just keep it all in the family, that's all. Why not?* Clara and Sam would do The Code. Perfect and simple and clean, and no need to worry about leaks from Gabby Hayes, or bad publicity or surprise articles in the student newspaper saying: *"President Parker Engaged in Occult Rituals in a Secret Chamber Under the Library."* Clara would do The Code with Sam.

Sam was happy as a salmon heading upstream for its yearly orgy when he heard of Clara's decision. He filled her in on each essential detail, gave her the low-down on what to expect. The dark altar room, the robes, her on the table, the whole shebang. He rather enjoyed talking about it. Clara Parker had been on Sam's bucket list of personal conquests for years. Just a year or two older than Sam, she kept herself in tiptop shape, though unlike Lenore, she had gone under the knife to get rid of those pesky crow's feet and the droop in the cheeks. Whoever had done the job, had done it well. It took a good six years off her age and gave her a bright and sharp appearance. She dressed like an ace. Like all the rest of Sam's clique, Clara was single, once married to an anthropology professor at Graebner. The marriage had fizzled like a sputtering sparkler. He had left Graebner to swim in deeper calmer waters elsewhere.

2

Clara Parker performs a Code with Sam

"I thought I knew everything about this old school," Clara Parker said as she looked around the altar chamber. She knew that Sam and Lenore had discovered the room with the help of Frank Cusimano, Sam's architect brother-in-law, but she had never ventured inside, preferring to stay as far away as possible. Clara thought about the early days of Graebner and its roots as Schulenmeister Theological Seminary. She knew few of the nasty details of what had happened there, however.

"You really think this will work?" Clara asked as she climbed off the altar.

"And so, judge not till ye has seen."

"That from the Bible?"

"Nope…it's from the Book of Sam."

The Code proceeded predictably, if not a little disquietingly from Clara's point of view.

Five days later, the vision came to Clara in her sleep, along with the words "Red Rover." She called Sam from home and delivered the information the moment she flew out of bed. Within ten minutes, he was at his desk buying a stock that made sports clothing. It disgusted Clara to give Sam the name Over The Top—a company with its flashy and popular OTT logo spread across its shoes and shirts and hoodies. A company that was one of the top outsourcers of clothing manufactured in the sweat shops of China and Latin America, the kind of thing an institution like Graebner led the way to expose. But right now, Clara was in desperate need for a big dose of outsourcing of her own—outsourcing for the endowment. Sam doublechecked with Clara. "You're sure about this, a hundred percent sure, a thousand percent sure. Right?" Then he sent four hundred million of Graebner's money in the direction of OTT. It was selling at $12.87 a share.

Sam had done this enough times now that he no longer checked into the stock he was about to buy. It made him nervous, nonetheless. Most of them were loosey-goosey stocks he normally would never have gone near. Certainly not with the amount of money he had been dumping on them. But so far, The Code had delivered, and delivered big. Yet he knew they were messing around with the occult. The worry of that never left him. More than once, he'd had a sleepless night, sitting in his darkened living room sipping oriental tea, imagining what would happen if The Code failed, if every penny he had went with it, if he had to peddle his entire net worth just to get out from under the bills.

Sam sat with eyes glued to the computer screen waiting for movement on OTT. It didn't budge a bit. Not an iota. For a long time, it sat stale and stagnant. Ten o'clock came and went, so did eleven.

Clara called periodically to see how it was going. Her voice quivered uncontrollably. She sat in her office at Graebner with strict orders not to be bothered. Bill Walker, her administrative assistant, built a rip-roaring fire for her in the fireplace. It crackled and sputtered joyously. It should have made her feel better, but it didn't.

From her desk, she could see the gray sky and thin motionless winter clouds, the naked branches of the silver maples and the sugar maples, the black birch. She rested her head in her hands and closed her eyes. There she was, a prisoner condemned to death waiting for the decision of the court—overturn the sentence or go forward with the execution. Could The Code overturn it?

Sam watched the computer screen, got up and paced around in anguish. The desire to win this one for Clara—for the Gipper—was almost greater than any of his previous dealings with The Code. Sam knew unequivocally the consequences of what The Code might or might not deliver. A thousand alternative possibilities raced through his head. What if Clara's 'vision' was no vision at all? Just a bad-ass dream from something that had been floating through her head in recent days. OTT would fit the bill for that pretty damn well. And so, what if he had bought four hundred million dollars' worth of a go-nowhere stock that they would have to bail out of sooner or later.

As Sam sat contemplating this, Lenore strolled casually into his office. Sam needed to be as normal as possible, but to look at him, he had the appearance of a man in need of a couple pints of blood.

That morning, Lenore had removed the stitches from her trepanation. With Victor Boudreau and Allison McClure gone, she'd had no choice but to do it herself. She'd bought a small pair of surgical scissors and a pair of forceps and a bottle of 70% alcohol from the local Rexall. She wetted and flamed the forceps, waited for it to cool, and one by one snipped the suture and pulled it out. Done like a pro despite her basic squeamishness for all things medical. With each suture she removed, there'd been a faint but sure odor, foul and rotted. It reminded her of the smell that had spread through the room during her trepanation. Holding a mirror over her head, she examined the wound in the bathroom mirror in front of her. The wound had healed, barely a scar, and the hair had grown back nicely. Smelled bad but looked good.

There was nothing but small talk between Sam and Lenore. She was bored. He was anxious to get back to the computer and follow OTT. *Come on, Lenore, give me a break. I don't have the time for this now*, came Sam's thought to Lenore.

Okay, fine, she thought and concluded he was up to no good again. She rose from the chair and left without saying much.

Sam went immediately to the computer. "Oh, God, no." OTT had dropped a couple of notches. He tried to find what was going on with the stock, but nothing came up. No bad news, nothing to be worried about. Clara called.

He mentioned the change but said not to worry. These things happen. She groaned painfully, thanked him, and hung up.

Sam sat with eyes tight on the computer, one hand gripping the other tightly. *Down two more points…then…WTF, up: two, three, four. It's moving, yes, yes, yes, it's moving, going up.* It crossed its original mark, finally going north into good territory. It hit $16.31 a share, stalled out for ten long minutes, then started moving again.

By two o'clock, it bobbled around at $20.66 a share. A tough choice faced Sam. He could unload now. They would not have reached the level they were hoping for but would have come home with a significant windfall. He did the calculation. The $400,000,000 was now worth $640,000,000 if he were to push the sell button this very second. Not what Clara wanted, but a win nonetheless…a bird in the hand. He sat broodingly at his desk, trying to keep his hand off the mouse, afraid he might spontaneously click the sell button.

He waited. He checked his pulse and took his blood pressure.

An hour went by. It happened, OTT hit $25.00 a share and kept going. There was no sign it was slowing. Sam waited as long as he could. As soon as it passed $38.00, he sent the signal to sell, his hand still trembling. Off went the sell order. This was a big pile of stocks to unload at once. It didn't go immediately. The minutes crawled by. Then, finally. The stock had sold. He made a quick calculation: one billion, two hundred and forty million dollars all told.

Sam did not call Clara to tell her of the success. He drove over to Graebner, almost blasting through two stoplights along the way. He went to the administration building. Parker's secretary nodded for him to go in the door. Sam raced in. Clara looked up with the jittery eyes of a relative waiting for the surgeon after a critical operation.

Sam began to laugh uncontrollably. Clara knew what it meant—the execution had been stayed. She raced over and gave Sam a huge hug and began to cry, then wiped the tears from her eyes. "How much?"

"A ton. All of what you had and then some." He told her how much.

Clara's legs became weak. She leaned on the desk, made her way to the sofa, and fell awkwardly down.

"Hey, babe, you're back in business," Sam said.

Clara buried her face in her hands.

"It's done."

"Oh, thank God," Parker moaned as she slumped on the sofa.

Sam laughed. "Thank The Code."

Clara looked at Sam in astonishment. Everything in the room took on a new and pleasant glow. The fire in the old stone fireplace snickered happily. Brisk sunlight—pale-yellow and warm—broke through the gray sky beyond the windows and cast a spark of light on the room. Clara got up and walked to the window. It was all hers again. Everything was back to normal. In five short yet pathetically long hours, she was back in business. She started to laugh, softly at first then uncontrollably as she leaned on the windowsill, watching students and faculty shuttle below. "I'm so hungry, I could eat a horse," she said, turning to Sam. "Let's go over to faculty dining and get something…courtesy of the endowment." She winked.

3

*Clara Parker connects Red Rover with the death
of Ira Pavlovich*

Clara Parker lived in a spectacular English Tudor house owned by the college a block and a half from campus. The lawn was immaculately cared for by the school landscapers in the spring and summer. The leaves were removed in the fall. The walks were shoveled and swept clean all winter. She had a housekeeper, a cook, and a maid. Parker's part was that of master-of-ceremony for the elegant and stylish dinner parties that always included a member of the board, a select faculty member or two, and the deep-pocket donors. But these were not meant as a dodge to squeeze money out of people. How crude that would be! Corner some rich bloke and make them pay up. No way. The good schools know better than to do that. It was a time for frivolity, a slightly bacchanal event depending upon who attended, good food and drink and lively conversation—laughter and fun.

The faculty for the events were carefully selected by Clara Parker. Always a spattering of the best and most important and the most elite: The school's world-famous American historian who had been a featured scholar in the PBS documentary, *The Immigrants*; the Russian poet who perennially topped the short list for the Nobel Prize for Literature; the chemistry Nobelist who no longer had to wait for that accolade; the professor of English literature whose books soared to the top of the New York Times bestseller lists time and again. Sam had been to these events more than once.

Though every aspect of the house was carefully and meticulously cared for by the house staff, some things Clara insisted be left untouched. She refused to let every aspect of her life be regulated and shrink-wrapped. At the top of the list was "Never throw away a newspaper or periodical until I say so."

Clara sat in the house's spectacularly decorated study. A stack of *The Covington Gazette* from the previous two weeks next to her. She was in search of one of the issues. It would be easy to find; on the front page would be the picture of happy smiling Ira Pavlovich and the detailed description of the murder. Yes, there it was. Clara read through it quickly until she arrived at the paragraph she was after—the mention of "Red Rover" scribbled above the bathtub. She read the article twice, then a third time, hoping to find a nuance that would help her solve her dilemma. From Clara's own experience with The Code, she now knew all too well about those words from the moment they had appeared in her dream along with the OTT stock.

So, if Ira Pavlovich had performed a Code with Sam, which Clara Parker knew she had, having been told this by Sam on more than one occasion, then the words "Red Rover" must have been written by someone who was also familiar with The Code. And whom might that be? Sam? Could Sam have killed Ira? Parker could not fathom that. That left one person and one person alone—Lenore Simenson.

Hence, one inscrutable fact was now clear to Clara Parker: Lenore had killed Ira Pavlovich. Exactly how much of that did Sam know? How much had he pieced together? Surely, if he were aware of it, he would want to act on it, report it to the police. Or was he protecting Lenore, his longtime friend and business partner? On the other hand, the Covington Police had their own investigation going; perhaps they were ahead of the curve. Perhaps they had Lenore in their sights right from the beginning.

4

There are many ways to destroy a person

Sam and Clara had conducted a Code. Lenore was pissed. This needed to be stopped, and she knew exactly how to do it. She made a key to the library and replaced Sam's copy in his desk. Now she could get into the library any time she wished.

She checked her calendar for the position of the moon. The quarter moon was still a week away. She could get in and get out with no chance of colliding with Sam, accompanied by who-knows-who on their way to and from a Code.

Lenore jammed an old bed sheet into a sack and headed for the library at one-thirty, just after the library had closed. She unlocked the gate, slipped inside, went up to the reading room, and proceeded down into the bowels of the building.

From the corridor that led to Parker's office, she piled the skulls that she herself had deposited there on the day prior to her trepanation. Pulling the corners of the sheet together, she hoisted the skull-packed cluster over her shoulder, looking like Santa Claus trundling off for a delivery into the inner-sanctum of Hades with the earthly remnants of many a lost soul.

Wiggling through the narrow passages and up the steep stairs, she emerged in the reading room. A hollow clunk rolled through the room as she set the makeshift bag on the floor. She sat in a chair catching her breath. With bag over her shoulder, she went through the library humming: "Zip-A-Dee-Doo-Dah, Zip-A-Dee-Aye...My oh my what a wonderful day...."

At ten minutes to six the next morning, Olive Mason, the staff librarian, opened the library doors. Three students waited behind her. One was Nick Sanchez. He would burn an hour of last-minute study before an eight o'clock test.

Seconds after turning on the lights in the entrance room to the library, Olive Mason let out a horrific scream that filled the air. Nick raced in. Olive clutched her hands tightly to her chest as she stared at a pair of skulls that greeted her from atop the circulation desk. She turned and ran wild and frantic from the building, hands waving in the air.

Nick continued in. He had a pretty good idea where the skulls had come from. Snapping pictures with his iPhone as he went, he passed from room to room through the first floor and then up to the second and third floor. There were scads of skulls on desks, skulls looking out the windows, skulls on bookshelves. In some rooms a half dozen skulls or more. Nick slipped his phone into his pocket and fled down to the first floor just as the campus police came tearing into the building.

Once outside, Nick sent the set of the photos to Alton Richter, his former roommate from his freshman year, now the editor of the Graebner newspaper—*The Daily Beacon*.

A volley of texts went back and forth:

Richter: OMG, where did ya get these?

Sanchez: Library. This morning.

Richter: You're serious.

Sanchez: Yep.

Richter: IN the library?!!

Sanchez: Yep.

Richter: You're SURE!

Sanchez: Was tired but not hallucinating. Yep, sure. Was there when they opened.

Richter: OMG!!!

Sanchez: If you use them, I'm out of it. K?

Richter: Done. Thanks!!

Nick omitted one picture from the series, however—a hand-written note in large block letters that had been left on the table in the main library room on the first floor:

MORS VITA EST
322

Nick knew the words all too well. He and Katy had seen them above the entrance to the Altar Chamber.

If Alton Richter was certain of anything, it was that Nick's photos were real and to be believed. Nick was a straight shooter, and Richter knew it. This was not the sort of gimmick Nick Sanchez would dump on him. Moreover, getting involved in something like this, even on deep background, was not Nick's style, but he felt compelled to do something, anything, rather than let the whole event disappear into the files of the campus security.

Nick stood in the bitter morning as the sunlight emerged from behind the buildings. Lenore watched from a distance. She saw the campus police enter the library and saw Nick, a hundred feet away, texting on his phone before he briskly took off down the path.

So how did the skulls get into the library, Richter wondered? Fraternity prank? Next to impossible. The library being the fortress that it was. And besides, what fraternity would have dozens and dozens of human skulls at its disposal? Even if they did, how could they sneak that many into the library without being seen during regular hours? Alton was at a loss, but it didn't matter. His job, as he saw it, was to report the news—good, bad, funny, stupid—to the students. He didn't need an explanation to print the images in *The Beacon*.

When Clara Parker heard about the security breach at the library, she was incensed. The campus police brought her to the library and showed her what they had found before the skulls were carted out.

As she walked through each room, all she could think was that she was forever grateful that no student had managed to see what she was seeing, that the damage had been contained.

The police took the skulls to the campus police station for safekeeping. Clara returned to her office and immediately placed a call to Sam and gave him the details of the morning findings in the library. She wanted to know if this lovely episode could have somehow been linked to The Code. Sam said he doubted it. Of course, he had a damn good idea where the skulls had come from and how they had ended up scattered about the library.

Sam wasted no time confronting Lenore about the matter, which she begrudgingly denied. But who else could have spread the skulls hither and yon throughout the library? Who else knew about them? The confrontation was pithy.

When the conversation settled down, Sam moved on to the topic of the downward slide of the investments at WSA, insisting he and Lenore needed to do something to rectify the problem, do it ASAP. It was time to quit dicking around and get back to The Code. Lenore sat stone-faced.

5

The pictures hit The Beacon

Alton Richter sat in Clara Parker's posh office. Parker's face was flushed with anger. She had placed a call to *The Daily Beacon* and ordered Richter to her office immediately.

Spread across her desk like a large nautical map was the morning's copy of *The Beacon*. For all Graebner to see were fifteen of Nick's photos, accompanied by a large article describing the 'finds' in the library, and a little speculation thrown in for pizzazz as to how they got there. As *The Beacon* saw it, this was not a prank or a joke. And it did indeed cause a stir.

Morning classes were full of students paging through the free newspaper that was stacked every day at the entrance to every campus building and outside The Whit—the student union. In actuality, most students found the situation funny, if not plain silly. The oldest building on campus—a bit of a medieval looking structure in its own right—being stuffed with human skulls.

But for Clara Parker, hoax or not, it was a nightmare. And now with the pictures and the article in *The Beacon*, there was little chance to undo the damage from them. Coupled with the recent nerve-racking Code performed by her and Sam, this had turned out to be a week laden with stress.

Parker tore into Richter the minute he set foot in her office. "You better have a good explanation for this, young man, and you better get ready to get your ass thrown right out of this school right now!"

"You can't do that, Dr. Parker," Richter said quickly. "I was merely—"

"I can do any damn thing I want to. I'm the president at this college, in case you didn't know." She slammed her hand down on her antique desk.

Richter stood his ground. "I didn't do anything that would cause me to be dismissed from this school," he said defiantly but calmly and logically.

"Don't get insolent with me, young man. You're not Ben Bradlee at the *Washington Post*—"

"And you're not Katherine Graham."

The words caused Parker to fume. "This is a college newspaper we're talking about…"

"I have a right to protect my sources just as I would at any paper big *or* small." He liked that thought. It made him feel like Ben Bradlee.

"You were granted this position to write fluffy stories about the school, the students, the football team, the basketball team, the faculty, the new buildings, not to publish pictures of human skulls in the library. Where the hell did you get those pictures."

If Alton Richter had wondered, even briefly, that the pictures he had been given by Nick might have been faked, seeing Parker's reaction convinced him otherwise. She wanted the source of the photos, which meant she knew the skulls had indeed been in the library. But Alton Richter remained true to his promise to Nick. At the *Beacon*, Alton and only Alton knew where he had gotten them. Once they had been transferred to the newspaper staff, he deleted the pictures from his phone. There was no trail—paper, electronic, or otherwise.

"And so tomorrow you will publish a retraction. Do you understand! You will say the whole thing was a stupid hoax and apologize for it."

"I can't and *won't* do that," Richter said. "It would be a lie…that would be the real hoax here. That would—"

"No newspaper publishes every piece of information it gets. Have they not told you that over there in the Communication Department? If not, I need to have a serious conversation with that bunch. Editors use discretion about what goes in and what stays out of newspaper. And this should have stayed out, and now *you* need to do something about it."

Alton Richter said nothing. His mind was made up. The further along this went, the more Clara Parker could tell that she had no chance of changing his mind. She rose from her chair and leaned menacingly over her desk. "That's it, young man. Go, get out!" she said angrily with a wave of her arm, as if she were talking to someone who had just pissed on the expensive Persian rug in her office.

It didn't take long for a copy of *The Beacon* to find its way to Winthrop Anderson, the Chairman of the Board of Trustees of Graebner College, and he was none too pleased. There was little chance of gathering the board for a meeting on such short notice. He drove across town for a private meeting with Clara. They sat at the long table in the conference room used by the board down the hall from Clara's office.

Anderson, a serious man with steely eyes and a jaw that had trouble with even the simplest smile, looked at Clara. "The skulls are rather sick and rather disturbing," he said in his New England accent. "But for the time being, let's just consider them annoying, albeit a rather lubricious joke on the part of someone or some group on campus. The real problem is the security in the library. And what I'm talking about, of course, is the Velvet Room and the Gutenberg Bible. If something ever happened to that, there will be two crucifixions—yours and mine—right out there on the quadrangle."

Looking into Winthrop's Anderson's hard eyes, all Clara could do was think: *God forbid if I were sitting here telling him that the endowment had almost vanished, that it had nearly taken a permanent vacation to Haiti or somewhere and wasn't coming back.* That catastrophe now averted, another landmine had exploded under her almost immediately.

Winthrop Anderson had been elected chairman of the board of trustees two years previously. He was by no means Clara's choice for the job, but she had little to say in the matter. The chair was selected by the other members of the board. Among his peers, Winthrop Anderson was well-liked and considered levelheaded and solicitous when it came to the future of Graebner.

Clara said, "No one can get into the Velvet Room, Winston. It's impossible, totally impossible. It's as safe as can be. Trust me, I will put my job on the line. If someone tried to get in there when the library was closed, a dozen sirens would set off, campus police would be there before the perps knew what hit them. And, in fact, the whole building would go into lockdown. That's how it's set up."

"Just the same, maybe it's time to relocate the Gutenberg."

"Relocate it where? What do you do with something that valuable?"

"There are places."

"It's one of the true treasures of the world, Winthrop...almost priceless not just in monetary terms but in terms of prestige. You know that as well as I do. Up there in the Velvet Room, it's protected from heat, cold, and fire...and, far as I'm concerned, from theft."

"We both better hope so. Far as I'm concerned, we should bring the matter up at the next full meeting of the board," Anderson said in a tone that was more than a mere suggestion. "This school has three things going for it." He held out his thumb and two fingers. "Academics: we're tops when it comes to that. The Gutenberg: show me another place that can boast having one of those! And an endowment that's second to none, one that will carry Graebner far into the future. And as chairman of the board, I plan to keep everything in A-1 shape."

The word endowment sent a shiver through Clara. "Okay, we'll put the Gutenberg on the agenda for the next meeting," she reluctantly agreed.

"And see what you can do about the pictures in *The Beacon*."

"I'm working on it," she told him. "I'm working on it."

Winthrop Anderson granted the weakest of all smiles, then got up and left.

6

Lenore strikes again

Some good news for Nick: when it rains it pours. But this was more than rain; it was a torrential flood, a hurricane, a tsunami.

On the same day, his mailbox had three letters. One from Harvard Medical School, one from Yale Medical School, one from Johns Hopkins Medical School.

He sat in his soft over-stuffed chair with the three letters in his hand, not opening them, just staring at the fancy embossed lettering in the upper left corner of the envelope and his name and address typed in the middle. Despite his sudden burst of anxiety, he couldn't bring himself to open them immediately. He needed to prepare himself if the worst scenario were to happen: a rejection from all three.

If that were to occur, it wouldn't mean his dreams were dashed. He still had seven other schools from which he had yet to hear. But the three letters in his hand were his top choices. After these came Stanford Medical, Duke, the University of Chicago, and the University of Pennsylvania.

From there the list tapered off to include his fallback schools: The University of Texas Medical School at Austin, Northwestern Medical School, and Baylor College of Medicine.

He pulled a letter opener from his desk. He would proceed from third choice to his top choice—Yale, Hopkins, Harvard, in that order. In reality, Hopkins and Yale were tied for second place, but Hopkins edged out Yale by a hair. It seemed like every book about the history of medicine he read, and he read a lot of them, mentioned some monumental achievement that had taken place at Hopkins. Surprisingly, being the newest of the three medical schools, dating to the 1870s, its ascent to the top, its string of accomplishments, were mind-boggling, in addition to the fact that it was one of the first medical schools to admit women, but only because a wealthy suffragette had bailed-out the early financially strapped school so long as it opened its doors equally to women. Gertrude Stein had been admitted in one of those first classes but had left after two years due to poor grades and a total lack of interest in medicine.

Nick gasped, slipped the letter opener in the corner of the Yale envelope, opened it and unfurled the page. He stared at the short but concise letter, at first doubting what he was seeing. "*No*...I don't believe it," he exclaimed with a burst of glee. He had been accepted.

Then the letter from Hopkins and once again, accepted.

Then from Harvard. This he didn't open immediately. He waited a minute, carefully sliced the top, and removed the letter and read it. *Oh my God! A hat trick*. He had been admitted to Harvard Medical School. He leapt to his feet. "*Woo-hoooo!*" he roared as he danced crazily about in his apartment.

He believed he'd had a shot at one of the schools. His grades were good enough, his MCAT scores were sky-high, his background and the circumstances of his personal life probably helped. They certainly didn't hurt his chances.

Barely able to keep his hands from shaking, he called his mother in Texas and gave her the great news. Yes, she knew he would get into medical school. Yes, she never doubted it. But the blind faith of parents can't by themselves work miracles.

Which one would he choose, she wanted to know. But all Nick could do was laugh. The information was too new, too unbelievable, to make that decision.

Nick called Katy. She was ecstatic. They would celebrate later that evening at The Rat with Nick's friends.

⚘

The Rat—dark and filled with rowdy, chatter laughter and bawdy jokes of the Graebner students—was the perfect place for a celebration. It was Wednesday, hump-day for most. Nick and Katy and their friends sat with pitchers of beer. Nick laughed gleefully at every comment they poked at him about his grand success.

Across the room just inside the entrance, Lenore stomped lightly, shaking a dusting of snow from her shoes. She looked around the dark room but could see little, her vision momentarily stolen by the bright glare of evening whiteness outside. Her plans were not to be there more than a few minutes. As her eyes adjusted to the dim light, she scanned the room until she lit on the table with Nick and his celebrants. That's all she needed. She turned, pulled her collar high, and promptly left.

Would the door to Nick's apartment be open? Lenore strolled casually down the hall of the building toward number 24. *Cripes, not again…unlocked. Kid didn't learn his lesson.* Anxious and happy, Nick had departed for The Rat without locking the door.

Lenore walked possessively inside. Nick wouldn't be back for a long time, she expected. She wandered through the apartment, opened the refrigerator, made a ham sandwich, and read his mail—the letters from Harvard, Yale, and Hopkins. *Ha, ha, ha, so that's it.* She checked her purse to make sure she hadn't forgotten the box of Benadryl.

It was barely eight by the stove clock in the kitchen. What was she going to do for the next several hours? A lot of time still. She slumped into Nick's soft, comfortable chair. The room was unnecessarily warm. She was uncharacteristically sleepy for so early in the evening.

Before she knew it, she found herself dozing off. Each time she pulled herself awake, worried that Nick would return and ruin her plans. Eventually, she fell into a deep sleep, only to be awakened by the sound of someone in the hall outside the door. She looked at her phone, one o'clock. Leaping up, she fumbled through her purse until her hand landed on the bottle of Benadryl. She removed a pill and dropped it into an open bottle of Evian water that Nick had left on the kitchen table. She gave it a fast swirl, then raced for the front closet, climbed inside, and buried herself under a layer of clothes that were spread on the floor.

Within seconds, the door to Nick's apartment opened. He staggered in. Party hearty, he indeed had done. Best of all, he was alone. If Katy had accompanied him home to finish off his day of celebration, Lenore's plans almost certainly would have been thwarted. She could escape, but the night would have been a total loss. To say the apartment was warm and stuffy was nothing compared to the closet. All she could do now was wait.

As luck would have it, the plan went according to Hoyle. Nick unscrewed the cap of the Evian bottle and took a huge swig, nearly draining it. He walked around the apartment unsteadily, then emptied the bottle and tossed it in the trash. The rest happened quickly.

Within twenty minutes, all activity in the apartment ceased.

Lenore cracked the closet door and peered into the room. Nick was slouched in his chair, head tilted back, mouth sagging to the side and snoring. He was out. She emerged, moved silently past Nick, and stopped and looked around. *Where is it, where is it? His phone, where is it? Oh, don't tell me, not in his pocket!* Then her eyes landed on the thin black phone sitting on his desk. With one eye parked on Nick, she stepped adroitly and softly across the room and picked up his phone. One last stroke of luck was needed now. She pushed the activation button and the screen lit. No password needed!

She went immediately to the Messages icon, scrolled through, and selected Alton Richter. *There they are, every freaking one of the photos he sent to Richter from outside the library.* She left the apartment, taking the phone with her.

By the time Gustav Becker in the reading room struck two a.m., Lenore had made her way through the library, past the altar chamber, down the Green Mile, through the Sick Room, and down the corridor to Clara Parker's office. She placed Nick's phone on Parker's desk so that it would be impossible to miss when she arrived bright and early in the morning.

⁂

As was her habit, Clara Parker opened the door to her office at eight o'clock the next morning. Bill Walker, her administrative assistant, stuck his head in. "A pot of fresh hot coffee is ready," he told her.

She hung up her coat and went to her desk. There in front of her was Nick's cell phone.

Bill brought in a cup of coffee.

"Where'd this thing come from?" she asked him, referring to the phone.

"Huhm, I don't know," Walker said as he picked up the phone and examined it.

"It's okay, you can leave it."

When Bill Walker left her office, Clara turned the phone on and examined its contents. She went to the Contacts icon. There were scores of names. She selected the one listed as Mom, which was linked to the name Karen Sanchez, the address 445 Goldsmith St, Houston, TX, and a phone number.

Parker went into her computer list of students at Graebner and selected Sanchez. There were only four, and only one from Texas—Nick Sanchez, premed, biology major, now a senior, a top-tier student. *How in Holy Hades did his phone get into my office?* Parker's mind trundled through a multitude of possibilities. Had he somehow managed to get into her office during the night? Seemed preposterous, and anyway, why? Had someone left it on her desk? Just as crazy, but what other explanation was there?

The day would be a busy one, Clara Parker had no time to spend playing sleuth about a lost cell phone. She would turn it over to security and let them worry about it. Before she abandoned it, she went to his photo album and began scrolling through. There were hundreds, literally hundreds, of photos—students, family, friends, a girlfriend no doubt (lots of selfies taken with her on campus, at Jake's, at The Rat, everywhere).

Then, suddenly, came a string of something unexpected—the pictures of the skulls in the library. Clara Parker pulled the dreaded issue of *The Beacon* from her desk drawer, opened it to the library photos, and compared them to the ones on the phone. No question, they were the same. *So this* is how Alton Richter, the editor of *The Beacon*, got hold of those photos.

She had all the evidence she needed. It was funny, though. When it came to Alton Richter, she wanted to nail his butt to the wall. Maybe that was what you do with someone you've given a significant dose of authority to, especially when it's a student, one of the drudges that have come to work on your plantation. Give them an inch and they'll try for a mile.

But for some reason, Nick Sanchez seemed less of an accomplice in all this and more of a disinterested party. That's what Parker preferred to believe.

And for that matter, she had not been able to get Alton Richter to place a retraction in *The Beacon*, as she had forcefully insisted. Now, as time passed, she knew none would be forthcoming. And her dealings with Winthrop Anderson wouldn't get any better no matter what she did. He was a pompous industrialist jerkoff, a rich old jock whose grandfather had made a fortune from a paper mill that Winthrop had inherited. Funny how money buys influence and authority and prominence for no truly justifiable reason.

Maybe, just to piss off Winthrop Anderson, she would not pursue the photo thing—would let it die. The skulls had been removed from the library. Pretty soon, even the students would forget about the whole episode, or would talk about it as a big joke months or years later. Besides, Parker had some pretty big fish of her own that needed to go into the skillet. She had some new plans for that.

7

Big worries in the Medical Examiner's office

The reports came back from the cultures from Victor Boudreau's and Allison McClure's lung and brain specimens. All clean as a whistle. No virus, no bacteria, no fungi, no parasites. How could tissue that looked as bad as theirs be that clean? Coombs sat in her office, considering the possibilities. So, what if it wasn't due to something infectious? *What if it was due to something caustic that could spread from person to person? A toxin, let's say. Something that could cause almost immediate destruction of the tissues. In the lungs first then up in the brain from the blood.* But since all tissues of the body are bathed in blood, that possibility didn't make much sense in and of itself. And anyway, she had taken a blood sample form Victor and Allison; both had come back negative.

Possibly, the answer to this would come from Oscar Delworth over at the state health department. He had taken tissues from Allison McClure for toxicology. They had the facilities to identify almost every known toxin that exists, and any they couldn't identify could be detected at the Center for Disease Control in Atlanta.

But her usually sleepy medical examiner office at Covington was now buzzing with activity. In any given week, she might get one case, and those usually consisted of nothing of any great mystery. A drug overdose, and more frequently than not, some form of accidental drug overdose. Two or three times a year, maybe, a suicide from an overdose. Small town, small cases. Easy cases.

Now Coombs was facing big-city stuff. Two ghastly unexplained deaths, and the death of detective Blum, who not only had been murdered in a motel room while on a morning fling had also been left without his ring finger. The cause of death was easy to deduce: blow to the head and suffocation. Coombs's role in describing Blum's death was done. What remained of the case was in the hands of the police.

What was going on in Covington? Coombs tapped her fingers nervously on her desk.

8

Clara Parker and Sam talk things over

After leaving Graebner at the end of the day, Clara Parker went directly to Sam's house. They sat in the living room. Sam poured two single malts.

Clara could drink like a pro. It was a strategic approach she had perfected over the years to deal with fat cats, the folks with deep pockets. She knew the game. You do "what's necessary…whatever's necessary" as Edmond Walker told Ned Racine in *Body Heat*.

Two items topped Clara's agenda that night. She started with the touchiest of the two. "I have to ask," she started, holding the glass of scotch, "this thing with Red Rover…." She hesitated, hoping Sam might jump in. He didn't. "The Code we did, the one you and I performed, and the dream I had and the Over The Top stock we bought, and the words…the words Red Rover I saw in the dream in great big red letters."

Sam sat quietly. He had a feeling where Clara was heading.

Clara looked at the glass in her hand several times as though studying it. She took a sip and said, "I knew I had heard something about the words from somewhere before, but I couldn't remember where. It's not a phrase you hear much these days, us old farts. Then it hit me. I dug through the back issues of *The Covington Gazette* and sure enough, there it was in the article describing Ira Pavlovich's murder."

Sam, of course, had known about the connection of Red Rover and The Code for many months. So, what to do? Pretend it was all news to him? There was no way he could do that; he knew he couldn't. Poker-faced, he sat calmly waiting to see how much she had figured out.

"As I read the article again, a chill ran through me. I thought, egads, was it…? Did Lenore…I mean is it possible that she, that she was the one…it's hard to even suggest—but you know what I mean. I never would have considered it had it not been for The Code, if I had not seen those words myself."

Sam faked surprise. "You're wondering if *Lenore*…?"

"Well, I know it's preposterous, but it does make you wonder. Doesn't it?"

Indeed, Sam had had the same reaction when he first read about Ira's murder in *The Gazette*. The coincidence was too great. At the time of Ira's murder, only Sam and Lenore had known about the phrase and its connection to The Code. Sam and Lenore and, of course Ira, too. But Ira took her knowledge of that with her to the promised land when she departed from the planet. But among the living, only Sam and Lenore, and now Clara, knew the connection to The Code.

"Somehow I think the police should be informed of this," Clara said.

This was not what Sam wanted to hear. His conundrum was that even if Lenore was responsible for Ira's death, focusing that kind of light on her was out of the question. "Oh Christ, Clara. That would open the flood gates, would get those buggers from the police department buzzing around all over our place again. Everyone there is still on edge. Consider, how would you like it if they were paying a visit here at your office day in and day out?"

Clara saw his point, but her concerns remained. "Sam, you have to let the chips fall where they may. This is serious stuff. Believe me, my life is one landmine after another. *You* know that. Maybe it's not always about something as big as this, but everyday someone drops a bag of crap outside my office door, and every day I step in it."

"Look...the guy who was investigating the case, a dude named Blum is...well he's off the case."

"Oh, really? Why?"

"It didn't make much of a splash in the paper. I guess the police don't like publicity, but he was, agh...killed. Murdered apparently."

"You are kidding!"

"Would I?"

"No, you wouldn't."

"A cop from the police department came to the office and told Lenore and me." Sam went into the details, what little he knew—the rendezvous in the motel and the fact that Ira's case had now been passed on to another investigator. "They're still working on it. That's all I know."

"Who would want to kill him?" Clara said.

"About a thousand people, it seems." Sam offered another defense. "Exactly how is it that you would approach the police with the Red Rover info? Don't forget, once you do that, the cat's out of the bag for good. They will want to know how *you* came to know about the words. And then you'll have to tell them what *you* know...about The Code, the dreams, the whole caboodle. Think about it. I thought your game plan has always been to keep the bad pub as far away from Graebner as possible. You start talking about Red Rover to the cops and some weenie reporter from *The Gazette* will get wind of it and we'll all hear about it in a big nasty article. Newspapers seem to be fond of doing that, I've noticed. First *The Beacon* here at Graebner, then possibly *The Gazette*, the paper every townie in Covington reads. You really want to risk it, do you?" Sam got up and poured himself another two fingers. "And like it or not, there's no way to know that the Red Rover thing on Ira's bathtub wall was really and truly left by Lenore. Okay, sure it looks suspicious," Sam conceded, "but who am I? A cop? The district attorney? No. Let them do their own snooping."

Clara didn't like that approach. A good college president needed a strong moral compass, and she had one. But the thought of possibly having to explain an article in *The Gazette* to the likes of Winthrop Anderson, the chairman of the board, and possibly to the entire board, was not at all a pleasant thought. Maybe Sam was right. Maybe she should let the dicks at the Covington Police Department do their own snooping. Or maybe the scotch had tinkered a little with her moral compass.

Thinking it through, Clara got up and walked casually through the living room, spending a few minutes by the original Frederic Remington sculpture above the mantle, the Pablo Picasso pen and ink on the wall, the Modigliani. Sam's collection was impressive. *My, how well the other half lives—the uber rich.* She turned to Sam. "Okay, maybe you're right. But there is another matter that's been chewing at me. We made barrels of money for Graebner off The Code. So, what I'm wondering is, what would be the chance of doing it again. This time with the hope of socking a gigantic load of new dollars into the endowment."

Money screams.

Sam flat out rejected the idea. It was one thing to invest personal money, or even to use money from his company— if The Code went sour and they ended up short, well, that's how it would be. His professional life had those kinds of ups and downs all the time. But money that belonged to Graebner?

"But let's say we were able to add another, maybe another five hundred million, to the endowment. Christ, it makes my head spin."

"Clara, I thought the plan had been to recover the lost money from your attempts to leverage the endowment. Am I wrong?"

"Yes, at first, but suppose we did it again and won big?"

"And suppose we did it again and lost big."

"Has it happened yet?" Clara asked. "From what I hear, the answer to that is no."

Sam chuckled. "Has it happened yet? Has California fallen off into the Pacific yet? No, but how many times have

I done a Code? That's the real question. Not very many. We have absolutely no solid information to make a judgement like that.

Clara took a sip of scotch and thought.

"Your sounding like the dicers out in Las Vegas," Sam said. "The ones who can't stop rolling even though they've lost the farm."

None of it fazed Clara. "I lost the farm when I was doing it myself. With The Code, we made more freaking money than I could possibly imagine."

"What if it all goes haywire and you end up with your own bad version of Red Rover?" Sam set his glass on the table and leaned forward. "I'm real serious here, Clara," he said, looking at her over the top of his glasses. "Let's not get twisted into the idea of double-downing our bet to make a lot of money just because we got lucky once."

9

Bye, bye Mr. American Pie

Putting his responsibilities as an educator, academic, and scholar aside, Byron Linkley had only one other duty at Graebner: to be gopher-in-chief for Clara Parker. And this he did well. Insecurity is a wonderful garb for a worried soul.

By now Parker knew The Code routine inside and out, having been through it with Sam in the moment of desperation when she needed to repack the College endowment she had so recklessly drained. Till then, she had known little and cared even less about The Code.

Linkley had been set up as a pair of eyes for Sam and Lenore. He'd charted the comings and goings in the reading room, which he'd reported periodically to Clara. But his role in the whole matter was that of an outsider, and he knew better than to so much as enquire what was taking place deep inside the library.

There were perks for this, of course. Clara Parker knew how to handle the Linkleys of the world. One hand truly does wash the other. Parker bestowed on Linkley special privileges. His teaching load was featherweight. He was vice-chair of the history department. Chair of the Appointment, Promotion, and Tenure Committee at Graebner—the most important and powerful committee on campus, the equivalent of the Ways and Means Committee in Congress. All faculty promotions or denials went through the APT committee. His life at Graebner was better than most—three squares a day, no heavy lifting, as they say. Everything was perfect, almost.

⁂

Saturdays on campus had but a sprinkling of activity. The crowded campus walks of weekdays were mostly vacant. Most students were holed-up in their dorm rooms, recovering quietly from a long night at Jake's or the Rat the night before.

Clara Parker pulled her car into the reserved parking slot in front of the administration building. Briefcase in hand, she scooted smartly up the steps of the building, went down the hall to her office, and let herself in. She set her briefcase down, hung her coat on a hanger, and shook snow from her gloves and off her hair. It was a good day to get some work done, quiet, undisturbed, and alone. A chance to make a dent on a manuscript that had been relegated to the back burner due to the assault on her time from school business during the past two weeks.

Clara closed the office door and turned toward the room. There before her, sitting in her chair, feet propped on her desk, was Byron Linkley, eyes bulging, tongue puffy and limp and hanging out of the edge of his mouth.

Covering her mouth in shock, Clara walked slowly over to Linkley. Her stomach knotted up. She felt her legs weaken. It was Byron Linkley, all right—right down to the plaid bowtie that was wrapped not around his collar but around his bare neck. And yes indeed, he was dead all right, dead as roadkill. How in the world did he end up in her office? At a loss for what to do, she picked up the phone and placed a call. "*Sam,*" she said in desperate urgency. "*You need to get over here immediately.*"

"Where are you?"

"Graebner."

"You okay?"

"*Just get over here!*" she said and hung up.

Clara looked out the window, waiting for Sam's arrival. It may have been minutes, but it seemed like hours. She turned periodically and looked at Linkley as though he might rise and take a big stretch and a yawn and deliver one of the corny salutes he always gave her when they passed on campus—and then with a wide smile walk amicably out of her office.

Sam swung his Mercedes into the slot next to Clara's and bounded two steps at a time up the front of the building. When he got to her office, Clara opened the door, pulled him in, and closed the door quickly. She pointed to the cadaver in her chair.

Sam walked over. "*Oh, my God!*" he blurted, in disbelief. "Linkley?"

"Linkley."

"Oh my God, how did *this* happen?"

"I have a damn good idea, Sam. A damn good idea."

Sam moved slowly toward Linkley but stopped well away from the chair and peered into his ashen face. The words Red Rover were written in jerky red letters across his forehead. He turned to Clara. "Lenore...is that what you're thinking?"

"Yes! Lenore."

Sam groaned. "Now what?"

"Oh, Sam, I don't know."

"Call the police," he said.

Clara sat on the edge of the sofa, face in hands. "We're in big, big trouble. How did all this happen. Big, big trouble, Sam."

"It's not your problem, Clara. Let the police figure it out. I mean, *you* didn't do this." Sam's words sounded more like a question.

Clara looked up. "*Of course I didn't, Sam! Why would I kill Linkley?*"

"I didn't say you did. I just said let the police deal with it. Let's be calm."

"*Calm? Calm?*" Parker glared angrily at Sam. "We can't go to the police."

Sam jammed his hands into his pockets and chewed nervously on his lip and paced across the room.

"If the police see this, I'm done for. And you're done, too. It will be front page in *The Covington Gazette*. No matter who did it, the Board would have no choice but to dump my ass...real damn fast. I'll be damaged goods forever. I'll never get job anywhere." She got up and double-checked the office door, making sure it was locked, going so far as to push a heavy chair against it.

"What are the options then?"

"We get Linkley's butt out of here."

"Out of the building, you mean? Off campus? How?"

"Just let me think," Clara said, returning to the sofa.

"Do you know what that means? If the police found out about it?" Sam argued. If we didn't report it, or tried to dispose of the body or something, we'd be accessories to a murder. Christ almighty, Clara!"

"Let me *think*, Sam. *Pleeez*!"

Clara sat motionless, staring at the carpet below her. Sam paced, looked out the window, glanced at Linkley, then turned to the window once more.

Clara said, "One thing for sure, you need to get control of Lenore before she strikes again. Woman's become a demon. Has issues, *big* issues."

"One thing at a time," Sam snapped, his frustration showing through his usually controlled demeanor.

"We get the body out of here, that's all there is to it. If you can't help, fine; I'll find a way myself." Clara's mind was made up. Linkley was going.

"How?"

"This evening. I know how."

10

A midnight mission

Clara was waiting in her office thirty minutes before Sam arrived at three a.m. The campus was devoid of people. Already, Linkley was beginning to reek. They would need to give the room a good airing out when this was done.

Sam had rented a pickup truck in the afternoon. He pulled up to the administration building and turned off the engine. From the back, he removed a large footlocker, a roll of heavy plastic, and a bag of duct tape that he had bought at Walmart. He scurried to the building, dragging the locker up the stairs behind him. Clara stood at the door to her office, all but pulling him inside as he arrived.

"Okay, let's get this dude out of here," Clara said coldly, then added, "I liked old Linkley but preferred him a whole lot more when he was breathing…and farting."

"Won't someone be looking for him, once they realize he's missing?" Sam asked.

"Linkley's a bachelor. I think his life ran a bit slow most of the time. We should have a pretty good window of time on this once we dispose of him."

Sam fitted a pair of latex gloves on his hands and gave a pair to Clara. He touched Linkley's limp body. The rigor mortis that had set in during the first twenty-four hours was now gone. Sam spread the plastic on the floor and lifted Linkley off the chair and curled him onto the plastic, turning him on his side in the fetal position. He dumped a handful of mothballs over the body to deal with the eventual odor, then folded the plastic around him and taped it in every direction, over and over and over. He shoved the body into the footlocker—a tight fit but with a little squeezing and tucking it went. Buckles and straps were secured.

"That's it," Sam said, standing next to the trunk that held Linkley's cold body. "No time to waste; let's go."

Clara opened the door and looked down the hall. Sam rolled the locker to the entrance of the building while Clara closed the office. She left the building ahead of Sam, checking the way. The night was cold, dark, and vaguely eerie, but there was not a soul in sight. She waved to Sam, who thumped the locker down the steps one at a time, wheeled it to the walk, and hoisted it up on the truck bed. He gave it a hefty push and pulled the gate up.

Sam climbed into the driver's seat; Clara rode shotgun. The easiest part was over. They didn't have far to go, but one bad stop, one wrong move on Sam's part, a row of flashing police lights in his rearview mirror, and….

Sam tried not to think about it.

The roads were deserted. Covington was sound asleep. A half mile away, Sam turned the truck into the Walgreens, dark and closed for the night, and pulled behind the building. He had scoped it out earlier in the day. The lack of security cameras and bright lights suggested there was little chance of people rummaging through the dumpster.

He got out and lifted the dumpster lid and looked inside. Ah, exactly what he wanted to see—a smattering of trash, empty shipping boxes, out-of-date frozen pizza cartons. The homeless population in Covington was almost nil; there were few dumpster divers to worry about.

He unfolded the gate and backed the truck up until it touched the dumpster, went around and climbed onto the bed, and dragged the locker to the edge of the gate. This wasn't going to be easy. He lifted one end of the footlocker until it rested on the rim of the dumpster and pushed hard. It teetered and careened inside. Like a squirrel hiding a nut, he buried it with an assortment of trash and garbage.

"Done!" he exclaimed, climbing back into the cab, breathing fast in a state of near panic. "Let's get out of here!" he said as he jammed the truck in gear and headed back toward Graebner. Barely a block from the store, they passed a Covington patrol car coming slowly down the road in the opposite direction. Sam let out a groan.

11

Gone at last

Sunday was the worst day of Sam's life, and not a bit better for Clara. Three times he drove past the Walgreens. So long as he did not see a half dozen flashing police cars and yellow police tape cordoning off the area, all was safe he figured. His only foray out of his condominium was to take the pickup truck to the U-Do-It-Jiffy-Wash, where he gave the back of the truck a power soak and wash.

Sam self-medicated with scotch late into Sunday night. Despite a prominent hangover, he was up early and out quickly on Monday morning. He parked across from the Walgreens. Time passed as if dropped into an impenetrable time warp. Three times, a Covington garbage truck passed the store and went on. At mid-morning an employee walked around behind the building and crammed a stack of boxes into the dumpster. Finally, at eleven forty-five in the morning, a garbage truck pulled behind Walgreens, hooked onto the dumpster, lifted it overhead, and deposited its contents thunderously into an open-topped truck.

This still wasn't good enough for anal-compulsive Sam. He cryptically followed the truck through its route for two hours until it headed out of town for the landfill. With a pair of binoculars, he watched as it dumped its load in the middle of a pile of trash of every imaginable kind. Scavenger birds circled through the air.

Sam gasped and rested his forehead on the steering wheel for several minutes, then turned and drove off. Linkley had been planted. Each day he would be covered by more rotting and decaying refuse—his whereabouts unknown.

12

Sam and Lenore agree to a Code

This was not the first time Sam had given serious thought to the possibility that he and Lenore might be consorting with the evil one. The idea had been floating through his mind for weeks. Why? Like Dr. Faust, had they sold their souls to the devil never to get them back? Impossible! They hadn't made a pact with anyone. They had merely stumbled onto a great secret. Everything was of their own doing and they could bail out any damn time they wanted—that free will thing, pure and simple.

Yet, Sam was worried. Lenore's persistent reluctance to get involved in another Code spoke volumes. If he knew anything at all about Lenore, it was that her instincts when it came to the important matters in life were spot-on. Most of the time, far better than Sam's. But, as it were, neither of them had a lick of experience when it came to matters of the occult.

So too, behaviors had emerged in Lenore that had never existed before. With each passing day, she become more edgy and moody. At first the changes were subtle, but now they were impossible to ignore. Was this the big change—the mid-life change? Possibly, Sam figured. But that's what men always think, isn't it? When a woman hits her forties, every little deviation from the norm is blamed on menopause. Yet from what little Sam knew about such things, menopause was still several years off for Lenore.

Then what, pray tell, was going on with Lenore? It was impossible for Sam to believe she had turned into a cold-hearted killer, a serial killer that stalked Covington, Vermont, ready to strike again in a flash. And he was still having trouble believing that Lenore was truly involved in any of the murders: Ira Pavlovich's, Blum's, Byron Linkley's. She could throw a tantrum good as a two-year-old when she wanted to, but so could a lot of other people on the planet who had never hurt a flea. But Sam had no plans to find himself trapped into cleaning up a nasty mess from Lenore—carting bodies out of buildings at Graebner or anywhere else.

And as Sam saw it, Linkley's death could just as easily been the work of Clara Parker. She knew all about the words Red Rover from her own experience with The Code. And, she knew Linkley far better than Lenore did. Had Parker and Linkley gotten into a tussle somehow and then right there in Parker's office she let him have it in a moment of rage and then tried to make it look like it was Lenore's doing? Clara Parker was no saint, Sam knew that only too well. She had a fuse just as short as Lenore's at times. She was a hard-driving women, as hard-driving as a sledge coming down on a ten-penny nail.

But did it matter now who had killed Linkley? He was dead; his body was gone, buried under tons of slow-rotting garbage. The real problem facing Sam was the investment profile at WSA. It was looking worse by the day, far worse than it had in a long time, and Sam could come up with no good reason for that.

His only solution, as he saw it, was to run yet one more Code. Lord, how he did not want to do that, but if they were to strike a big vein of gold, they could shut down the whole decrepit business of The Code once and for all. At this point, he had come to be exactly like Clara Parker, whose life had come crashing down around her when she'd squandered away the college endowment only to be bailed out by Sam and The Code.

All day Sam's stomach was tight as a knotted washrag. He pumped down Tums like they were candy mints. Then he loaded himself up with coffee, even more than his usual eight to twelve cups a day, all of which had the effect of tightening the knot even more.

He accomplished little as he sat numbly at his desk, now and then getting up and staring out the windows at the fluttering bursts of snow that filled the streets and sidewalks and blurred the distant landscape across the dormant Vermont farmlands.

Late in the afternoon, Lenore stopped by Sam's office.

"I guess you know what day this is?" she said.

Of course he did. His desk calendar had been marked weeks before. His Outlook calendar kept reminding him from the multiple entries he had made. Every ten minutes it seemed, but actually on the hour, his Outlook reminder pinged and flashed the word Code in a corner of his computer screen.

Lenore's sudden burst of enthusiasm for conducting another Code was surprising, a total and complete reverse of her attitude on it for the past ten days. Perhaps Sam's subtle and constant promotion finally had its effect. He kept telling her, "We'll hope for the motherload of all Codes." Then he would add, "I for one am looking forward to life the way it had been…following stocks, searching, digging, buying, selling. It was once a lot of fun, wasn't it?" He damn well meant it.

The Midas touch, which wasn't a particularly good description of The Code, but close enough nonetheless, was beginning to feel like a curse, just as it had become for Midas.

Sam loved WSA. He loved the staff meetings, the strategy sessions, the occasional afternoon stop at Clara Parker's office at Graebner, listening her to carp about her troubles. He vowed to never, never, never again let things get to the point of dumping two-day-old bodies into the Walgreens' dumpster in the middle of the night.

It had taken a full two weeks of late-night scotch-rocks to blow that image from his memory, and even then he hadn't succeeded very well. He woke up at night from dark dreams of himself dragging Linkley's body out of Parker's office like some grave-robbing ghoul and loading it onto the truck. And as everyone knows, dreams don't always follow reality. How often have we found ourselves walking through town stark naked and wondering how we got there and where our clothes are. These dreams of Sam's were no different than those except that they were replete with heart-pounding scenes of Linkley suddenly coming to life, screaming and scratching frantically on the side of the trunk as Sam slipped it into the dumpster. Dreams where Clara Parker, sitting shotgun next to Sam in the truck, suddenly morphed into the Covington Chief of Police, who stared silently at Sam as he drove through the dark streets of Covington on that dreadful night from hell.

"Why the sudden change of heart?" Sam asked, surprised.

"Your point is correct. We get what we can from The Code, put WSA back on track financially, and get out. Makes sense."

Sam sighed enthusiastically. "Makes a lot of sense...a lot."

13

Lenore has a flashback

With another long night and another Code still ahead that day, Lenore decided to catch a few hours of sleep before she would meet Sam at the Graebner Library at two in the morning. As she lay in bed, everything focused in sudden perfect clarity, as though each neuronal connection had been reset. It was perfectly clear to her that she had, with her own hands, stolen life from Ira. And that she had sent Blum's tarnished soul to its ultimate reckoning without so much as a *mea culpa* or a Hail Mary for all his hot and illicit moments in cheap motel rooms.

With shades drawn, she closed her eyes. Her plan was set. She was still fuming from the knowledge of how Parker and Sam had used The Code to save Parker's ass from total disaster as president of Graebner. Her anger towards Parker reached new heights.

Tired and exhausted, Lenore fell into a sleep filled with a shattering re-enactment of an episode of which she had no memory whatsoever.

⚜

Friday night, nine-thirty, Lenore walks into the reading room. The room is empty but for bowtied Byron Linkley, nerdy middle-aged professor, book opened on the table in front of him.

Linkley looks up and watches as she saunters over to his table and sits across from him.

"Dr. Linkley," she says in a low voice like Bacall speaking to Bogie.

A bare smile emerges on Linkley's face. He knows exactly who Lenore is, yet he waits for her to speak.

"I'm Lenore Simenson," she tells him.

"Professor here at Graebner?" His foolish comment fools neither of them. At a school as tightly shrink-wrapped as Graebner, every member of the faculty knows everyone else.

"No…but you are," she says. "I know all about you. I know you're very tight with Clara Parker."

"Fine. What can I do for you?" he says, as though addressing a distraught anxiety-packed student on the night before a looming test.

"It's not what you can do for me. It's what I can do for you."

"Oh! Really! And what might that be?"

"The Code. Ever heard of it?"

No point in deking. "I have…yes."

"From Dr. Parker?"

"From Parker."

"What do you know about it?"

Linkley thinks for a second, then decides to speak the truth. "I am an academic. Academics are naturally curious. That's why we are not bookkeepers or lawyers or bankers…or anything else. I found out a lot about The Code once I learned what Clara and you, and Sam, your buddy over there at your shop," making it sound like WSA was some kind of transmission repair business, "were up to."

It occurs to Linkley that he may be divulging more than he should, but he keeps talking. Something about Lenore prompts him to speak freely. The loneliness of the night perhaps, or Lenore's eyes—soft, warm, and tender—and green, his favorite color in a woman's eyes. Even Byron Linkley has human passions.

But then in the snap of a second, her eyes flash deep red—fiery sapphires, glowing. Not in the iris, not those thin thready arteries that occupy a tired and weary pair of eyes, but the entire eye. Linkley blinks and flinches and pulls back in his chair. *It could be the light through the stained-glass windows*, he thinks. Possibly. It happens so fast, he's not sure.

"Admit it, you have a lot of curiosity about what goes on down there, don't you?" Lenore nods toward the panel door.

"*That* is none of my concern, not in the least. I come here to read and study…read and study, that and nothing more. Look at this place." He points to the bookshelves, the windows, the table lamps, the Gustav Becker ticking away slowly in the corner. He plunks his hand lovingly down on the volume in front of him. "*This* is why I am here."

It's total baloney and Lenore knows it. "And if I offered you a chance to go down and see what's really happening there," nodding again toward the panel, "You wouldn't pass up an opportunity like that, would you Professor Linkley?"

"Why the big offer?" Linkley's hand moves nimbly across his bowtie, checking by habit the angle of it. He leans forward and locks an eye on Lenore and waits for an answer.

"There's a good reason, but unless we go and until I show you, I cannot divulge the reason. You'll have to see it firsthand."

Linkley shakes his head; it sounds way too fishy. "Well, I'm sorry, but I'm rather busy, as you can see." He points to the book and the writing tablet next to him as evidence. Gustav Becker sends ten melodious notes throughout the room. "And it is Friday and I am feeling a whole lot more tired than adventurous right now. I was about ready to leave and—"

"It won't take long. What would you say if I told you Clara Parker asked me to do this?"

"She could have told me directly. I see her all the time in and about campus."

"She doesn't go down there," Lenore says. "Only we do. Me and Sam…Sam from the shop as you say."

"That's not totally true. Nick Sanchez and Katy Malone know about it, two students here at the school. They've been down there, too, on more than one occasion. I'll bet you know that, don't you?"

"No, I don't know. You're the eyes up here so I'm told." Lenore thinks momentarily, then says, "Do you academics turn every conversation into a bloody debate?"

Linkley laughs curtly. He leans back, folds his arms, and laughs again, then returns to the table.

"So, you know about the…uhm, what should I say, the ceremony that's being performed down there?"

"I know that it's tied to the occult and that you're trying to use it to manipulate stock markets or some such thing." He chortles quiet and mockingly, and says, "Frankly, I don't believe any of that gibberish. Practitioners of the occult have been around in one form or another for probably two thousand years or so. History is replete with examples of how people attempted to use it—use it to control the weather, to get rich, to fight disease, to gain immortality. But show me one example," raising his index finger in defiance, "one example in history of where it really worked. You can't. The occult is mankind's attempt to connect with the spiritual world in the hope that they, those who have departed, will bestow on those that remain some special knowledge that no one else has." Linkley's lecture continues for a full three minutes more, each statement becoming more gesticulated and animated. You can take the professor out of the classroom, but you can't take the classroom out of the professor.

Lenore pretends to be listening to Linkley's silly diatribe, though she has no intention of letting him derail her plans. When he finally hits a pause, she says, "Then you be the judge. We go?"

With a surprisingly fresh and lively face, invigorated perhaps by his own lecture, he methodically closes his book and sets it on top of his tablet.

Lenore leads the way to the panel door, carrying a large bag. Opening the door, she offers Linkley black stillness and grim darkness. They step inside. She pulls the door shut.

"We will do this properly." She retrieves two thick twelve-inch-long candles from her bag, lights each, gives one to Linkley, and keeps one for herself.

"Just follow me," she says. "Go slow, there are several sets of stairs to negotiate, so be very careful."

Upon arrival at each tier along the way, Linkley stops and views the inner structure of the old edifice. As a historian, he is as much interested in old buildings as he is in theories of whether Lee Harvey Oswald was the lone assassin of Kennedy, or whether it was a big elaborate conspiracy.

They arrive at the altar chamber. Lenore places her candle in a holder on the wall. Linkley does the same on the opposite wall. Choleric light quivers from the tapers, weak as the first glimpse of illumination at Lauds coming in through an opaque monastery window.

"Did you folks put this here?" Linkley asks, looking at the heavy stone altar.

"Did we put it there? No. It was here when we came in the first time. That's all I know."

"It's from the old seminary, no doubt. Regional marble from Vermont probably. Very pretty stuff, huh? The skulls, though, were carved into it later. They don't quite go with the design, the basic motif." He chuckles, then looks at

Lenore, then back at the skulls. "I heard about the seminary and its demise from one of the other historians who knew quite a bit about the ontogeny of Graebner and the school that was here before it. Things at the seminary went haywire...not sure why that was, but they did. It all began down in some underground room on campus. See what you found, you and your buddy Sam?" Linkley's eyes focus on the stone slab.

"No one really knows the whole story, that's what I'm told anyway," he says. "Something nasty happened. It's been written up in a few of the anthologies, but it's the work of amateur historians, not scholars. You can't take that stuff seriously." He walks past by the Stations of the Cross as he talks. "But one look at all this and you could get yourself to believe just about anything, couldn't you? I also heard that Graebner seriously engaged in discussions about demolishing the library, but its beauty and historical significance saved it." Linkley talks with great enthusiasm, as though he's visiting the Chauvet Caves in France or something.

But Lenore has work to do, and all this jabber is getting in the way.

Linkley circles the room and stands next to Lenore. As he glances at her, both of her eyes flash bright neon red, causing Linkley to recoil quickly back. *No reflection from a stained-glass window this time.*

"Are you all right?" Linkley asks.

"Me, I'm fine. Why?"

"Your eyes, geez...good grief, they were...." He clears his throat. "Well, I think we've been down here long enough, don't you? I'm not so sure what the big deal was in the first place. The occult might be fascinating to some people, but it's needlessly irrelevant in today's world. I'll leave it to you and your gang to explore it. It's of no interest to me."

"Hold on, not so fast," Lenore prompts. There's one more thing."

Linkley moves impatiently about the room again, ending up by the small door on the far wall. He bends over and gives an uninterested tug on the ring.

At that second, Lenore reaches into her bag, grasps the handle of a ballpeen hammer, lifts it high, and with a mighty heave-ho brings it straight toward the side of Linkley's head. Linkley turns just in time to see the mallet coming down on him. He pulls his hand up to shield the blow. Knuckles and fingers snap and crack. He pulls his hand in pain to his chest. Lenore loads up and comes down again, this time delivering a square hit on Linkley's temple. He collapses on the floor.

Lenore looks down on Linkley. His chest rises and sinks in irregular shallow breaths. She loosens his bowtie, slips it off from around his collar, and wraps it like a tourniquet around his neck until his breathing stops. Her mind races fast and crazy. She lets out a deep maniacal gasp, then stoops over him and presses two fingers against his neck in search of a pulse. Nothing, still as a dry garden hose.

Part A done.

With a hand under each of Linkley's arms, she drags him into the Green Mile step by step. Tug and rest, tug and rest. The dusty foul air, undisturbed for decades, fills her lungs. Halfway down, she drops Linkley's body on the floor, steps clumsily over him, returns to the altar chamber, and retrieves a bottle of Fiji water from her bag. She sucks in three long gulps, then returns to her task. Part B is proving to be a whole lot more difficult than expected.

Onward she goes—tug and rest, tug and rest. Breathing deep and hard, she arrives at the Sick Room. She pulls Linkley past the operating table and enters the long dark corridor to Parker's office. This is not going to be easy. She feels her energy slipping away, the corridor to Parker's office is as belligerently foul as the one she just came through. She stops and arches her back. *Persist, persist, persist*, she tells herself.

At long last, she arrives at the stairs that lead to the closet in Parker's office. Now for the real challenge. Getting Linkley through a long flat corridor is bad enough but getting a hundred and seventy-five pounds of dead weight up a set of stone stairs is something else.

She looks at her phone: eleven thirty. Lots of time. To be on the safe side, she climbs the stairs, quietly enters the closet, and gently opens the door to Parker's office. *Pray tell, what if Parker is working late? What if security or housekeeping is in there hiding out, playing poker, screwing away on Parker's sofa?* But the room is dark and empty, lit only by spent light that sifts in through the large windows.

Lenore returns to the stairs and looks down at Linkley's, body slumped awkwardly at the bottom of the steps, head tilted to the side.

"You dork," she grouses, as if blaming him for the events of the evening. "You just wait, I'll get your butt up these stairs yet."

She hobbles down to where Linkley lies. "Here goes, Herr Professor." She puts her arms under Linkley's. "One step at a time, old boy. That's how we do it." She gives a huge tug upward and parks Linkley's butt on the second step. Taking in three deep breaths she yanks and pulls again until she rests him on the third step. Then the fourth, then the fifth, then the sixth, and the seventh and eighth.

There he is, spread out on the closet floor.

She goes into Parker's office and sits on the sofa for a moment, breathing heavily. *Almost there,* she tells herself. *Almost there.* She hears a noise outside the office. She listens carefully. Someone is in the hall. The *second to last* thing she needs is to be caught in Parker's office. The *last* thing she needs is to be caught in Parker's office with a dead body. The voice fades away.

Almost ready for Part C, but not quite there yet.

She leans back on the sofa, stretches out, and looks at the ceiling and the ornate crown molding that trims it. *Nifty place*, she thinks. Closing her eyes, she rests motionless and weary and tired for a minute. She tells herself not to fall asleep. She tells herself to get this mofo job done.

Returning to the closet, she looks at Linkley as he lies on his back in the doughy darkness, turned partly to his side exactly as she left him. Or had she? She steps back a half step. *He was on his back when she dropped him on the closet floor, wasn't he? Don't get crazy now,* she tells herself. Just to be sure, she reaches down and places two fingers on the side of his neck in search of a pulse. Nothing.

Get with it, she tells herself. With one gigantic grinding burst, she pulls Linkley non-stop out of the closet into

Parker's office. She's breathing hard. She pushes Parker's large leather executive chair over to the wall and secures it tightly in place to keep it from slipping, then drags Linkley over and, with every ounce of strength left in her, she plunks his butt in the bucket of the chair and wheels it over to Parker's desk.

One by one, she lifts Linkley's feet, props them on the desk, and ties his bowtie into a crude bow around his bare neck just above the collar of his rather unpleasant salmon-colored oxford shirt. Linkley's head is tilted back, eyes open to the ceiling, tongue hanging out the left side of his mouth.

Part C, done!

She looks at the time. *Almost half past eleven. Plenty of time to walk casually out of the library.*

⚲

One minor little detail about all of this never made it onto Lenore's magic retroactive radar system. What didn't show up in her mysterious dream was that, on the night she slaughtered Linkley, Nick had been on the second floor putting in an hour of hard work before heading over to meet Katy and friends at the Rat.

He had looked up just as Lenore fled down the corridor on her way past the room in which he was working. She never turned toward him, never saw him. Without doubt though, she was coming down from the reading room a floor above. Nick knew that Professor Linkley had been up there. The reading room was always Nick's first choice for studying at the library, but on that night, seeing that he would be alone with Linkley, he opted for one of the rooms on the second floor.

Out of sheer curiosity, Nick left his books and climbed the flight of stairs to the third floor. The reading room was empty. Linkley's book and notepad were spread on the table. Detecting the faint odor of burning candles, Nick walked to the panel door and breathed deeply through his nose. No question, someone had been down there very recently. *Must have been what's-her-name*, he surmised. But fearing that Linkley might return at any second, Nick left and returned quickly to the floor below.

14

Devastation

By two fifteen in the morning, Sam and Lenore were creeping down the stairs into the Altar Chamber. The environment seemed more ghostly dead than ever before, as though most of the air had been sucked from the stairways and the chamber, leaving little to breath. They felt the need to pull in deep breaths every few minutes to fill their lungs with the stagnant air just to keep from fainting.

Sam checked and double-checked everything, making absolutely sure all was in order before they started. He wanted no slip-ups this time. His plan was for The Code to work perfectly and then to have the room sealed off. Maybe even filled with concrete so all temptation to return to the psycho-demented place would be thwarted. He had talked about this with Clara Parker. She was anxious to accommodate him, given the tenebrousness of having to cart off Linkley's cold dead ass from her office late at night. Having suddenly gone missing, his disappearance had yet to raise an eyebrow among his colleagues. Only the smallest rumblings had occurred on campus as to his whereabouts.

The candles were lit, the robes were donned, the moment of The Code was at hand. They passed the Stations of the Cross and returned to the altar, Sam leading the way. But on that night, Lenore had a surprise in her bag.

Sam swiped his hand across the altar, sweeping away a thin sprinkling of dust that had gathered on the beautiful old marble. Sam's hopes were that in an hour they would be done and on their way out of the building. As he turned toward Lenore, from her bag she pulled a twelve-inch butcher knife, one of the mementos that she had taken from Nick's apartment the night she had slipped him the Benadryl and taken his phone. She stood, arm raised, knife over Sam, her eyes fiery red. She let out a bone-chilling shriek.

Sam leaned back. "*Lenore!*" he yelled. "What's going on!" As she brought the knife down, he leaned to the left in just enough time to avoid having his carotid dissected from his neck. The blade of the knife screeched across the marble altar.

Sam backed off. "*Lenore!*" he yelled again.

Lenore's face had taken on an evil and sickly stare. Her teeth had changed to pointed black spikes. Her eyes blazed in glowing red. Putrid breath poured from her mouth, as if gushing from a pair of decayed and rotted lungs. The skin on her face was thin and translucent and gray. A voice, pitched and high, came not from her mouth but from somewhere deep in her horrid body.

"Saaa-mee boy." The words filled the room. "I've got just the thing for you, my buddy, my friend. It's the investment of a lifetime." The knife slashed back and forth through the air in front of him. He stepped back, dodging each swipe. "You'll never have another opportunity like this, Sammy. Never! It's the chance of a lifetime!"

She backed him against the wall. As she pulled the knife overhead, he slammed his fist into her face, knocking her jaw to the side but leaving her unscathed, undamaged. He slid away from the wall, grabbed a burning candle from a holder, and jammed it into her face. The skin of her cheek sizzled. Lenore laughed gleefully. "Hee, hee, hee," she yelped, her skin unaffected by the assault. "You're *always* so much *fun*, Sammy. That's what I like about you. What would I do without you?"

Sam backed away. If he could get to the stairs, he could outrun her, charge up and out of the building. He made it to the doorway, ready to bolt. But as he arrived, Lenore suddenly appeared before him—mouth open, black spiked teeth gnashing up and down. Her body had been transformed across the room, blocking his egress. She slammed the knife down on him, catching him on the forearm, cutting deep into the flesh. He yanked his arm quickly back. He was trapped.

There was one last chance. He ran to the altar, holding his bleeding arm to his chest. Grabbing the black wooden cross that hung upside down above the altar, he ripped it from the chains that strung it to the ceiling. Turning it right-side-up, he held it in front of Lenore. She screamed and screeched at an ear-piercing volume.

Sam moved closer, one safe step at a time. Closer and closer, holding the cross in front of him. She moved back, cowering until she was hunched in a ball near the wall. In a weak and sickly voice, she beseeched, "The Code, Sam. We must do The Code. Don't you think? That's what we came for." She repeated the words over and over, her voice lowering with each word until it was little more than a garbled, grizzly, growl. "The Code, Saaam. The…Code…Saaam."

She curled on the floor, looking helpless and drained. Yet in one last burst of energy, she leaped to her feet and lurched, attempting to skewer Sam with the knife. He held the cross in front of him and, with a ferocious blow, kicked the knife from her hand, grabbed it off the ground, and swung it across her, catching her on the throat, cutting halfway through her neck.

The room lit in blazing light—deep and rich and impossible to tolerate. A blast of rancid air belched out of Lenore's severed neck. Her body exploded in a flash of fire. Sweltering heat filled the room hot as all of Hades.

When Sam looked up. Lenore was gone. He was alone. An unbearable odor filled the room. One slow step at time, like a small child, he made his way up the stairs to the reading room, slammed the panel door, and lumbered from the building.

15

Red Rover, Red Rover

Two days later, Sam sat in Clara Parker's office. He had awakened that morning exhausted but knew he had to go talk with Clara and tell her what had happened with Lenore. Then he would try to push every memory of it from his life forever.

Sam sat in a chair in front of Clara Parker. He talked in a slow droning monotone, spilling out the details of the ungodly events of the night in the altar chamber with Lenore.

"She's gone," he said, with more than a little sadness. Sad for what had come of his adventure with Lenore. He wished he had never heard the word Code. But no matter, it was over now.

Clara sat motionless, mesmerized. As he continued to speak, she leaned slowly forward. "Are you sure you're okay, Sam?" she asked.

"What? Am I okay? Why do you ask?"

"Your eyes, Sam…I don't know. For a second, they looked red, bright, bright red…glowing red."

Made in the USA
Middletown, DE
08 November 2021